In High Cotton

by

Ane Mulligan

HERITAGE BEACON
FICTION

IN HIGH COTTON BY ANE MULLIGAN
Heritage Beacon Fiction is an imprint of LPCBooks
a division of Iron Stream Media
100 Missionary Ridge, Birmingham, AL 35242

ISBN: 978-1-64526-268-8
Copyright © 2020 by Ane Mulligan
Cover design by Elaina Lee
Interior design by Karthick Srinivasan

Available in print from your local bookstore, online, or from the publisher at:
ShopLPC.com

For more information on this book and the author visit:
https://anemulligan.com/

Brought to you by the creative team at LPCBooks:
Eddie Jones, Shonda Savage, Denise Weimer, Steven Mathisen

Library of Congress Cataloging-in-Publication Data
Mulligan, Ane.
In High Cotton / Ane Mulligan 1st ed.

Printed in the United States of America

PRAISE FOR *IN HIGH COTTON*

Mulligan pens a story full of Southern charm with a cast of characters in a cute Georgia town you won't easily forget. Makes me want to sit down with the lot of them for a glass of sweet tea.

~**Rachel Hauck**
New York Times bestselling author

In the tradition of *Steel Magnolias* and *Fried Green Tomatoes*, Ane Mulligan creates a cast of seemingly incompatible characters and brings them together into a family the likes of which I wanted to belong. Maggie is a delightful, relatable heroine, and I cheered for her through every page of this well-written, delightfully insightful, and descriptively captivating story. Be transported to the small-town South during the Great Depression and grow along with Maggie as she battles challenges and emerges triumphant thanks to faith and with a little help from her friends.

~**Kim Vogel Sawyer**
Bestselling author of *Bringing Maggie Home*

[With] the perfect marriage of Southern charm and dramatic tension, author Ane Mulligan takes the reader by the hand, immersing you in a story world you won't want to leave. The women of *In High Cotton* are strong, brave, and compassionate, role models from the past who are every bit as relevant to women today. Personally, I think this is Ane's best work ever!

~**Michelle Griep**
Christy Award-winning author of *Once Upon a Dickens Christmas*

Ane Mulligan's writing *sings* in this moving tale of friendship and heartbreak. I haven't enjoyed a Depression-era novel more since I read Steinbeck's *Grapes of Wrath*.

~**Elizabeth Ludwig**
USA Today bestselling author

I am not generally the biggest historical fiction fan, but this book has so much action and intrigue that it kept me captivated throughout. I was on the edge of my seat through most of this book. There is a subtle but meaningful spiritual thread throughout the book that focuses on trusting God to bring a person through hard times, and that God's timing is always perfect, even if we think otherwise.

~**Melissa Parcel**
Top Goodreads reviewer

I was privileged to receive an advanced copy of *In High Cotton*. [The author] brought together such a unique group of characters who bonded so tightly, it gives a new meaning to family. I found it hard to put down. I stayed up way too late one night because I just had to read one more chapter. I binge-read the rest of it today because I just had to find out how it was going to end! You need to read this book! You will not be disappointed!

~**Lynn Baker Worley**
Goodreads

I enjoyed this fun-loving cast of Southern women in rural South Georgia during the Great Depression. Maggie Parker, widow and single mom, captured my heart as her faith is tested in surprising ways, as she remains hopeful, naturally pressing into the arms of Jesus. This story has it all: characters to cheer for, mystery, suspense, a splash of wholesome romance, heartache, and well-timed humor. This author pens a beautifully written story of hope and healing and shows the meaning of family through the lives of her fun-loving, complex cast of characters.

~**Nora St. Laurent**
The Book Club Network Blog

Ane Mulligan has a knack for creating colorful characters with emotional depth and sharp wit. *In High Cotton* is a heart-warming story of what it means to be family and the sacrifices we make for those we love. Mulligan weaves together sensitive and tender moments, delivering a flawless tale of faith, understanding, and perseverance.

~Kellie Coates Gilbert
Author of the Sun Valley series

Acknowledgments

No book is written by the author alone. It "takes a village," and my village consists of my critique partners Michelle Griep and Elizabeth Ludwig. Without you, this story wouldn't be what it is today. You encouraged me, offered suggestions, and brainstormed. When I had to set it aside for a few years, you mourned with me. And you cheered at its resurrection. Thank you. You're the best writing buddies in the world!

Another brainstorm partner is author Patty Smith Hall. Patty, you made sure my historical details were correct and provided insight on customs and traditions in Georgia. You selflessly shared your own research and time with me. Thank you, my friend. This journey is more fun having you alongside me.

Many thanks to Lynn Bowman of the Buford Museum and Brandon Hembree, Sugar Hill city councilman and enthusiastic history buff. Gentlemen, your help provided vital historical details for this book. Thank you!

I have two beta readers, Ginger Aster and Gail Mundy. This is their favorite of all my books. Thank you, ladies, for your eyes for detail, your suggestions, and your encouragement.

There are several other authors who probably don't know they influenced my writing. Besides Michelle Griep and Elizabeth Ludwig, those are Janice Hanna Thompson and Annie Barrows. Thank you, ladies. The way you incorporate humor in your writing struck a chord within me.

Then there's, my editor, Denise Weimer, who took the final product I submitted and made it better with her suggestions. We were new to each other, and I entered the editor/author relationship with enthusiasm ... until she pulled out her red pencil, to which I screeched and kicked the heads off a few wildflowers. Then I took a deep breath, reread her remarks, and realized she was right. Next time, I'll skip over the angst and go straight to fixing. Thank you, Denise, for not giving up on me.

Finally, yet most important, is the Author of my soul. Thank you, Lord, for whispering stories to my heart. Thank you for leading me down this path of creativity. It's beyond my dreams!

Dedication

To Ginger Aster and Nora St. Laurent

Your support and friendship mean the world to me,
not to mention your love of books.
May God richly bless you both.

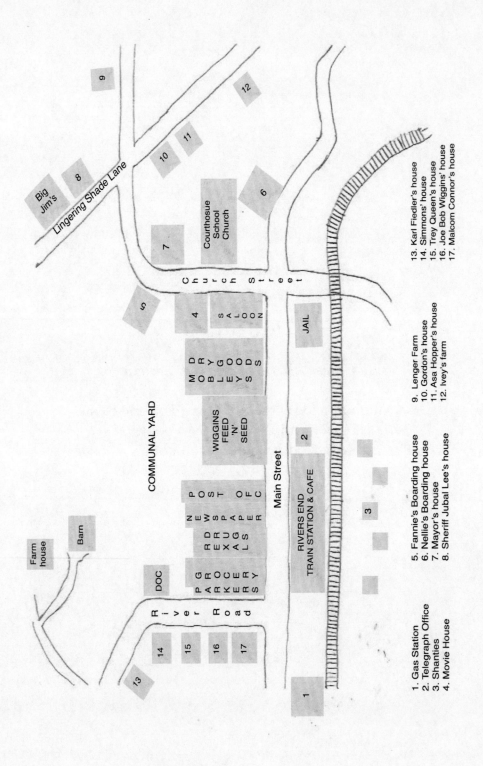

CHAPTER 1

October 28, 1929

Sadie always says, "Southern women may seem as delicate as flowers, but we've got iron in our veins." I long to be like her—a lone Yamasee Indian rose, whose thorns protect her better than any man could. But it's hard when every day is a struggle to make ends meet for myself and my son.

"Mama?" Barry pulls on my sleeve. "Can we buy these?" He bounces on his toes, his nutmeg eyes pleading with me over a pair of black high-topped, canvas athletic shoes.

I tousle his golden-brown curls, so much like mine, and pick up the price tag to consider. Mobley's Dry Goods has them on sale, marked down from $1.39, but the ten cents saved won't be enough. My heart cries to fulfill my baby's wishes. In my own defense, I've done a respectable job raising Barry by myself while keeping Parker's Grocery afloat, but our bottom-line hangs on a precarious black edge, teetering way too close to red for comfort.

I blink away threatening tears and stroke his smooth cheek, hoping his just-turned-seven-year-old heart will understand. "I'm sorry, sugar. You'll have to make do with the tennis oxfords for now. Look." I hold the tag for him to see. "They cost half of those, and with you growing so fast, they're all we can afford right now."

He nods and squares his small shoulders. "Okay, Mama. The oxfords lace up quicker, anyhow." My sweet boy puts the high-tops back on the shelf.

I turn to search for the owner's middle-aged wife. I spot her salt-and-pepper topknot as she bends over the counter. "Ida Clare, can you measure Barry for these shoes?"

"Certainly, Maggie. Have him bring them to me."

I give my boy a squeeze, and he carries the canvas oxfords to Miss Ida Clare. While she measures his foot, I wander to the front of the store and a display of aprons. I pick through them, looking for one with a little personality in a cheery yellow or royal blue, shades that work well with light-brown hair. In these dark financial times, a bit of color helps—lifts a gal's spirits like a new lipstick.

A train whistle blows, and the wheels clickety-clack on the tracks, vibrating the wooden floor. My heart skips a beat. Someday, I'm going to be on one of those, going somewhere. I turn to see if Barry heard it. He has and darts to the window. Anything to do with trains or airplanes draws him like a fly to butter.

"That's the ten-ten, Mama. Right on time." He peers past a set of fingerprints that are eye level with the dolls. I can't help but wonder if some little girl's mama feels the heartbreak I do as she stares at the dolls, knowing she can't afford one for her little girl's birthday.

"Is Miss Ida Clare finished with you, son?"

"Yes, ma'am. She's got 'em at the register."

I stand with him a moment. The train has one of those private passenger cars hooked on the end, in front of the caboose. We don't see many of those. Mostly it's freight cars that rumble through Rivers End, hauling crops or lumber. I wonder where it's going and who's on it. I sometimes wish I could step onto that train and simply roll out of town, leaving my worries behind. But then, of course, I'd also be leaving Barry, my friends, and the town I love. And so I stay and fight. We all do.

Dreams aren't fulfilled in times like these, and I need to pay for those shoes. While the apron is a bargain at twenty-five cents, I daren't fall a quarter short on the upcoming tax bill our state legislators voted in that says I owe $273.42 on the grocery store. How can that be? Might as well be a million dollars. Where am I going to find an amount like that? After all the expenses of the store, my annual income barely peeks over the seven-hundred-dollar mark.

The apron I hold will have to wait. I lay it down.

"Here you go, sugar." I pull a wrinkled dollar from a timeworn wallet I should have replaced a year ago and hand it to Barry. "Now bring me the change."

After he pays, we leave Mobley's. The leaves are starting to turn, and there's a crisp feel to the air as we walk back along Main Street to the grocery, four doors down. To say Rivers End is a small town is an understatement. Established to serve the outlying farms, it amounts to a block-and-a-half of stores, a theater, a library, one bar-slash-gas station, and a couple of churches—the Methodist and the Catholic. The Baptist preacher is a traveling one, so most of the Baptists worship with the Methodists—strange bedfellows, but it works in Rivers End.

Still, we're a tight-knit community, especially the merchants who live and work in the town. Between Mobley's Dry Goods and my grocery, there's the newspaper, the *Farm Whistler,* that runs my columns, Wiggins Feed & Seed with its sorry sun canopy tattered by a storm two years ago, and Hampton's Drugstore, which also houses our tiny post office. The druggist, Beau Hampton, is our mayor and postmaster who was responsible for the town getting electrified three years ago. Now Parker's has an electric refrigeration room for storing meat and dairy goods. No more ice to contend with in the grocery.

Across the street, behind the train station and the row of shanties that look like old men leaning over a checkerboard, the Oconee and Ocmulgee rivers converge into one, becoming the Altamaha. The Yamacraw Indians called the place "where rivers end," giving our town its name. If Sadie is right about me having iron in my veins, then somewhere in the vortex of those rivers there must lay a giant magnet. And it's pulling me under.

"Mama, can I go over to the train station and show Ozzie my new shoes?"

"Of course, but don't you go bragging."

His eyes grow large at the hint of offending his best friend. "No, ma'am. I won't. But he got a pair 'zactly like mine yesterday."

As soon as he scampers safely across the street to the train station, where Ozzie's daddy, Wade, works and has one of the town's two private telephones and the only pay phone, I step inside the grocery. Immediately, the scent of old wood and dirt clinging to the potatoes lays an olfactory rug beneath the citrusy tang from the oranges I displayed last night.

The grocery store, bearing my late husband's family name, Parker's, still flourishes with me at the helm. Well, *flourish* stretches it a mite, since the 1920s haven't been very profitable here in Georgia. The rest of the country may be roaring through the twenties, but here in Rivers End—all of Georgia, really—we've been squeaking through. We're still climbing out from the War of Northern Aggression, which ravaged the land. Then came the boll weevil that killed King Cotton, leaving the farmers dirt poor. And when the farmers are poor, we all suffer.

Still, I put food on the table and shoes on my son's feet. That counts for something, doesn't it? Don't ask Big Jim for his opinion, though. My late husband's daddy is pushing me to get married again, but I like things the way they are, like being in charge of my life.

I lift my chin and my resolve, nodding hello to a farmer's wife—whose name I can't remember—inspecting the catfish laying on ice. I cross my fingers behind my back and hope she buys some.

Sadie, a few wayward strands of her salt-and-pepper hair escaping the knot on the back of her neck, enters the grocery. Though older than my mama, she stepped into the role of friend the day I arrived in Rivers End as a new bride, and then later as mentor on the day my husband died.

She hovers at the meat counter with Cal, my store manager, watching him count off some sausages. Her scowl deepens, turning the fine line between her brows into a deep crevice. "You keep your finger off that scale, Cal Llewellyn."

I hide a smirk. She trusts few men, and he isn't one of them. Cal lays the last sausage on the scale and holds his hands in the air like a man under arrest.

I set my pocketbook beneath the cash register and stroll over to greet her. "Mornin', Sadie."

A smile replaces her frown. "Mornin', yourself. Where've you been?"

Sinking. I straighten a box of Quaker Oats someone has left too close to the shelf's edge. "Over to Mobley's to get Barry shoes. That boy grows faster than monkey grass."

Cal hands her the butcher paper and twine-wrapped sausages as Sadie nods a thank you. She counts the change, tucks it into a small red coin purse, and slips it in the pocket of her trousers. She's raised many an eyebrow in Rivers End since she took to wearing those.

Linking arms with me, she guides me toward the front door. "Did y'all figure out what you're going to do about your tax bill?"

I glance back at Cal, but he's weighing the farm wife's catfish. *Thank you.* Not everyone is the good fisherman my Barry is. "What *can* I do but pay it? Only, I'm going have to get creative to figure out how. I'm hoping the *News Standard* up in Lawrenceville will buy some short stories. They pay more than the *Farm Whistler.*"

Sadie leans close enough for me to smell the cloves she's chewed. "You know, if you come up wanting, I have a little set aside and would gladly lend—"

"No." Bless her heart, she can't have much laid aside. I pat her hand to take away the sting of my refusal. "I thank you kindly, Sadie, but no. I have to do this on my own. Besides, I've written four of those little bedtime stories the newspapers are finally running." I'd been trying to convince my editor to run the stories for three long years with no success. I don't rightly know what changed his mind, but I'm not questioning my good fortune.

"You're a true Southerner, Maggie Parker. But just remember, accepting a little help isn't a sin."

It is for me—or feels like it. It's giving up my self-reliance, my independence. I step outside with her, blinking against the sunshine. Fat clouds drift across the sky, playing hide-and-seek with the sun. "I know it's no sin, but it's hard to explain without tarnishing Jimmy's memory."

Sadie looks me up and down with those piercing hazel eyes of hers, so in contrast to her father's. She does have his Yamasee dark-brown skin and high cheekbones. A half smile twists her lips. "I understand more than you think. Knew your Jimmy from the day he was born. He was smack like his daddy."

Part of me wants to blurt out I'm thankful someone understands. But the other part wants to banish old disappointments and cherish only the good memories. Barry looks so much like the daddy he never knew. It saddens me that Jimmy passed on before he knew I was expecting. Though my Jimmy was a century behind on his thinking about women, I loved my husband. Still, there were times when I wanted to jerk a knot in his tail. Some of his decisions defied logic.

A dented, rusty farm truck with wooden sides holding in bushels of apples and onions backfires as it pulls into the gas station cattycorner across the street. Half its back bumper's gone, and the cab barely misses the edge of the marquee's sagging roof.

I pull my gaze back to Sadie. "It was so frustrating." The words gush out of me like groundwater from a pump. "He never let me make a single decision beyond what to have for supper or which of his shirts to iron first. And he certainly never discussed business with me."

We step to the side of the doorway as Cora Cook and her bucktoothed daughters approach the grocery. She still considers me an outsider and Sadie a half-breed. Sadie's looks display her Yamasee heritage, but she's a Georgia peach in my book. Biggity attitudes like Cora's put a knot in my knickers.

Still, I give them my best smile. They're usually good for fifty cents. I certainly hope so today.

"Morning, Cora. Hello, girls."

The girls giggle, but Cora simply nods.

Sadie follows them with her eyes, waiting until they go inside to resume our conversation. "Neither Jimmy nor his daddy believed women had the brains for business." She chuckles, her low voice raspy. "You should have seen Big Jim when he first learned I was working in the bank. He got so riled he nearly withdrew his money. Big Jim told old Mr. Hardee that the day he hired me, his cheese done slid clean off his cracker."

Leaning down and picking up a gum wrapper someone dropped, I can well imagine Big Jim saying that. Besides being prejudiced against anyone not like him, my father-in-law pitches a conniption fit if somebody's opinion differs from his. "When Jimmy was courting me, I had no idea—"

Sadie lifts her chin, peering over my shoulder and squeezing my arm in warning. "Shh. Barry and Ozzie are headed our way. We'll talk later." She smiles brightly and offers a cheery wave as the boys jump up the curb and onto the sidewalk. "Mornin', boys. Come give me some sugar." Her tone changes faster than the weather.

"Morning, Miss Sadie." Their two young voices chirp in unison. Barry, who idolizes her, kisses her cheek. Ozzie's ears turn pink as ripe rhubarb. He's always been slightly awed by the legends surrounding Sadie, but he kisses her, too, then the boys run upstairs to our apartment to play.

At the street door to the stairs up to the apartments, I bid Sadie adieu. When I open my front door, a folded paper miraculously still clinging to the mail slot after the boys banged into the apartment flutters to the hardwood floor. As I bend to retrieve it, my breath hitches, my heart pounds, and dread sours my stomach. The dark scrawl of my name on the front reveals the sender—Big Jim. My father-in-law. Straightening, I draw in a deep breath.

He's just trying to call my bluff. He can't sell the store because Jimmy left it to me. But as his threats have grown, so has my fear.

With shaky hands, I unfold the note, and as my eyes fly over its content, dread turns to alarm. Just as he's sworn to do so many times before, he's finally spoken to a lawyer.

CHAPTER 2

With my stomach churning, I read over the ultimatums in Big Jim's letter one more time. His menacing tone and accusations reveal a side of the man I don't want Barry seeing. I wad the note and stuff it in my pocket, planning to take it to the burn barrel in the backyard later. I take some deep breaths to slow my heartbeat and calm myself before my son sees me.

Dear Lord, help me.

I don't have money to hire a lawyer to fight Big Jim. I don't even have the money for my tax bill. The living room begins to blur as my eyes fill, but the boys' laughter from Barry's room stops me. I draw on that iron Sadie keeps saying fills my veins. Maybe she'll have an idea for me—a way to counter Big Jim's threats.

For now, there's nothing I can do, and I have a son to feed. And maybe an extra boy too. With one more prayer and another calming breath, I knock on Barry's bedroom door and open it. The boys are on the floor, so intent on an advertisement for a model airplane, they don't even look up.

"Ozzie, doesn't your daddy work late tonight? Would you like to stay for supper?"

The boys whoop like Indians, and Ozzie grins. "Yes, ma'am. I'd love to."

"What do you boys think of tomato soup and grilled cheese sandwiches?"

"Yippee!" They both shout.

"Thought so." It's their favorite. "You two run over and tell Mr. Wade, then come right back and wash up. Oh, and don't forget to tell Louella she can go on home. You can stay here until your daddy gets off work." It's nice having Wade and Ozzie live in the apartment above the drugstore, next to us. Wade and I help each other out with the boys, especially when his housekeeper is not around. Have ever since my Jimmy died. I'm thankful for his influence in Barry's life. He's a good friend.

"Yes, ma'am." The two sets of rapidly growing feet scramble down the stairs, pounding loud enough to set the wall sconces to rattling. The door at the bottom bangs shut. One day, the glass in that door is going to break.

Downstairs in the kitchen, I slice off quarter-inch-thick squares of soft Velveeta cheese to make sandwiches. Jimmy had added the kitchen next to the back porch when he asked me to marry him. It would be more convenient to have it on the same level as the rest of the apartment. I can't complain, though, since I don't have a mortgage, which I would if we'd have bought a house. Besides, I get my exercise this way. I don't snack if I'm writing, even if I do get hungry. It's too much bother to go down.

I open the can of tomato soup, blessing Mr. Campbell for coming up with twenty-one varieties. They make my life easier since my boy likes most of them, with the exception of the asparagus. With the fragrance of buttery bread making my mouth water, I keep one eye on the sandwiches sizzling in the frying pan as I stir the soup.

On the kitchen table, leering at me, is that tax bill. The one I don't have enough money to cover. I balance that nasty bit of bureaucracy against what little I have inside the cookie jar hidden in the cupboard. And it holds more crumbs than dollars. Between Big Jim and the tax bill, I may not be able to feed my son much longer.

Since I refuse to borrow from Sadie, my options are woefully few. My writing helps, but it only brings in about three dollars a week—respectable but not a living wage by itself. If the *News Standard* buys all four of my stories, it will only bring another two dollars.

It isn't anywhere near enough. I have to sell something. I have my wedding ring, my last link to Jimmy, but I can't bear to part with it. The only other jewelry I own of any value are family pieces I inherited from my grandmother, and it's a wonder she never sold them. I close my eyes, envisioning the sacrifices she must have made to keep them after the War of Northern Aggression.

I'd prefer to keep Meemaw's jewelry as an inheritance for Barry, but saving the family grocery is better than a brooch. Besides, the proverbial "roof over our heads" also covers said grocery, and I'm determined to keep both. I'll send them to my sister, Duchess, to sell.

The boys return just as I'm dishing up the soup. After supper, we move into the living room to play Go Fish. While not expensively furnished, it's cozy and inviting, with a burgundy velvet overstuffed chair and the old green davenport. Jimmy wanted gray, but I held out for the colorful one—even if it was a cast-off of Big Jim's. Then, in a moment of whimsy, I made drapes out of a tropical print with bright green ferns and red, blue, and yellow parrots. Sadie says they suit me. I don't know about that, but they make me smile and spark my creativity. My writing desk sits nearby where I can see the drapes and the world outside my window.

We sit on the floor around the coffee table, and Barry deals the first hand. All too soon, Wade's special knock the boys taught him echoes in the hallway. Like the little man he is, Barry answers the door, but his boyish enthusiasm takes over, and he grabs Wade's hand and pulls him inside.

"Play one game of Go Fish with us, Mr. Wade. Please?"

Wade's thick, wavy hair adds another inch to his six-foot-plus height. It's red like Ozzie's, and when he takes off his stationmaster cap, it leaves an indentation on the sides. He hangs the cap on a hook on the hall tree, then slides his fingers into his hair, giving it a good ruffling.

"How can I refuse?" His merry brown eyes crinkle when he smiles at the boys.

"Just one game, boys." I shake my finger at them, trying not to smile. "It's nearly bedtime, and Barry has a pound of dirt to wash off."

Wade sits on the floor between the boys.

"Want a bowl of soup?" I ask, gathering the cards and passing them to Ozzie.

He shakes his head. "No, thanks. Louella brought my supper by the station on her way home."

Ozzie shuffles the cards and deals.

"Whose private car was that on the ten-ten, Mr. Wade?" Barry asks while we organize our hands. I slip the jack of hearts next to the jack of diamonds.

"Governor of New York, hurrying home from Warm Springs."

I don't believe it. *Franklin Roosevelt?*" I rise up on my knees. "Did you meet him?"

"No opportunity. He kept to himself."

"Do you have any jacks?"

Wade tosses me the jack of spades and grins at Barry. "Got any threes?"

"Go fish," Barry hollers. He adores Wade, and I let him get away with the shout, imagining how he might have interacted with his daddy. It brings a smile to my face. I think Jimmy would be proud of our boy.

Once Barry wins the hand, they go home, and we go down to the kitchen. Barry pulls out the tin tub from the storage closet. After I fill it with water from the stove's reservoir, he jumps in, splashing a little onto the wood floor. He grins at me and starts warbling "Singing in the Bathtub." Oh to be a child again, full of hope instead of worries. While he washes and plays a bit, I pick up the tax bill off the table and slip it into my pocket, where it rubs against Big Jim's note.

I'm eager to get the jewelry ready to send to my sister, who lives in Atlanta. Her husband, Mr. Alden, is Yankee rich, and they know folks who will buy jewelry. When Duchess married Mr. Alden, Mama forgave him for being a Yankee, saying that's the only sin money *can* forgive.

I pick up Barry's towel and hold it out. His off-tune crooning of "In the Jail House Now" makes me smile. "Come on, sugar. It's nearly your bedtime, and if you want to read a bit, we'd better get a wiggle on."

"Do you think I can be a singer like Jimmie Rodgers?"

I help him get his towel wrapped around him. As usual, he forgot his pajamas upstairs in his room. "I thought you wanted to be a pilot."

"I can be a singing pilot." He flashes a saucy grin, and I grab him in a hug, tickling while I rub him dry.

After he's dry, we head back upstairs. One day, I'd love to be able to afford real indoor plumbing. My Jimmy wanted to put in a bathroom with a sink and bathtub for me, but he died before it became a reality. Truth is, there's no way I can afford it now, but it purely would be a luxury to not have to bathe in the kitchen.

With Barry in his room donning his pajamas, I quickly clean up the cards, then, not wanting to alert him to my mission, I tiptoe past his door. For a six—I mean seven-year-old—he's mighty intuitive. He sees trouble coming like a hound catching a scent.

I retrieve the broach, a sizable amethyst ring, and the diamond stickpin from the bottom of my lingerie drawer—the one that sticks and needs a hard jerk to open. My narrow gold wedding band is in my jewelry box. I pull it out and stare at it in my hand, running my finger over its slender, smooth edge. It isn't fancy and probably wouldn't bring a lot, anyway. Sending a prayer heavenward for a generous buyer for Meemaw's things, I slip it back inside its home in my jewelry box.

I carefully wrap the other jewelry in a hankie and then tissue paper. Once the parcel is laid in a box along with a letter explaining my need, I get a piece of butcher paper, wrap it, and address it to Duchess. My fountain pen stops on *Atlanta*.

What if the package gets lost in the mail? Or worse, no one wants the contents, or they don't fetch enough? My poor Barry doesn't have a daddy. Am I going to have to tell him he may not have a home either? If this doesn't work, we could end up having to live on Big Jim's charity. That thought sends a shiver up my spine. This *has* to work. I write *Georgia* with a flourish and tie twine firmly around the parcel, cutting off the excess with scissors.

"Mama?" Barry stands in the hallway, his towel haphazardly wrapped around his waist.

"Yes, sugar? And why haven't you put on your pajamas yet?"

"I was picking out a story and forgot. Are you coming to read to me?"

I lay the parcel on the coffee table, where I'll see it in the morning and remember to carry it to Beau Hampton to post for me.

"I surely am." I pick up my Bible as he scampers off to put on his pajamas.

His room is painted blue and decorated with airplanes, his passion. He likes trains, but his allegiance changed to aviation when he found his daddy's newspapers from the Great War. Today's paper is strewn all over his bed, and next to it, his damp towel lays on the floor beside his baseball mitt. He's wearing only the bottoms to his pajamas.

"Whatever are you reading about?" I pick up the towel and rub his damp hair.

His eyes sparkle. He pulls away from my ministrations and points to an ad for a large toy airplane. "It's a triple engine, Mama. I'm saving my money to buy it." He reaches for his piggy bank. "When do you think I'll have enough?"

The ad says the toy costs $3.48. Fissures crack across my heart, and I paste on a smile I hope he'll believe. Taking the piggy in one hand, I weigh it. It's painfully light. I didn't want to discourage him, but I thought he'd saved up more.

"You keep doing chores for Doc and Mr. Wade, and it may take a while, but you'll get there." I give his head a final vigorous drying with the towel. "I have faith in you. Now …" I run a quick comb through his hair and help him slide on his pajama top. "Give me the papers and find the story you want."

I drop the towel and the thin newspaper on the floor. My daddy always said you could gauge the economy by the thickness of the want ads. It's plumb sorrowful how few there are. Less than a half page and then only two columns. Four years ago, there were three pages' worth. There's more laying off than hiring in 1929. I'm hoping next year will be better.

"What did Granddaddy say in his note, Mama?"

I cross my fingers beneath the Good Book, hoping God will forgive me. "Not much, leastwise nothing worth repeating." I don't want my son to be hurt, and he will be. He's a protective little bear. "Let's read about David and Goliath."

Barry opens my Bible and finds the well-loved story. I'm glad I didn't suggest a different one. Right about now, I can use a dose of David's courage.

CHAPTER 3

The mouth-watering aroma of bacon sizzling in the skillet wakes up my taste buds and warms the kitchen against the morning's chill. I didn't sleep much last night, worrying about Big Jim's letter. He's hinted that his lawyer found some loophole that could give him control over the grocery. How can that be possible? Surely, he's bluffing.

I'm standing at the stove, flipping flapjacks when two small arms wrap around my waist. Barry's cherubic face tilts up at me. The joy in his sleep-filled eyes empowers me. All is right in my little world. I can take on Big Jim.

"Happy birthday, Mama."

I'd forgotten today was the twenty-ninth of October. In one fluid movement, I lift the pan to the warming shelf and pivot to hug him. He squeezes me tight, wiggling and giggling.

"What's got you so tickled?"

"Your birthday present. It's upstairs." He squirms out of my embrace and pulls me by the arm. "Come on."

I let Barry lead me to the apartment. Morning light streams into the living room from the three tall windows overlooking Main Street. When the electric company ran wires for the store, they wired the apartment too. The exposed wires are visible running up the wall, but the convenience is worth it. Barry likes to lie on the floor in front of the radio to listen to the *Amos and Andy* show and *The Adventures of Helen and Mary*. When my sister visits, we roll up the carpet, and she teaches me the latest dance steps. Rivers End is a far cry behind Atlanta for those things.

This morning, a rumpled-but-gaily-wrapped package, looking

suspiciously like a book, sits on the coffee table next to my package for Duchess. Barry fairly dances with excitement over my present while seeming oblivious to the one for my sister. Thank goodness.

"Open it, Mama. Hurry! Miss Sadie helped me pick it out, and Ozzie helped wrap it."

We sit on the old green davenport, avoiding the spot where the broken spring pokes through. Barry bounces on the cushion next to me while I slowly open his present, savoring each wrinkle in the paper as I imagine the two little boys, intent on their surprise. It *is* a book and one I've been dying to read—a leather-bound collection of H. G. Wells' short stories. But the price ... my heart squeezes. It was $2.35. My boy's lightweight piggybank comes to mind, and guilt over the cost nearly steals my joy.

I turn and gaze on my precious boy, his cute face blurring as my eyes fill. "Oh, Barry. You took the money you've been saving for your airplane, didn't you, sugar?"

He fidgets, staring at his toes. "It's from both me and Miss Sadie, Mama." His little brow puckers. "You like it, don't you?"

I hug my little man, the book sandwiched between us. Somehow, I'll find a way to get him that airplane for Christmas. "I love it. I've been wanting it for so long. We can read it together." I kiss his cheek. "Thank you, and I'll be sure to thank Miss Sadie too. Now, we need to hurry and eat our pancakes. It's almost time for you to leave for school, and I need to get to work in the grocery."

Before we go downstairs to eat, I grab the parcel for my sister off the coffee table. I need that money more than ever.

Helen Ivey wrings her hands as Cal rings up her groceries. Poor as Job's turkey, the years of working beside her husband on their hardscrabble farm have stolen her beauty. In a threadbare dress made from a White Lily flour sack, she looks rail thin, and worry lines her face. Stringy, dishwater blonde hair, parted in the middle and pulled back into a bun at the nape of her neck, does nothing to flatter her. She'd only been a year ahead of me in school but now looks twenty years older.

With a nod acknowledging my arrival, Cal finishes tallying up her flour, cornmeal, and sugar, licks the end of a short, stubby pencil he keeps behind his ear, and writes her total in the ledger. With the *fwop* of the ledger book closing, I see dollar signs winging their way out the door. Grunting, Cal squats and lifts Helen's fifty-pound bag of flour to carry it out to her old rusty Chevy truck, parked in front. I don't know how he can carry that weight. He's so skinny, if he stood sideways and stuck out his tongue, he'd look like one of those new-fangled zippers.

While he makes three trips helping her, I grind chuck for hamburger and ponder our policy of extending credit. It's how business has always been done here, and most customers pay their bills on a monthly basis. However, Helen's account is in arrears. How much I'm not sure but plan to find out as soon as Cal returns inside. Wondering how many others have slipped into that state, I toss another few chunks of beef into the grinder and crank the handle, letting the grindings fall onto a sheet of butcher paper.

I had Cal take over most of the grocery's business for me when I gave birth to Barry. That included doing the books. Since he'd worked for years for first Big Jim then Jimmy and had always been trustworthy, it had been a relief not to have to do the math. Numbers stifle my creativity.

I lay the ground chuck in one-pound, loaf-shaped lumps like a mountain range in the meat case, putting a sprig of parsley between them to mark the pound increments. After I wash my hands to get rid of the fat and the smell of raw meat, I jot a note on the blackboard for Cal to cut half a dozen steaks for the bank president's housekeeper. They must be having a dinner party. He's the only person in Rivers End who ever orders steak.

After a quick survey of the cooler, I add another note about the need for a hog butchering. A lone smoked ham hangs from the overhead rack. Later, I'll go over to the train station and use Wade's telephone to call in an order to my distributor for the other things we need.

When the front door next opens, Cal makes a show of holding it for Myrtle Davis, our town librarian, followed by Ida Clare Mobley. Both ladies nod to Cal and make their way to different aisles to shop. Myrtle looks smart this morning in a bright red blouse beneath her suit jacket. She always adds a bit of dazzle and pizzazz to the library, and the color helps disguise the threadbare condition of her jacket's elbows. Ida Clare wears her daily uniform of a brown skirt and white blouse. If a stranger were to see them, between the two, they'd pick Ida Clare to be the librarian.

Smiling at that thought, for Ida Clare dislikes reading, I take a position behind the meat counter while Cal works the front, lifting, carrying out, and loading groceries. The farm wives love his service. Even though many of them are stronger than he is, a few actually simper as they follow him. Silly women. I never can understand why they hide their strengths.

One of that ilk is Nellie Taggart, who comes in pulling her son's little red wagon. Its high wooden sides make it easy to carry grocery bags the two blocks home. She owns the boarding house where Sadie lives.

While Nellie stops at the door to chat with Cal, I begin stacking a display of Campbell's Soup cans near the front of the store. It's always been a tradition at Parker's to have an owner's birthday special, and mine is Campbell's Soup—three cans for thirty cents. I already have the first row set in a two-foot circle when a shadow falls across my shoulder.

"Now, missy, I'll handle this." Looking down his nose, Cal stands over me. "I was a-plannin' the special on sugar. Why don't you go write your little household hints column whilst I take care of it? I know the ladies always look forward to reading those."

What they look forward to is seeing if I use their tidbit of advice and their name in print when I give them credit for it. Cal's attitude is another matter. No doubt, in his mulish mind, Jimmy is still his boss. My Jimmy has been dead for eight years. Why do men insist on living in the past? He might even consider Big Jim the boss.

That's going to change right now.

From my position kneeling on the floor, I peer up at him. "Cal, this is the *owner's* birthday special. I'm the owner. It's my birthday. I'll decide on the special."

He throws up his hands. "Now, missy, don't go gettin' your feathers ruffled. Didn't mean nothin' by it."

Did too. I take a deep breath. "I chose Campbell's Soup because it's a cheap meal, quick and easy. And more nutritious than sugar." Why am I explaining to this man?

He folds his arms. "Might be, but sugar's a necessity for pickling."

He thinks I'm a Dumb Dora. "Pickling's over for this year, Cal."

He chews on that for a moment. I know that mind of his. He's searching its empty space for another argument. Not finding one, he harrumphs. "I'm going to cut those steaks. Clearly, you don't need me to stack cans."

"Now you're on the trolley, Cal." I *don't* need him, although I could have used the opportunity to ask about—I rise to my feet. "Cal, how far in arrears is Helen Ivey?"

The electric saw grinding through meat and bone drowns out his answer.

Well, I can outwait Cal Llewellyn. I sit on the floor again, returning to my birthday sale display. I reach for another case of soup when a foot plants itself right next to me. I jump and nearly knock over my tower of cans.

"Maggie Parker, what are you doing sitting on the floor like a sla—"

"Don't you go there, Big Jim. I don't want to hear it."

Wearing gray slacks and a tweed jacket, my father-in-law is putting on airs. Trying to impress that lawyer? My stomach clenches.

"Well, somebody better say it. If you're going to be on your hands and knees, it should be on your own kitchen scrubbing the floor and not in public. It isn't fitting." He slaps a folded newspaper in front of my face. My column in the *Farm Whistler*. "And neither is this drivel. Why do you have to go stirring up women like this? I swear, you don't have enough brains to give yourself a headache."

I count to ten like Daddy always taught me before I turn my tongue loose. "Because it's better for a woman to work than have her children go hungry. How would Barry eat if I didn't work?"

"That don't carry water. Y'all know full well we'd feed you." He looks around the store, then leans in close. "I'm warning you, Maggie. You stop writing like some Bolshevik Communist. Otherwise, you can vacate this store and move to California where they tolerate anarchy. Now … where's Cal, and why aren't there any sale posters in the window?"

Big Jim changes the subject faster than green grass through a goose. I bite my cheek and count. "I've got Cal cutting steaks for Malcom Connor."

"You shouldn't coddle the help, Maggie. He can do this work as well as cut the meat. I swear, you aren't fit for employing anyone but a housekeeper or a cook."

Why Cal stays loyal to Big Jim defies logic. Why I even *tolerate* him defies logic. If it weren't for Barry and Faylene, my sweet mother-in-law, he'd be banned from the store. "Is there a reason you came in here, beyond expressing your opinion of what I write and the way I run *my* store?"

"Your store?" Suddenly, he's trembling like the devil's on his tail. "*Your* store?" His face turns redder with each syllable. "Parker's has been in my family for three generations, girlie."

"Kindly lower your voice."

My own face heats as Myrtle rounds the end of an aisle and glares at Big Jim. She looks ready to come to my defense when the door opens and Doc's wife, Clara, enters with a wave. "Happy birthday, Maggie."

"Thank you." As she joins Myrtle, I rise and turn my attention back to Big Jim. I stand straight, as close to nose-to-nose with my father-in-law as I can be with the six-inch difference in our heights. Unfortunately, this time my mouth overrides my brain. "I'm well aware of the lineage of this store. I'm also aware that you're retired, and my late husband left it to me."

The word *loophole* jumps out at me from yesterday's note. My stomach sours.

His mouth opens, then clamps shut. His brows dip to meet the bridge of his beezer. Any lower and his eyebrows could shake hands with his nose hairs. Big Jim is sore in need of Rivers End's sole barber, Asa Hopper.

Big Jim's eyes narrow. "Maggie, I'm warning you. You'd better stop this trash"—he throws the paper at my feet—"and think about doing your duty to your family." He stalks out the front door.

My duty? I stand there, staring at his retreating back. I swanny, if it weren't still morning, I'd think Big Jim is ossified, but he never imbibes before five o'clock. He's got his nerve. My son is healthy, clothed and shod, and well-fed. Why, I even keep Big Jim and Faylene in groceries without charging them.

Myrtle and Clara rush over. "Forget that old goat, Maggie-girl." Clara pats my shoulder. "We women think you're a wonderful example."

From the checkout counter, Nellie Taggart glares at us. Her mouth draws into a pucker as tight as the permanent wave curls in her hair. She picks up her four bags of groceries and sets them in her little red wagon.

I rub my nose to hide my smile. "I don't think Nellie shares your good opinion of me, Clara."

"Aw, she's an old Mrs. Grundy, stuck in the last century. Did you know that Nellie threw tomatoes at Sadie when she marched for the suffragettes?"

"Really?" I can't imagine priggish Nellie Taggart throwing tomatoes at all. I knew Sadie had a part in the suffragette movement, but Nellie opposing it? Sadie never told me that. I have to wonder if Nellie's husband knew about the tomato incident. He was sweet on Sadie at one time.

"Did Sadie retaliate?"

Clara laughs. "Maggie-girl, you should have seen her. Sadie never flinched. With tomato dripping down her chin, she held her head high and continued marching." She looks over her shoulder, then back at me. "Ah, but then they turned around to make another circuit, and when she passed Nellie, she swung her sign to her other shoulder and smacked the old bat upside the head. Nellie went down like a felled tree." Clara bends over laughing and slaps her knee.

When I can catch my breath, I ask, "Then why does Nellie rent to Sadie?"

"Her husband made her. Nellie's always been a judgmental gossip. It's my opinion her husband looks up to Sadie for taking her down a peg." Clara touches a hankie to the corners of her eyes. "Can you imagine the atmosphere there? I declare, they almost don't need electricity."

I'm glad to know some of the ladies support me. I get enough grief from Big Jim. After bidding Clara a good morning, I return to my project. When my birthday special display is finished and towering eye level, Cal's wife, Anna, arrives for work. She's been with us part time for about a year and gives me a little more freedom for writing. Though tall and angular like her husband, Anna puts me in mind of a mouse. Her nose even twitches when she thinks. I assign her the task of the special poster for the window. She's good with things like that.

I wave goodbye and head out to see my mother-in-law. Faylene's had a cold, and I worry about her. She'd been a lively woman when I first met her, but right after Jimmy's and my wedding, she went to New York City to visit her sister, not hearing there was the polio epidemic. Rural Georgia tends to be behind in receiving national news. Now, let there be a locust infestation, and we hear the first chirrup. In any case, Faylene caught the polio, and now the poor dear is confined to a wheeled chair.

Their house on Lingering Shade Lane, a fifteen-minute walk from Main Street, is my favorite in all of Rivers End. It has a wide porch that wraps around three sides of the house, shading the windows from the hot sun. Big Jim needs to freshen up the white paint, but its shutters are still a beautiful dark green.

Clutching the mums and purple pigweed I'd got Ida Clare's permission to cut on my way, I knock on the front door. Perhaps Faylene can give me some insight into what Big Jim is planning. They say forewarned is forearmed, and I need as much arming as I can get.

CHAPTER 4

When no one answers the door, I open it a crack and lean my head inside. By the savory aroma of pork chops drifting into the foyer, Faylene's maid, Bessie Mae, is in the kitchen. The smell makes my stomach rumble, and my taste buds stand at attention, reminding me it's noon.

"Yoo-hoo, Mama Faylene? Bessie Mae? It's me, Maggie."

"Out here, sugar." Faylene's voice, soft and lyrical, floats from the back of the house. I pass through the foyer and out to the sunroom, where she spends her days. Much of the house is no longer available to my mother-in-law, being stuck as she is in that wheel chair. When she arrived home from New York, Big Jim turned the front parlor into a bedroom for her. He still uses the master bedroom upstairs.

"I brought some flowers to brighten your day." Handing them to her, I bend and kiss her cheek.

"Thank you, dear. Bessie Mae? Will you please put these in some water?"

The cheerful colored woman comes from the kitchen, greets me, and takes the flowers. Her dress, a green, flowered cast-off of Mama Faylene's, pulls tight across her ample bosom beneath the white bib apron. "My, my, these are a welcome sight, Miss Magnolia." Bessie Mae never uses nicknames. "I'll put 'em in water."

I pull a chair up next to my mother-in-law, noting her pallor. "How's your cold, Mama Faylene?"

At fifty-two, she is still a lovely woman. Though her legs are puny from the polio, her arms are firm, and her face remains unwrinkled. Bessie Mae still fixes Faylene's hair in a Gibson girl style. It's out of date but suits her. Today, she's wearing a yellow, low-waisted dress with a V-neckline that ends in a soft bow. The color accentuates her paleness. Some Southern women still hold to the ideal of pure white skin, but I don't. A little sun gives a healthy glow.

"It's much better. Nearly gone, dear."

"Even so, you need some sunshine." I get up and go to the back door. I tap my foot, thinking, as I stare at the three steps down to the lawn. The loading ramp my supplier uses for his truck comes to mind. I return to my seat.

"I know just the thing. I'm going to make you a ramp that Bessie Mae and I can use to wheel you down to the lawn and back up when you've had enough fresh air."

Her eyes light up. "Maggie, dear, I'd purely love that. I haven't seen my flowers in forever. Bessie Mae is"—she lowers her voice—"getting too old to tend the garden, and you know Big Jim won't touch it. I'm sure it's languishing for lack of attention."

I don't see how she could do any gardening from her wheeled chair, and that just breaks my heart. "Then Barry and I shall take on that duty. We'll make it a lovely place for you to sit."

"I'd be beholden, sugar."

Now, how to broach the subject I came over to discuss? Head on is usually best. "Mama Faylene, Big Jim is on me to sell the grocery. Do you have any idea why?"

She blinks and tilts her head, considering. Finally, she shrugs. "I can't imagine why. Parker's has been his pride forever." She clears her throat. "I know how he feels about you running the store, Maggie. It's not personal, only because you're a woman, you know."

Not personal? It's about as personal as it can get. Bless her heart, Faylene doesn't understand. I glance at her. She's wearing a sarcastic smirk. Or perhaps she does.

"You can outsmart him, dear. I have faith in you."

I'm glad someone does. Bessie Mae returns with the flowers and Faylene's dinner. I leave her to it and follow Bessie Mae back to the kitchen.

"How is Mama Faylene's health? I'm concerned she's not getting any exercise."

Bessie Mae turns on the water and soaks a dishrag. "Her doctor done tole me how to move her legs to keep from getting them blood clots, and I does it every day. Twice, morning and evening, Miss Magnolia. I ain't letting my Miss Faylene get none of them clots."

Bessie Mae had been Faylene's nursemaid and then, when she grew up, her maid. She loves my mother-in-law like she's her own child.

"You know if anything goes amiss, you can send for me. I'm not sure ..."

Bessie Mae nods and lowers her voice. "I knows what you're about to say, Miss Magnolia. I don't trust Mr. Parker any further than I can throw him."

I reach over and squeeze her hand. "I know you'd defend Miss Faylene with your life, and we both love you for it. But you let me know if I need to come for *any* reason. Including if Big Jim gives you any grief."

"Yes, ma'am, I surely will."

"It's your bid, Maggie. Where are you, girl?" Sadie taps her fingers against her teacup, her normal patience deserting her. When we decided to learn bridge, the new card game sweeping the country, she took to it like a pig to swill—not a flattering analogy but apt. Under normal circumstances, I struggle with the bidding. Tonight, I'm the hostess, and Sadie's my partner. Problem is, I've got trouble on my mind.

In the space of just a week, Big Jim has sent me a second letter. Sometimes I wish he would talk face-to-face, but he'd have to be here to do that, and he's always over in Jesup or somewhere. He's been rebuking me for every sin imaginable since the day Jimmy died. He blames me for that too. Says since I nursed Sadie through the Spanish flu at our place, that weakened Jimmy. The man is crazy. My husband died in a different influenza epidemic, two years later. But this new note carries an ominous threat to take Barry away from me. I'm not sure if he can actually do it or not, but the very thought immobilizes me.

"I'm sorry. One diamond."

"Maggie." Ida Clare drops a sugar cube into her tea and stirs it. "You'd have to say two diamonds. I bid one spade."

Play I can do, but this part confuses me. "I swanny, I wonder if I'll ever cotton onto this bidding. Okay, two diamonds."

Bobby Mobley, Ida Clare's irascible husband, harrumphs. "Is that how many tricks you can take, or how many diamonds you've got in your hand, Maggie?"

It had been Bobby's idea to learn to play bridge. Poor man can't find another male who wants to learn, so he's stuck with us, at least until he talks Beau Hampton, our pharmacist, into it.

Ida Clare swats his hand. "I'd be careful if I were you, Bobby. You're the same sex as Big Jim, and right about now, she's not too partial to him."

Sadie wins the bid, and we play out the hand. Ida Clare and Bobby win, probably due to my bidding, and as they leave, she promises next time we'll change partners.

Sadie stays to help me wash up the dishes. "Unburden yourself. What's weighing on you, girl?"

I dip a teacup into the sudsy water, and thankful to share the load of worry, let it spill out. "Big Jim is threatening to take Barry away from me. Tried to say I wasn't providing a good home for him." I hand her the cup to dry. "I'm doing as well as anyone else, aren't I, Sadie?"

She snorts. "Of course, you are. He's a blowhard, trying to make himself sound important. He just wants y'all out of the store and taking over his responsibility for Faylene. Have you figured out what takes him over to Jesup all the time?" She reaches for the last plate and dries it as I empty the water from the dishpan.

"No, I haven't bothered. I don't rightly care. It's nicer when he's gone."

Big Jim travels a lot and always has. When Jimmy first took over the store, his daddy did the buying from farmers and the like. After he retired completely, he kept up the travel routine, although I have no intention of asking why so long as he keeps out of my business.

Sadie folds the dishtowel and lays it on the counter. "It's such a shame, the polio leaving Faylene dependent on a husband who doesn't have a compassionate bone in his body. Did I ever tell you I was sweet on him once?"

My mouth drops open in my shock. "I swanny, you never told me that."

"He was a handsome man back then before his narrow, pig-headed views overshadowed his looks." She tilts her head and peers at me. "You sure you want to hear this ancient history?"

"I'm looking for anything that might help me understand him." And build a defense. We sit at the kitchen table.

"Do you know the story of when Mr. Sam—I didn't know then he was the bank's president—found me and took me in?" Sadie's mouth turns up on one side in a little smirk. "His missus decided it was their Christian duty to educate me. Had she told him I needed to fly to the moon, he'd have agreed. He loved her so much, he couldn't say *no* to her. Anyway, I was saying, Big Jim was a looker back then. I caught his eye at school one day, but as soon as he opened his mouth, I saw the light and skedaddled."

"What did he say?"

I love Sadie's indignant snort. "He asked me why I was there. Said girls, especially savages, didn't have the brains to get an 'edgymacation,' as he put it."

I clap my hand over my mouth to keep my horror from spilling out.

"A lot of men still have that same feeling, Maggie. Especially in hard times like these."

The outside door buzzer makes us both jump. She turns wide eyes to me. "You expecting someone?"

I shake my head. "It's nearly nine o'clock. Come with me."

We go open the street door. There on the sidewalk stands my sister.

"Duchess?" My tall and willowy, blonde, beautiful sister. The daughter on whom our mother pinned all her hopes. The sister who married money. The one who could take Mama back to the world of plantation owner. The one who didn't disappoint.

"Well, don't just stand there staring at me like a fence post. Bring me inside, Magnolia. Hello, Sadie."

And the sister I love. She looks wonderful, although a little pale. Her navy-blue suit has a smart peplum, and a matching hat sits at a jaunty angle, tipping low over her right eyebrow. I rush to pull her into a hug. "Where's Mr. Alden?" I look over her shoulder for her husband.

"He's ... he's ...." She bursts into tears. "He ... he ..." She clouds up and lets loose a gullywusher, sobbing hard.

I don't know what it is, but it's bad. Duchess never loses her composure. "Sadie, help me get her inside. You take her. I'll get her suitcase."

Duchess' hand waves over her shoulder. "There's ... there's"—her breath stutters—"mo-mo-more."

Lashed to an old, beat-up Dodge at the curb are four steamer trunks. How long is Duchess staying? A weed of apprehension sprouts in my belly. I follow her and Sadie up the stairs. I'll deal with the trunks later. Right now, I want some answers. Like where is her new Cadillac, not to mention her chauffeur? And for that matter, whose old motor car is she driving?

I leave her suitcase in the hallway and bring a box of those new Kleenex disposable hankies. Duchess sounds like she'll need them. Sadie puts on the teakettle while I sit beside my sister.

"Duchess, what's wrong? Why are you here alone?"

Without a pause in her bawling, she reaches for her handbag, pulls out an envelope, and hands it to me. With a frown, I open it. It's filled with money. Understanding dawns. "For my jewelry?"

My sister nods and hiccups. I have to know how much. Lord, forgive me, I pull out the money and count it. It's enough. I exhale a grateful breath. I'll be able to pay the taxes and get Barry that toy airplane. I return the money to the envelope and set it on the coffee table. I need to focus on Duchess. I can't understand why bringing the jewelry money is making her cry.

Sadie brings in a tea tray, bless her heart. She knows how to dispense comfort. She sets it down on the side table and quietly leaves. I'll see her in the morning. Right now, I need to get to the bottom of my sister's crying jag.

"Duchess, honey, can you compose yourself and tell me what's wrong?"

"Oh, Maggie, it's terrible, and I'm so sorry it ... it ... it happened on your birthday." She wails. "My d-d-dear husband is g-gone." She buries her head in my shoulder and sobs.

"Gone? Sugar, what do you mean *gone*?" Mr. Alden adores, no, worships my sister. "Darlin', he wouldn't leave you." I hold her, patting her back for a long time, my mind whirling, trying to think of where Mr. Alden could have gone *to*.

Barry pads into the living room, rubbing his eyes. "Mama? Is that my Auntie Duchess?"

"Yes, sugar, but she's not—"

Duchess sits up, leaning forward. "Is that my sweet Barry Boy?" She pulls one of the Kleenex hankies from the box and dabs her eyes. She takes a deep, shuddering breath. Barry runs and leaps into her lap. He throws his little arms around her neck and squeezes her. For all her sophistication, my dear sister adores her little nephew and doesn't mind a bit if his affection renders her disheveled.

"Don't be sad, Auntie Duchess. Mama will make it all better."

"I know she will, sugar. That's why I came here the first moment

I could."

Barry looks around. "Where's my Uncle Will?"

Tears well in my sister's eyes again, but she holds them back for Barry's sake. "He's ... he's with Jesus, darlin'."

Barry leans back and puts his hands on the sides of her face. "Like my daddy?"

My fingers fly to my lips to smother a cry. *No!* But Duchess nods.

"What happened?" My words come out in a whisper, and my own tears sting the back of my eyes.

Duchess gives a tiny shake of her head and kisses Barry's nose. "I'm sure he's teaching your daddy to play golf up there, don't you think? Hand me my teacup, sweetheart. My throat is parched. Did you know I drove all the way here from Atlanta? All by myself?"

Barry, his eyes open wide, carefully hands her the cup and saucer. "You drove? I didn't know you knew how."

"I don't like to, but I know how."

Barry runs to the window, pushes the drapes aside, and looks out, but quickly turns back. "I only see a Dodge. Where's your big Cadillac?"

"I drove the Dodge. It's ... it's borrowed." Sister sniffs.

Time to intervene. "Barry, sugar, you have school tomorrow. Auntie Duchess will be staying for a while, I'm sure. You can see her tomorrow afternoon. Scoot on back to bed now."

He kisses us both and goes to his room. I swanny, he's got the understanding of an adult. Not a peep of objection out of him. That's not to say he isn't all boy and gets into his share of mischief, but he's intuitive.

We sip tea in silence for a few moments. If her husband is really dead, why is she here? She could have mailed the money. I mean, I'm glad to see her, but—I glance at her. She doesn't know how to do anything but host teas. What am I going to do with her?

Finally, I set my cup down and take my sister's hands. "Now, tell me what happened. Is it true? He ... he's really ... dead?"

Duchess nods, dabbing her eyes. "Sister, he took his own life."

I can't process what she's saying. It's unimaginable. "What do you mean?"

"He killed himself."

"How? I mean ... why?"

She wrings her hands. "He lost all our money. It's all gone. But I would have loved him anyway, Maggie." Her tears spill over. "He didn't have to ... do that." She wads her tissue against her nose. She clenches her teeth, and she narrows her eyes. "I can't believe he had the audacity to kill himself. It's so humiliating. But ... but ... Oh, Maggie. I miss him."

"Of course, you do, but how did he lose all your money? I can't fathom it."

"The stock market crashed. Didn't you know?"

I shake my head. I don't know much about the stock market at all. "Things are slower here, Sister, you know that."

"I guess I do." She sighs deeply, so deep I want to cry for her. "The bottom fell out of the market two weeks ago, on your birthday. I managed to sell your jewelry a few days before that, thank the good Lord."

"That saved the grocery for me, Duchess. I can't thank you enough." Now I feel guilty for my earlier thoughts. "When ..." I lick my lips, hating to form the words. "When did Will ..."

"The next morning. He must have stewed all night long. His assistant found him in his office. He"—she shivers—"shot himself." Her lips thin to a narrow line, marring her beauty. "He couldn't face me, the coward."

"Now, Duchess, you don't mean that."

"I do." She frowns, and her lips turn down, then a second later, her face crumples. "No, I don't." Her eyes flood and her nose runs. I hand her the box of tissues. One by one, she pulls them out, mopping her unending tears. Poor thing.

For the next hour, she cries and sips tea.

While she's crying and sipping, my mind is trying to get a handle on what this stock market crash might mean for Rivers End. The South has been poor since the War of Northern Aggression, and the only markets folks hereabouts invest in are farmers' markets. But I remember my daddy talking about a trickling effect or some such thing. I guess we're about to find out.

Finally, Duchess' tears begin to slow. Sure she'll collapse any moment, I steer her to my bedroom. My sweet Barry has brought her suitcase into my room and laid it on the other twin bed.

"Duchess, let's get you in bed."

"Can I take a bath?"

"Are you sure you're up to it? Remember, mine isn't like yours in Atlanta." She has a real bathroom—or had one. Mine is the tin tub we fill in the kitchen.

With a sad little smile, she nods. "I forgot that."

I help her undress, then I tuck her in the other twin bed—her bed now.

"Thank you, Maggie. I didn't know what to do other than come to you. I've lost everything but my clothes. I even had to borrow the car to get here. Can I stay?" Bless her heart, she's like a lost lamb without Mr. Alden.

"Well, of course, sugar." I hear my tight budget squeal, but this *is* my sister, so hang the budget. "You don't even need to ask."

We'll manage ... somehow.

CHAPTER 5

"Magnolia? Are you still awake?"

My sister's whisper from the other twin bed calls up memories of our childhood. I smile though she can't see me in the darkness. "I am now."

"Do you remember when we were little, how we'd sneak out the window at night and sit on the roof and dream?"

"Mm-hmm." Sleep pulls at me, and I struggle to hear her.

"You always dreamed of being a writer, and now you are."

"A household tips column and a few short stories. Not much to speak of."

"But you're a writer, and you're working on a novel. You shared some of it with me. Although it's pretty controversial, it's good. You're accomplishing your dream."

I'm wide awake now. I've always wanted my big sister to be proud of me, and hearing her say it is so gratifying. I bunch my pillow under my head. "Women are working in every city in America, and they want to read about other women who work. I try to encourage them."

Duchess sighs. "I know. I'm just saying, be careful."

The moon is bright, and tree shadows dance across the wall above Sister's bed. "I'm used to raising eyebrows. I've been doing it since the day I was born. Or at least soon after."

Sister giggles. "You surely have. I remember one time Mama had you all dolled up in a frilly dress with a pink bow in your hair. She turned her back to get her hat and pocketbook, and you tore that bow out of your hair, ripped the dress off, and had overalls donned before she could stop you."

I dislike disappointing anyone, but I'm not cut from the same cloth as my sister. I fidget in frills. "Poor Mama. I was such a disappointment to her. It's a good thing she had you first, or you might not be here."

"She was still proud of you. And Daddy? Why, he thought you set the moon and stars."

I roll over onto my side, propping one hand under my head. "Oh, sugar, *you* were his delight. Do you remember when you first began playing the piano for church? Daddy puffed his chest out so far, I thought his suspenders would snap. He kept telling everyone, as if they didn't know, you were his daughter." I also remember being jealous of her and pulling the ribbon out of her hair.

The moon hides behind a cloud, and I have to strain to make out my sister. She's on her side and facing the wall. Did she go to sleep on me? I lay my head down on my pillow and roll onto my back, closing my eyes.

"Sister, I'm scared."

Duchess? Scared? I can hardly believe it. What would I see written on her face if I turned on the light? "Of what?"

"I've never had a dream like yours. I don't know how to *do* anything but play the piano and serve tea. How am I going to earn my keep and not be a drain on you?"

My big sister by twenty-two months is now my dependent. I swanny, if Mama were still alive, I'd wring her neck for not teaching Duchess anything but manners. But it's never too late. I throw back the covers and climb out of my bed and sit on hers.

"Roll over. I'll rub your back. That's how you used to put me to sleep when we were little, remember?"

She turns onto her stomach, her arms cradling her head on the pillow. "I do. You'd be so wound up from helping Daddy birth a calf or something you couldn't fall asleep."

"Now *you* need to forget your worries and go to sleep. I'll find something you can do, and I'll teach you the rest. You're my sister, and I love you." *So very much*.

She sighs a goodnight, and it isn't long before her breathing is even and steady. I start to crawl back in bed when I remember I forgot to bring up water to wash with in the morning. I check Barry's room first to see if he has his, which he does. Down in the kitchen, I set the pitcher in the sink, and working the pump handle, I fill it with water, then take it back up to the bedroom.

Finally, in my own bed, I pray for the good Lord to help me. I can't for the life of me imagine Duchess working. However, she's an intelligent woman and can learn. I hope. As I drift off to sleep, my last thought is the extra set of hands could be a blessing. I might find a little more time to work on my novel.

The next morning, Duchess is already up when I awake. That's a surprise. I pour some water into the washbowl and clean my face. While I'm washing, I hear muffled crying in the living room. I hurry to finish and go comfort her. There she is with another box of Kleenex and a pile of used tissues beside her. Did I tell her those cost sixty-five cents a box? That's more than the cost of ten pounds of sugar. Even if I am just trying them out for the store. I put my arm around her and pull her close, waiting until her tears finally slow.

"Duchess, honey, my heart's breaking for you." I take the box of Kleenex and hand her a soft cotton hankie. "Why don't you come into the kitchen, and I'll show you how to make coffee?" Doing something will take her mind of Mr. Alden.

She sniffs. "Okay. I've never made coffee. We always had ... had—" A wail takes the place of whoever, or whatever, she was about to say. She holds the hankie beneath her nose and sniffles.

Barry pads into the kitchen, rubbing the sleep from his eyes. "Morning. Auntie Duchess? Are you still sad?" My little man puts his arms around her, trying to pat her back. Sister dries her eyes and bends down to kiss his cheek. Barry's good for her. I'll have to see that she spends time with him.

He gives me my good morning sugar and a hug. "Flapjacks or oatmeal this morning, son?"

He glances at my sister. "I want whatever Auntie Duchess wants."

"Sugar, you need more than toast, and you don't drink coffee." I bend to whisper to him. "Besides, with Auntie feeling so sad, she isn't eating." Duchess has lost weight. More than she needs to. "Let's see if we can entice her with a bowl of oatmeal. Maybe if we put a little maple syrup on it, she'll like it." I wink at him.

"Like a duck does a June bug," he says, spinning in a circle.

With her nose wrinkled up, Duchess looks dubious but shrugs. "I'll try it for Barry."

"Well, first let's start the coffee. Barry, wash your face and get dressed. Duchess, fill the coffee pot two-thirds full with water." I put wood in the firebox and stoke the flame. How I wish for a gas stove, but there isn't money for one. I suppose I wouldn't know how to cook on it, anyway. After adjusting the draft control, I pull out a can of Maxwell House from the cupboard. "Put the pot on the stove, and put in three scoops of grounds."

Duchess frowns in concentration as she works the pump handle. Just then, Barry hollers for me.

"Get the coffee going. I'll be right back."

I go help my boy, who's gotten himself tangled in his shirt. I try not to laugh as he twists, struggling to get the shirt over his head. Angry tears of frustration fall down his cheeks.

"Hang on, sugar. The problem is this shirt's too small now. I'm afraid it's time to send it on to someone else. You're growing so fast, I can hardly keep up with you." I kiss his cheek.

Duchess screeches. Barry and I look at each other for a second. His eyes grow wide, and his lips stretch. "Uh-oh."

Barry grabs another shirt, and we both run downstairs to the kitchen, where Duchess is indeed in trouble. The lid isn't on the coffee pot, and it's spouting coffee and grounds all over the stove. Hopefully, the mess hasn't drowned the fire. I grab a towel, pull the pot off the stove, and set it on the table. "Where's the lid, Duchess? Why didn't you put it on?"

She's wide-eyed like the engine's running but nobody's steering. "Don't you have to let it breathe like wine?"

I cover my mouth. I don't want to hurt her feelings by laughing at her, bless her heart. "No, it doesn't need to breathe. Let's clean this up and start over. It's my fault for leaving you." I glance at Barry, still clutching his shirt. "Why don't you help your nephew get his shirt on?"

After his shirt is on, Barry hugs her. "I'm sorry, too, Auntie. Mama, you do the oatmeal, and I'll make coffee." He jabs his thumb in his chest. "I know how, you know."

Yes, he does indeed. My little man is quite resourceful. After breakfast—which thankfully, Duchess eats—and Barry leaves for school, I decide to teach my sister the rudiments of housekeeping. I hand her a broom and dustpan since quite a bit of coffee grounds ended up on the floor.

"I had a hard time getting the grounds through that little hole, Maggie. How do you manage it?"

"What are you talking about?"

She gets the pot to show me. I declare, she didn't put the grounds *in* the basket but into the stem of the percolator basket, which deposited them into the water. "Honey, that was cowboy coffee you made. Sweep up the floor, and I'll show you how to do it right."

Watching Duchess sweep makes me want to grab the broom and do it myself, but she has to learn. We don't have any servants and aren't likely to get any in the foreseeable future.

"Sister, don't swish the broom so high after each pass. You're only sending the dust into the air." I take the broom from her and demonstrate. "Like this, dear."

I hand it back. She wrinkles her nose at me and sweeps the coffee grounds in my direction with a fast, lifting motion. Bits hit my apron, and I stare at her grin.

"Why you ..." I grab the broom and send the grounds back at her.

Soon we're laughing and battling like we did when we were little girls having a pillow fight. Our early morning ends with her successfully making a pot of coffee. As we sip, I can tell she's proud of herself.

Once we're dressed for the day, I take her down to the grocery and make her familiar with the layout. As we walk down the aisles, Duchess frowns and worries her hankie.

"Don't fret, Sister. I have the perfect job for you. Since you're a wonderful, accomplished hostess, it's my intention to have you greet our customers and help them find what they need. That will help us compete with the larger markets over in Hazlehurst and Jesup."

My sister is the perfect one for the job. I offer up a quick prayer of thanks for God's fortuitous decision to send her to me. Even though I'm sorry for the reason, I'm really glad she's here.

She brightens. "I can do that."

The front door opens, and Nellie Taggart enters. Duchess puts her hand on my shoulders, turning me toward the office. "Now y'all go do what you do. I'll help Nellie, then memorize where everything is. This is no different than memorizing the guest list to a charity gala. Easier. For that"—she bends toward me conspiratorially—"I had to know who did what, lived where, and was related to whom, so I wouldn't seat the wrong person next to the governor or whomever."

Since it's Wednesday, I need to finish my column and turn it in. I head to the office located near the register, where I can keep one eye on Duchess and Cal through the transparent mirror I had installed four years ago.

I slip a new sheet of paper into the typewriter and begin to transpose my notes to a publishable column. The keys are tapping, and my mind is whirling when my sister catches my eye through the mirror, going to the front door. Is she leaving? I start to rise but stop when I see her open the door for Bessie Mae and Louella. My mouth drops open, and Nellie Taggart's eyebrows nearly switch places over her nose as she stares from the meat counter. Her eyes narrow, and she huffs. Her mouth is moving, and it can't be good. She doesn't think servants should even shop at the same store as her. I'd better get out there. As I open the door, I hear Duchess and pause just outside the office.

"Mrs. Taggart." Duchess drapes her arm around Nellie's shoulders. "Come see the discount we have for a few *very special* customers."

My sister amazes me how she remembers everyone in Rivers End from her few visits. She walks Nellie over to the baking aisle and leans close.

I follow but stay out of sight. I have to see what Duchess will do. And Nellie.

"I know how much baking you must do with feeding all your boarders. Just for you today, you can take two cents off any two items in this aisle."

Why, that sly thing. Duchess has disarmed Nellie. Instead of walking out in a huff, she's debating which items she'll take to save a few cents. It's worth it to keep her happy.

Back at my typewriter, I shake my head. Not here twenty-four hours, and Duchess is already sovereign of her grocery court.

CHAPTER 6

I'm taking a rare morning to work on my household hints newspaper column. I need to have several ready. If I can sell these to the Lawrenceville paper, I'll be able to bring in a little more money to offset the expense of my sister being here—although I would never say as much. She's lying on the floor, writing a letter. It reminds me of when we were schoolgirls. I hadn't realized how much I've missed her until she arrived.

Now I can't imagine being without her. In the two weeks she's been here, changes in her are blossoming. She's taken to working the grocery like Barry to fishing. Her help is invaluable. She charms the grumpiest of shoppers. Even Cal can't figure out how to tell Duchess *no*. Her presence at Thanksgiving soothed the rough waters between Big Jim and me. He hasn't cottoned on how to overcome her graciousness. And her presence has given me extra time to work on my novel. As if feeling my scrutiny, she looks up and smiles at me.

"What? Did I get ink on my nose?" She checks her hands for telltale signs.

"No." I pull my finished column from the typewriter. "Remember you met my editor, Karl, from the *Farm Whistler*? He came by yesterday to tell me he heard from Mr. Evans at the *News Standard*. He gave me an appointment to see him tomorrow afternoon. The *News Standard* is a larger paper than ours here, and it pays more. I'm hoping he'll buy my column and bedtime stories." I used the telephone at the train station earlier to make a phone call to my cousin Gracie, who lives in Lawrenceville. I asked if I can stay with her and her husband tomorrow night.

My sister folds the letter and sits up. "That's a fine idea. I haven't seen Lawrenceville in years. When do we leave?"

I shake my head. "*We* don't. I need you to stay here with Barry. He's got school."

"Oh, well, of course. I'll be glad to." She sets her pen on the coffee table, then looks me up and down. "And don't you even think of wearing one of your dresses. You'll borrow something of mine. You want to make a good impression, don't you?"

I do, and her wardrobe is way nicer than mine. "Thank you."

Duchess drags me into the bedroom and starts flinging hangers back and forth in the small closet. Her dresses are beautiful and expensive. It will be fun to wear one.

"Voilà!" She pulls out a hanger with a lovely long-sleeved dress that's deep blue with a light-tan collar and a soft, lacy necktie to offset its severity. Below the drop waist, the skirt has small pleats. Thank goodness, there's no frills.

I take it from her and hold it up in front of me. "It's perfect." My sister's face quickly changes from admiring to calamitous. "What's wrong? I don't have to wear this one."

"Oh, no, no, it isn't that. I just thought of something. What are Barry and I going to do about eating while you're gone?"

Relieved it isn't about the dress, I hang it on the back of the closet door. "You, my dear sister, are going to learn how to cook a few basics, and we're going to start with fried chicken. Come on."

"Can't I just make do with the leftovers from yesterday's chicken?"

"No, you can't. There isn't enough. I don't know why, but on Thanksgiving, we all overeat."

I pull her downstairs to the kitchen. I'd already taught her how to lay the wood and kindling in the stove, light it, and adjust the heat. She mastered it quickly, to my surprise. But then, she's very smart.

I point to a canister on the counter. "Bring the flour and the lard."

While Duchess grabs those, I take a cleaver to the chicken, laid out on the table. With a couple of hearty thwacks, the legs and thighs separate.

Duchess jumps and squeals, hiding her eyes. "That's a bit brutal, don't you think?"

"How do you expect me to fry it if it isn't cut up?"

"Well ... I thought they just came that way."

"Oh, Duchess. You gathered eggs with me back on the farm. You saw the chickens running around. When we ate Sunday dinner, didn't you realize it was one of our own?"

Her eyes widen, and her mouth forms a perfect O. "You mean those were—"

I suck in my lips for a moment. I swanny, my sister is so naive. I blame Mama. "They were. Daddy wrung their necks, and I plucked them so Sally could cut them up and cook them."

Duchess puts her hand on the side of her face. "Well, my, my. I never made the association." She laughs. "I must have had my head in the sand or the clouds. So what's next?"

The one thing my sister isn't, is self-absorbed. "Normally, I marinate the chicken overnight in buttermilk, but we don't have time. I'll add the buttermilk to the egg. Then I put some salt, pepper, and garlic powder in the flour and mix it up."

Duchess makes notes on a recipe card. I'm glad she's taking an interest in cooking. It will help me if she can do some of the meal preparations.

After I season the flour, I pick up a thigh. "Take a leg, dip it in the egg wash, then the cornmeal." I show her how, then indicate she should take a turn.

Concentrating on the chicken, Sister wrinkles her nose, and using two fingers, picks the leg up by the tip of the bone. Her hold is so delicate the leg slips from her fingers and lands with a splash into the buttermilk.

"It's a bit slippery, isn't it?" Her face is puckered up in distaste, making me wish I owned a Brownie camera. She lifts the leg out of the egg wash and sets it in the bowl of seasoned flour.

"Now coat it." I try not to roll my eyes as she dredges the chicken leg, but then she always did hate to get her hands dirty. She's got to learn, though, so instead of taking over, I stand back. "Now set it on the wax paper. When all the pieces are coated, we'll put them in the skillet."

Normally, I coat and drop the pieces right into the hot grease, but in the time it takes her to get one ready, the first piece would be done. While she finishes the preparation, I drop lard into my cast-iron skillet, letting it melt. I show her how to set the pieces of chicken into the hot grease instead of dropping them. Soon, they're sizzling away, filling the kitchen with a mouth-watering aroma. Too bad they don't look as good as they smell, but they're edible.

After a while, Duchess asks, "Is this done yet? Can we take a tea break now?" She lifts the back of her wrist to her brow in a dramatic flair.

I show her how to check a leg by piercing it with a fork. The juices run clear. "It's done. Use the tongs and set each piece on the cooling rack." Some of the coating drops off the chicken, but all in all, she's done a good job.

She stands staring at the chicken and sighs. "Well, it doesn't look as pretty as yours does, but I did it, didn't I? I actually cooked fried chicken."

Bless her heart, she's proud of herself, and I'm proud of her. "You did a credible job for the first time. I remember when Sally tried to teach me. Mine was overdone on one side and half raw on the other. She had to throw it out."

"Now what?"

"When the chicken cools, we'll put it in the icebox. Meanwhile, we'll fix a meatless loaf. You can bake it the next day. I'll be back on Saturday. You and Barry can have the chicken tomorrow at noon for dinner and then make sandwiches with the leftovers for supper. I'll mix up some batter for flapjacks and leave it in the icebox for Friday morning. Saturday, Barry likes corn flakes. You already know how to make grilled cheese sandwiches, and there's always soup. You'll be fine."

"You'll only be gone the two nights?"

Lawrenceville is a little over two hundred miles from Rivers End. "That's it." I begin to worry she might not be able to handle it, but Sadie will watch out for her, and Barry will be all right. "If you have any questions, ask Sadie."

"My nephew and I will be just fine, Magnolia. Don't you worry."

I believe her. She's discovering that she's quite capable of more than being a socialite. While she truly grieves for Mr. Alden, she's starting to like a bit of independence, and she enjoys working in the store. I only hope it's not just play to her and that she'll get tired of it.

Back in the bedroom, I try on the dress. My sister's a little taller than I am, but since hers are the new shorter styles, it doesn't matter as much. I slip it over my head, and my breath catches as the cool silk slides into place on my body like a soft summer breeze. I wink at myself. "That's puttin' on the Ritz."

"Turn around."

I pivot to find Duchess in the doorway with a bag in her hand. "You're lovely. That editor won't be able to say *no*."

"I hope not, but I'm depending on my writing and not my looks."

"Oh, I didn't mean it that way, honey. But that color makes you glow. After I take this trash out, I'll get the hat. It's a cute cloche, and you'll look so professional and up-to-date."

When she leaves to take the bag to the burn barrel in the commons yard out back, I step out of the dress and hang it up. My old broadcloth housedress sure feels rough compared to the silk. I pull out my suitcase and begin to pack.

"Help! Help! Fire!"

I run to Barry's bedroom window, which overlooks the yard. Smoke is rising from the porch. My heart beats loud in my ears. I race down the stairs and out the back door.

Sparks from the burn barrel have started a small blaze on one of the porch pillars. It's happened before, and because of that, Doc keeps a full bucket of water next to the barrel. But Duchess isn't reaching for it. She's dancing around and screaming, her hands fluttering in all directions.

The back door to Doc's house bursts open, and he runs across the yard, meeting me at the bucket. He lifts it and slings the contents on the fire, quickly extinguishing it. He refills the bucket from the yard pump and gives the pillar a second dousing for good measure.

Unfortunately, Duchess' screams bring out the neighbors too.

"It's just a small fire, no danger," I tell them. The way gossip flies in this town, if I don't stop it here and now, by tomorrow it'll be a three-alarm blaze with half the town up in smoke. "See? It's already out."

My sister, no longer screaming but clearly undone, approaches Doc. Her hair, which normally rolls away from her face in the latest style, flies about her cheeks and in her eyes. She pushes it back in a futile attempt to regain her dignity.

"Doc, thank you for saving our home. I am so sorry."

He pats her hand in his best bedside manner. "That's all right, my dear. I'm always at the ready. Why, I've watched over Maggie for years. One more of the MacBride girls won't put a quiver in my liver."

Duchess tilts her head as she tucks a strand of hair behind her ear. "I didn't realize you knew Daddy."

"I did. When the Spanish flu hit the county, I traveled a fair piece more than I do nowadays."

I look up from inspecting the pillar to see how deep the fire went. A few neighbors continue to watch them. I clear my throat. Doc glances over at me and then at their audience. He waves them away.

"Go on home now, y'all. Show's over." He winks at Duchess, then fills the bucket once more and places it next to the burn barrel.

"Next time, remember this is right here."

"Now listen, Barry." I squat in front of him. My suitcase is beside the door. I still have to don the adorable cloche Duchess is lending me. "You be a good boy for your Auntie Duchess. I'll be home Saturday afternoon."

He nods, his little face solemn. "I will, Mama, and I'll take care of her."

I hug him. I haven't spent a night away from my dear boy since he was born, but I need to do this. I kiss his cheek and rise.

Sister hands me the cloche. It's tan to match the collar and lacy tie on the dress. I set it on my head, and as I glance at myself in the mirror, I look like some rich man's wife.

"You look lovely," Duchess says.

Barry nods and grins at me. "You're beautiful, Mama."

"Well, then, I'd better be off before somebody figures out this isn't me."

He frowns. "What do you mean, Mama?"

"I simply mean this isn't the real me."

He cocks his head. "But I think you're always pretty."

I place my hand on the side of his face. "Thank you, sugar." I turn my gaze to Duchess and raise one shoulder. "Now why would a woman need any other man in her life?"

As I step out the apartment door, Duchess' arm is over Barry's shoulder, and he leans against her. If anything ever happens to me, he'll be in good hands. She adores him. They follow me downstairs.

At the outside door, a hand reaches around me and takes my suitcase. "Just where do you think you're going?"

I recognize the gruff voice immediately. "Not that it's any of your business, Big Jim, but I'm going to Lawrenceville to see the editor of a newspaper. He's interested in carrying my Helpful *Home* Hints column." I emphasize *home* so he won't start a tirade in front of Barry.

Big Jim glances at Duchess and dips his chin in acknowledgment. She raises hers. I almost feel sorry for him—almost. He doesn't know what to make of my sister.

He turns back to me. "You need—"

Wade is crossing the street, and Big Jim hushes. Wade holds out his hand. "I'll take that for Maggie. Thanks, Big Jim."

My father-in-law hasn't much choice but to release my suitcase to Wade. I stifle a grin and nod to them. "I'll be home Saturday afternoon."

Big Jim harrumphs. "Y'all been sniveling about the shortage of money, and you're spending it on a wasteful train ride?"

I have him on this one. "No, I'm not. The *News Standard* is paying for it. Tell Mama Faylene I'll see her when I get home." I take Barry's hand, and with Duchess following us, we cross to the train station. Some of the mortar has come loose from between the bricks and fallen out, giving the old place a gap-toothed appearance.

As soon as we're inside, Wade grins. "I'd like to throttle that man, but for the sake of peace, I restrained myself."

I can't help myself—laughter bubbles up. Even Barry is grinning, which is most likely the reason Wade said it.

In the station, only a couple I don't recognize occupies one of the three benches. We don't often get strangers here, and my writer's curiosity begins to give them a story. The train pulls in, so we go out to the platform. Wade has my overnight case next to the train.

"Thanks, my friend." I kiss Barry and Duchess and board the train.

It will be nice to get out of Rivers End for a change. I can't remember the last time I've been farther than Grizzles' pond. I feel quite the adventurous woman. It's a good day to pretend I don't have Big Jim's threats hanging over me. I still have no idea what loopholes he means, and his lawyer hasn't sent me a letter. Could he be bluffing? I wouldn't put it past him.

Through the window, fat clouds are playing tag across the sky.

This would be an ideal time for the dear Lord to send me some help.

Are you listening?

I need a defense against Big Jim's scheming, and if it doesn't go against God's design, the editor of the *News Standard* buying my bedtime stories and Helpful Household Hints column will help significantly. Not that I'm ungrateful for everything the Lord has done. He's done plenty, keeping body and soul together for Barry and me. So, having laid my burden at the Lord's feet, until I'm back in Rivers End, I'll forget about Big Jim. The sun is shining, the air is cool, and I'm riding on the train, which I haven't done since my honeymoon to Savannah.

The train is Scheduled to arrive in Lawrenceville at one-fifty-eight. That will give me time to freshen up at my cousin's house before my four o'clock appointment with the editor. I settle back and watch the countryside pass by.

As we're closing in on Lawrenceville, I discover somewhere during the ride, butterflies snuck onto the train and have taken up residence in my stomach.

CHAPTER 7

My cousin Gracie's house is on East Oak, a quiet street two blocks from downtown and the train station. It's a cozy, two-story bungalow, painted light gray with dark wood and green trim, the kind of house you could grow old in and never once notice you'd aged. Gracie throws open the door before I can knock and pulls me into her arms.

"Magnolia, I'm so glad to see you. It's been forever." She pushes back, holding me at arm's length, and looks me up and down. I must pass inspection, for she reels me in, squeezes once more, then releases me. "How's little Barry?"

I pick up my suitcase and follow her inside. "Growing like kudzu."

Gracie laughs as she holds the door open. "I can well imagine. He's such a cutie. Well, I know you have that appointment, so let's get you to your room to freshen up. We can catch up later, when you get back." She leads me right on through the dining room to her guest bedroom on the first floor. "The bathroom is just here, next to your room."

I peek in as she pushes the door open. I can see why she's proud of it. It has an indoor toilet and a bathtub. I can't wait to tell Barry this piece of news. Our toilet is in the courtyard outhouse, and we share it with Doc and Clara.

My jaw slowly starts to drop. "Is this new wallpaper?" I stare at a likeness of trees as tall as the wall. There is a pagoda painted around the mirror over a pedestal sink. And a Chinaman standing by one of the trees. I'm not sure I could take a bath in here without covering myself up.

"Yes. Do you like it? Britt put it up before Thanksgiving."
She rubs her fingertips over the Chinaman. Gracie always did like
bragging on her husband. Britt's in advertising for the Bona Allen
Company, and from her demeanor, it doesn't appear this stock
market crash has affected them all that much. I don't have time to
dwell on that, though, so I search for a diplomatic answer.

"I've never seen anything like it."

"Do y'all have time for a cup of coffee before you go? The
newspaper office is only around the corner from the next street
over. You can walk there in five minutes."

It might help settle my nerves. "Thank you, I'd love one."

While she makes the coffee, I wash my face, then join her in
the kitchen. It has one of those single French glass doors out to her
backyard, where dogwood, oak, and crepe myrtle compete for the
sunlight. Their leaves are starting to turn now that the nights are
getting cold. It makes a lovely backdrop for our chat comparing
life in Lawrenceville to life in Rivers End.

She's properly shocked over Mr. Alden's demise. "I simply
cannot imagine Duchess working in your grocery."

I assure her that my sister is already an asset, but all too soon,
I need to leave.

I walk over to the newspaper office, following Gracie's
directions, and arrive right on time. The office is in one large
room, not at all lavish, but it is filled with the clatter of typewriters
and ringing telephones, sounds that energize me. I sometimes wish
Jimmy had been a newspaperman because then I'd be the owner of
a paper instead of a grocery store.

A young woman sitting at a switchboard looks up as I enter.
She slides off her headset and gives me a welcoming smile. "Are
you Magnolia Parker? Mr. Evans is expecting you." She points
toward a walled-off area in the corner of the large room. The door
placard says "Editor."

I have my hand raised to knock when the door opens. Does
everyone in Lawrenceville anticipate arrivals?

A tall, middle-aged man with thin, light-brown hair and chewing on a stubby cigar nearly plows me over. "Oh, sorry." Waving a slip of paper, he looks past my shoulder. "Harris, come get this. There's a fire over at the Bona Allen tannery. Cover it." After Harris takes the assignment, Mr. Evans turns around and heads to his desk. "Well, come on in. Don't stand on ceremony. Let's see what you've got."

I suppose it's the urgent nature of the job, but are all newspapermen as gruff? I don't think I've met one yet who isn't. I hand him a copy of the *Farm Whistler* containing my column and three of my bedtime stories. I manage to speak through tense lips. "My Helpful Household Hints column runs biweekly in the *Farm Whistler* and the *Savannah Morning News*."

He slides his glasses from the top of his head to his nose, takes the paper from me, and reads. When he's done, he lays it aside. "Hattie Wakefield is retiring next month. The replacement will need to be in place soon. This Helpful Hints column would work. I'll let you know." He pushes it off the edge of the desk and onto the floor, where four other newspapers lie. Then he picks up my bedtime stories. "Now, what are these?"

"They're short stories for children. I believe the *News Standard* could sell more copies if you printed them. When times are hard economically as they are now, mothers don't have an extra twenty-five cents to buy their children a book. But if a three-cent newspaper carried bedtime stories, she'd buy it."

Mr. Evans looks over his cheaters. "That's a pretty good argument, young lady, but before I say yes, I want to test your theory. I'll buy *one* of these. I'll run it and see what happens." He leafs through the three I brought, chooses one, and then with his hands clasped on his desk, he looks me in the eye. "I've heard that you write social protest articles too. I haven't read any, but I'd be interested in seeing some." He pulls his cigar stump out of his mouth. "I'm not saying I agree or disagree with you, but controversy sells newspapers."

"I'll put one in the mail as soon as I get home. If I may ask you a question?" I pause and wait for his approval. When he nods, I ask, "Where do you stand on women working outside their homes?"

His chair creaks as he leans back. "I have a daughter who's twenty-three. If she'd gone to college like I wanted her to, she'd be a teacher. Instead, she has three children under the age of four and is exhausted, taking care of them and a husband who lost his job." He stood. "I agreed to see you because of what the editor of the *Farm Whistler* told me. I like forward thinkers."

Is that what Zeke told him about me? When he doesn't say any more, I rise and hold out my hand. "Thank you for your time, Mr. Evans. I'll look forward to hearing from you."

"Right. Leave a phone number and your address with Phoebe, our receptionist, before you leave."

On my walk back to Gracie's house, I'm fairly confident Mr. Evans will syndicate me, but I won't count on it yet. Daddy always said, "Don't count your eggs before you collect 'em."

When I get back to my cousin's house, her husband, Britt, is in the living room reading his newspaper. He folds the corner down and looks over it when I come in. His whole face turns down, as if he's sucked a lemon. He's never held me in high esteem, and his welcoming harrumph confirms he hasn't changed his mind. Still, I'm here on his begrudging kindness, so I'll do my best not to antagonize him.

"Maggie." He gives a slight dip of his head. "The grocery must be doing well to afford a train ticket."

Why do men think they have the right to question a woman like they do? I know what he's really saying is *why aren't you staying at a hotel instead of mooching off us*?

"The ticket was paid for by the *News Standard*."

"Must be nice."

"Indeed, it is. The editor is thinking about carrying my column, which will help pay the bills."

"Humph. He like your Bolshevik ideas?"

I yank off my hat and sit on the davenport. "Britt, believing that women can help their families during this time isn't a Bolshevik idea. It's simply practical."

He snorts.

"If you lost your job and Gracie could get one, would you refuse her? Risk losing your home for your pride?" The moment the words leave my mouth, I knew I shouldn't have said them.

He throws down the newspaper. "The man's the head of the household and the provider. Pride has nothing to do with it. Encouraging women to work outside of their own kitchen is un-American, and it's ungodly. Her place is taking care of her children."

"Exactly! And if her husband is laid off, she can bring home a paycheck and buy food to fill their bellies."

With his face redder than a sugar beet, he leans forward and shakes his finger at me. "I'd never let any wife of mine work, no matter what. Children are better off with her at home."

I hold up my hands. "Look, Britt, I don't want to argue with you. We obviously don't agree, but I'm curious. What would you have these families do? If the husband can't get work, and the wife is willing to clean houses or cook for a school or somewhere, why shouldn't she?"

"Her place is cleaning and cooking for her own family."

This isn't going anywhere. He's too stubborn to see clearly what I'm trying to say. Besides, poor Gracie's in the doorway wringing her hands.

I pick up my hat and stand. "We aren't going to solve the world's problems tonight. I think I'll go change my clothes." Britt harrumphs and disappears behind his newspaper. I send Gracie an apologetic grimace.

As I pass by, she whispers, "He'll never change, Maggie. Don't bother yourself. He'd have us starve before he'd let me get a job." Out loud, she says, "Supper in ten minutes."

Britt's a city boy. He has no earthly idea how hardscrabble life is in Rivers End. Anywhere in the rural South, for that matter. Farms are sharecropped—even Daddy was a sharecropper. That doesn't leave money for anything but feeding one's family. And that barely. Now … well, now with the banks failing, farmers can't borrow money for seed. The price of cotton is falling faster than autumn's leaves.

I don't know if we'll ever climb out of this.

In the guest room, I slide off Duchess' dress and hang it up. I get so angry with men like Britt, I could spit nails. Why do they feel so threatened by a woman working? I don't advocate all women go to work. But for goodness' sake, what would have become of Barry and me if I hadn't? We'd be living with Big Jim, that's what. I shudder to even contemplate that existence.

For Gracie's sake, I'll keep to stories of our childhood during supper.

As I arrive back in Rivers End, Barry and Ozzie are standing on the platform, fishing poles in hand. Are they coming from or going to the river?

After I hug him, Barry's little head tilts. "Did the man buy your bedtime stories, Mama?"

"He bought one, and he said if his readers like it, he'll buy more."

"Then he'll buy more, 'cause they can't help but like it, Mama!" Barry thrusts his pole at Ozzie and grabs my suitcase. That's when I see the two fish in his basket.

"Thank you, sweet boy. And what wonderful fishermen you two are. Now give me some sugar." I lean down and turn my cheek toward him, then laugh as he gives me a raspberry.

Duchess must have been watching through the front windows for me because she runs out the door and across the street to greet me.

"Well? How did it go, Sister? Is he going to syndicate you?"

"I think so. Let's get inside, and I'll tell you all about it. How did everything go here?"

Duchess takes my arm, and we follow Barry, who insists on carrying my suitcase. It bumps each step behind him as he hauls it up the stairs. "Finer than frog's hair. And that meatless casserole dish with the peanuts? My word, it's delicious. There's leftovers for supper."

"Good. I'm hungry. We can fry Barry's fish to go with it."

We're halfway up the stairs when the street door opens and Ozzie pops inside.

"Miss Maggie, there's a phone call for you in Daddy's office."

Who would be calling me on Sunday? My heart thumps an extra beat. Maybe it's Mr. Evans with his decision. "Duchess, you and Barry go on up. I'd better see who that is."

"Did you catch anything today, Ozzie?" I ask as we walk back across the street to the station. He tells me about losing his only catch then stops and opens the station door for me.

"Thank you, sweetie." I nod at Wade, who's helping Mrs. Grizzle with her suitcase. I'd heard her sister in Chicago just had a baby. She must be going to see her. In the office, the receiver is laying on Wade's desk. I pick it up.

"Hello?"

"Magnolia Parker, what in heaven's name were you thinking? You don't need another mouth to feed, let alone one who's so empty-headed as your sister. I hear she set the grocery on fire. What kind of environment is that for my grandson? You're risking his life. Why, I ought to call my lawyer—"

"Slow down, Big Jim." I swanny, that man fell out of an ugly tree and hit every branch on the way down. "That fire was an itty-bitty one from the burn barrel. You know those happen all the time, and Doc put it out right away. It didn't even leave a scorch mark on the pillars. And while we're at it, I don't need you or anyone else telling me whom I can or cannot feed. I'll thank you not to insult my sister."

"You better listen to me, Maggie. You don't have an ounce of common sense in that head of yours. Leaving the boy alone with your sister is outright neglect. I thought she was goin' to take him to Faylene to watch. It's as thoughtless as that writing of yours, encouraging women to anarchy."

"What? First of all, I never said Barry was going to Faylene. Secondly, anarchy? When did I ever do anything of the sort? You're talking crazy." My hand grows clammy, and I tighten my grip on the receiver.

"You need to get married and take care of the boy."

"The boy has a name. It's Barry."

Big Jim snorts so loud, I pull the receiver away from my ear. "I know his name full well. You'd better remember his last name is Parker. You need to get him a father."

"He had one. And I'm doing fine on my own. Why, look at Sadie. She never married, and she's done all right for herself."

"Don't you compare yourself with that renegade half-breed. She's no example to follow. That's what I mean. Your thinking is catawampus, and you're endangering my grandson. If you don't come to your senses, I'm going to have my lawyer do something about it."

"What do you suggest? Throw my *sister* out on the streets? It's unchristian, and it's downright unconscionable of you to even suggest it."

"Un—wha?"

I can always take the air out of the old windbag when I use words he doesn't understand.

"You'd better find someone to support her. And you. I'm warning you, Maggie. I'll report you to the Child Protection Agency."

"What Chi—"

The line went dead. I drop the phone into its cradle as if it's a snake. Child Protection Agency?

Whatever it is, it can't be good.

CHAPTER 8

"Mama, why is Granddaddy always so angry?"

I nearly jump out of my skin and spin around. "Barry, you scared the fire out of me." I hang up the phone. "Don't sneak up like that, sugar."

My little boy is wide-eyed and trembling, so I pull him into a hug. Outside the office in the main station, Wade examines the silver luggage tag on a suitcase and points to the schedule board. The station is busy this morning for a town as small as Rivers End. A half dozen passengers wait to board the train.

"Now, darlin', you know your granddaddy. He blusters like a winter storm, but it always blows over. This will too." I hope. "Tell you what." With my hands on his little shoulders, I turn him around and move him toward the door. "Let's go get Auntie Duchess and have story hour. We haven't had one since she arrived. It's time we get back to it." A bit of normalcy will do us all good. "Now, tell me about the new fishing hole you and Ozzie found."

That brings a smile to his face, and the sparkle returns to his eyes. Wade salutes goodbye to us as we leave. While we cross the street, Barry chatters about fishing, forgetting his grandfather for the moment. How I wish I could. The word *lawyer* keeps my stomach in turmoil over Big Jim's ugly intentions. I've never had any dealings with lawyers, except when my Jimmy died, and that one only read the will. I follow Barry up the stairs.

In the living room, my sister is sitting on the davenport embroidering a sampler. Surely Mr. Alden, God rest his soul, dealt with lawyers. Maybe Duchess will have some advice for me. I'll ask her after Barry's gone to bed. For now, I grab my Bible, drop into the arm chair, and search for a story. For selfish reasons, I choose one in Daniel about Shadrach, Meshach, and Abednego in the fiery furnace. I feel flames in Big Jim's threats.

Duchess lays her embroidery in her lap, her hands idle, while Barry hops onto the davenport beside her, snuggling against her arm. She kisses the top of his sweet head. "What are we doing?"

"It's story time, Auntie."

I draw up my feet, tucking them beneath me as I smooth the thin pages of the Bible. Duchess frowns slightly but doesn't say anything about my sitting position. Her legs are crossed at the ankle like a proper lady. She settles back, and I begin reading. Growing up, our mama didn't read the Bible with us. She told us stories but left the reading to our Sunday school teachers. I secretly thought perhaps she couldn't read. I don't remember ever seeing her pore over a book or magazine, or a letter, for that matter.

I've always dramatized the stories for Barry, making them come alive to draw him in. I hope Sister doesn't mind.

"Tonight's story is about three men, Shadrach, Meshach, and Abednego." I begin to read, paraphrasing. "There was a king, King Nebuchadnezzar, who fancied himself a god. He had a golden statue made of himself and said when the people heard the trumpets sound, they all had to bow down and worship his statue."

By my sister's confused expression, she doesn't know this one. Her head tilts, and a slight dip appears between her brows. Barry, however, is on his knees and fully enthralled.

"But the king found out that three men—Shadrach, Meshach, and Abednego, whom the king put in charge of the province of Babylon—refused to bow down. King Nebuchadnezzar flew into a rage and ordered the men brought to him." I pause for that to sink in.

Barry pulls his little face into a mask of anger and growls at Duchess. For his benefit, I'm sure, she screeches in mock horror. He giggles, and I pick up where I left off. I need to hear the end to remind myself that God is watching over us.

As I continue to read, Duchess picks up her embroidery and stitches rapidly. I doubt she will be able to keep it without ripping much of it out because her eyes are on me and not her work. I'm delighted. Not about her stitchery but about her reaction to the story.

"The men are brought to the king, but they still refuse to bow down to anyone but the one true God whom they serve. They believed God would save them, but even if He didn't, they refused to bow down to the false god, the golden statue."

By the time the king orders our heroes to be thrown into the fiery furnace, Sister's hands give up trying to stitch, and her work lies beside her. Her feet are drawn up onto the davenport. Avoiding the flames?

"'Look!' Nebuchadnezzar shouted. 'I see four men, unbound, walking around in the fire unharmed. And the fourth looks like a god!'"

Duchess leans forward. Her embroidery is in a forlorn ball in her lap, forgotten. "Is that truly in the Bible, Sister? Or are you making it up?"

Barry shakes his head. "She never makes it up, Auntie Duchess. It's really in there."

Sister hardly blinks as she watches me read. We are coming to my favorite part—when the three come out of the furnace and there isn't even the smell of smoke on them. Barry cheers at that, throwing his fist in the air. I pray God will deliver us from Big Jim's threats as well.

When I finish, I ask Barry a couple of questions to be sure he understands. As he often does, he surprises even me with his insight.

"I think it was Jesus in that furnace with them."

Duchess smiles down at him, squeezes his shoulders, and drops another kiss on the top of his head. "I'm sure you must be right."

After I tuck Barry into bed, I return to the living room. My sister has the Bible in her lap and is turning its pages. She raises her head as I come in.

"Maggie, I find myself woefully inadequate in Bible stories. I thought they were all about the queens and princesses. At least, that's what Mama always told me about."

I settle back on the davenport. "I'm not surprised. All Mama thought about was returning to the 'royal life.' Grandmother Cora filled her head with stories of living on the plantation as a girl."

Duchess sets the Bible on the coffee table. "And mine. While I worked on my stitchery lessons, Grandmother would tell me about the balls and the ladies' gowns." She runs the material of her skirt between her fingers. "I used to imagine myself dressed in one of those big old hoop skirts." She giggles. "Truthfully, I prefer our styles to theirs, as gorgeous as they were. I shudder at the thought of wearing a corset laced so tight you can scarcely breathe."

"Corset or not, I can easily picture you in a great ball gown, flirting behind your fan, Sister."

Her eyes well with tears. "I was only sixteen when I married Mr. Alden. He caught my fancy and stole my heart in one fell swoop." She lifts her hankie to her nose. "I can't believe he's gone."

Before I can offer any sympathy, her countenance changes, and her tears dry up. "And I can't believe Mama allowed me to grow up with nary a skill other than embroidery and playing the piano. How am I going to earn my keep, Maggie?" She looks around the apartment. "I suppose I could dust for you."

That surprises me. Does she even know how? "I thought you had servants to dust and clean."

She gives a halfhearted nod. "We did. But how hard can it be?"

My thoughts drift back to her sweeping skills, and I hide a smile. How hard, indeed? "Don't you worry, I'll teach you anything you need to learn. You're much more capable than you realize, sweet sister." I unfold my legs and rise. "Besides, you being in the store is already helping with our customers. I heard Nellie tell someone about you—said you're a good addition."

Duchess sighs and picks up her stitching. "I hope so."

"I think you know more than you realize. You've just never had an outlet for those skills, other than managing a large household."

"I can play a mean hand of bridge too."

"The sarcasm doesn't mitigate how smart you are, Duchess." We need to liven up this evening. "How about we listen to the mystery hour?" I cross the room to the radio and turn it on. "Then after that, we can put on some music, roll up the rug, and dance."

Her face brightens. "Now we're hitting on all sixes."

Why, all she lacks is self-confidence. Amazing.

My eyes narrow as I watch her roll the other side of the rug in preparation for our dancing. She's organized too. She doesn't waste time. My mind begins to perk with ideas for my dear sister to earn her keep. While we listen to the mystery hour—rather, while Duchess listens—I'm forming a plan.

For too long, I've had suspicions about the store's finances. Even with hard times, I know what inventory I purchase and for what amount it's sold. Yet the final income always seems to come up short. I'm not quite ready to blame my store manager, but there's no one else who has access, other than Big Jim. That gives me a moment's pause. He hasn't been asking for money lately. Cal bears watching, and despite my sister's lack of practical education, she's a whiz at numbers. Poor old Cal Llewellyn won't know what hit him—if it is him—when I turn Duchess loose on the books.

CHAPTER 9

A s soon as Barry is off to school the next morning, Duchess and
I unlock the store. I shiver as I insert the key. The weather has
turned, and the nights are cold enough for hog butchering, which
we will start later today. Cal hasn't arrived yet, and that's why we're
here now.

"Duchess, I want you to look over the books and see what you
can find. You've always been much better at numbers than I am."

Sister clasps her hands beneath her chin, and her whole face
smiles. "I'll be glad to. Mr. Alden used to have me look over what
his accountant gave him. It was interesting, and I learned a lot
about what to look for in case somebody was playing funny."

Her desire to be useful makes me glad I asked her to do this.
While raised a princess, she somehow avoided the "I deserve it"
mentality. Opening the office door, I can't help notice she still calls
her husband "Mr. Alden."

"Did you never call Will by his first name?"

A wistful smile plays across her beautiful face. "Normally, I
called him Will, but remember, he was fifteen years older than me.
When I first met him, I naturally called him Mister Alden. On our
first wedding anniversary, he teased me about it. After that, I took
to calling him Mister instead of sugar or honey. It took us both
back to when we fell in love."

"That is so romantic. I may have to use it in a book."

"Well, not in the accounting ones. Let's get to it."

Once I settle her at the desk perusing the books, I go open the
boxes from the delivery that arrived yesterday afternoon. There's a
case of Campbell's chicken noodle soup and one of pork and beans.

The next crate holds sugar, flour, and cornmeal.

"Maggie, your hogs are here." Cal stands near the butcher counter, hands on his hips and looking none too pleased. "The half-breed is in the back in the commons. Says she's here to help."

How long has he known Sadie? At least as long as he's been the store manager, which is years longer than I've known her. "She has a name, Cal. I'd be obliged if you'd use it. And don't use that term around me again." Why some people insist on holding onto prejudice, I just don't know. We live in the twentieth century now. Time to bury those outdated, ridiculous ideas.

"What are you muttering about, missy?"

That does it. "Cal, if you can't remember that I'm your employer and refer to me as either *Maggie* or *ma'am*, I may forget to cut you a check come payday." I turn and stalk out the door. I don't want to see his expression.

A large crew is in the communal yard behind the grocery. Each family around the yard has brought out a table in preparation for eating dinner. Yesterday, Doc oversaw the fixing—to make everything ready for today. I trade him meat for doctoring. It's a good barter in my opinion, especially with a young, active boy.

Five tripod structures are waiting to hang the hogs after killing. I always buy two extra hogs to pay the helpers and Doc. There are plenty of men here to work—several from the shanties behind the train station. Fresh meat is enough pay and gladly accepted by their wives. I always invite a couple of farmers' wives who I know are struggling. All in all, we have thirty-four people. With the scalding, scraping, shaving, and finally butchering these animals, we'll all be working hard for the next two days.

While the men take care of killing the hogs, I run upstairs to change into bib overalls. Sadie has the fires going so we can scald the animals as soon as they're ready. I stop on my way back out to check on Duchess and let her know what I'm doing.

A shot rings out as the first hog is killed. Duchess startles, then eyes my attire with one raised eyebrow. "Those look rather comfortable." She smiles, but it quickly fades. "You've got a problem." She moves so I can see over her shoulder. I lean in as she points to a place on the page. "There are several poorly disguised changes in the records, Sister."

"What do you mean?"

"See this one? How it's been erased?"

It does look smudgy and not real clear. "I see, but if someone inverted a number, they'd have to erase it to fix it. Right?"

"Yes, and that was my original thought. So I went upstairs and got your personal order book." She picks up my order book and opens it to July's entries, pointing to the nineteenth. "What do you see here?"

I peer at my own handwriting. "I ordered fifteen ten-pound bags of sugar, thirty fifty-pound bags of flour, and forty-five of cornmeal."

"Now look at this entry in the accounting book."

For the same date, the sugar ordered and paid for is—"Twenty-two bags of sugar?" My voice ends in a squeak as I drop into the chair beside her.

"He paid the delivery for fifteen bags and pocketed the difference of $2.52. That's not the only one." She points to two other entries, tapping her pencil next to one, and makes a face. "He tried to cover up by erasing and reentering a few others, here and there."

"That dirty polecat."

Duchess twirls a strand of hair around her finger. "Each time, he varied the amounts, but they always raised the price you paid. And since you pay for your deliveries in cash, it's easy for him to skim it off and change the amount after the fact. How often do you rectify your books?"

"Not often enough." My stomach is sinking. I haven't rectified those books in a few years. I didn't think I needed to. *Oh, Maggie. You're going to prove Big Jim right. You don't have a head for business.*

"I think he most likely went back at a later date and changed them, and with customers on credit accounts, you wouldn't have noticed that sales didn't add up to what you expected. He could hide it. I think if we went back farther, we'd find more. But it doesn't matter. We have the evidence."

We might have the evidence, but what am I to do with it? Voices raised in thanksgiving for the hogs filter through the window. "What should I do?"

"Well, first, I'd try to make certain it was him."

"Duchess, nobody else has access to the books or the money."

She raises one perfectly drawn eyebrow. "No one?"

"Big Jim? Why would he—" Why indeed. "To force me out of business? But he built this business with his father. Why—"

"To prove a woman can't manage." Duchess narrows her eyes. "You and I, my dear sister, are going to show that man what two women can do. I've got a plan."

"And I want to hear it, but right now the yard is full of people who are here to help butcher hogs. Do you suppose you can make fried chicken for dinner?"

Her face blanches but, bless her heart, she nods. "How many?"

"Only two, sugar. Several others are also cooking." She rolls her eyes heavenward at that, making me smile. "And I know you won't want to help butcher hogs."

Her eyes startle wide, and she shakes her head vehemently. I laugh and hug her. "Duchess, you are definitely earning your keep. You are now my accountant."

"Really?" She smooths her hair, pushing it off her face. "Mr. Alden always did say I understood business. He taught me so much and always shared what he was buying and selling with me." She rises and links arms with me. "Just wait. We'll show those men they can't intimidate us. Or beat us."

I hope she's right. Big Jim's words about lawyers send a shiver down my spine as I return to work. Big Jim or Cal? Which one is it? Both? I can't figure it out. Big Jim doesn't have the access to the books that Cal does. No lights have been seen in the grocery at night, so my father-in-law isn't sneaking in. No, I'm thinking the culprit is Cal. But I know as well as I'm alive, Big Jim has his hand in the till one way or another.

In the commons, Sadie is splitting up people into five teams, one for each hog. I'm glad Cal isn't out here to raise any objections to her leadership. Sadie has plenty of experience, and the men from the shanties have little to none.

We have hours of scraping ahead of us. We won't actually butcher the meat until tomorrow. The carcasses need time to firm up, and that will happen overnight, now that the weather is cold enough. I pull on a pair of gloves and grab a scraping tool. Who says women don't have muscles? I smile as I walk outside to the yard, thinking about a column I should write on the subject.

After several hours' worth of work, a parade of ladies with platters of fried chicken and bowls of corn, potato salad, beans, biscuits, and other delicious-smelling offerings arrive. They lay the food on one long serving table. I glance around for Duchess, but she's not here.

"Sadie, I need to go check on my sister. She's supposed to have fried up a couple of chickens for us." Sadie nods and goes back to her scraping.

Just then, Duchess shoulders open the screen door and comes down the steps. In her hands is a large platter of very respectable-looking fried chicken. She's got flour in her hair and a smudge beside her smile. I can only imagine what my floor looks like, but by the way she carries herself, I can tell my sister is pleased. And she should be.

She sets her platter on a table and sits. She lends an elegance to the farmers and merchants, yet she's relaxed and comfortable with them and they with her. They aren't intimidated by her. How can that be? For the past seventeen years, she's graced the tables of Atlanta's wealthiest hostesses. Why, she and Mr. Alden even hosted a prince and the president in their home. Yet she speaks with Sadie and Clara like old friends and introduces herself to folks she doesn't yet know, treating them as her equals. I'm very proud of my sister.

And a tad envious of her grace.

I fill my plate with her chicken and a portion of potato salad Bessie Mae sent down from Faylene. The chicken is as good as any I've eaten. Finding her watching me, I wink, then lick my lips. Her smile is my reward. Wait until Barry hears about this. I'll save him a piece of his auntie's fried chicken.

Barry. Big Jim's words about loopholes, lawyers, and that new agency for children's services pinches my insides. Suddenly, I'm no longer hungry. I push a chunk of potato around my plate. My only hope is that my sister's right, and we can somehow bamboozle Big Jim—catch him at his own game and show them all what a couple of women can do.

Duchess and Sadie have their heads together like a pair of conspirators. Is Sister drawing Sadie into our plans? A Scripture verse comes to mind. One about a cord of three strands.

"Mama? Are you and Auntie Duchess almost ready for story time?"

Barry's voice floats down the stairs to where Duchess is massaging my shoulders as I soak the soreness from my muscles in a bath. I glance up at her. "I think we'd better get me out. I'm almost jelly. Your hands are strong, sugar. Where'd you learn to massage like that?"

"We'll be right up, sweetie," she calls to Barry. "My husband didn't like to have anyone but me massage his neck and back. Over the years, my hands developed the strength."

She holds up a towel for me as I stand. "I'd like to borrow some of that strength to stand up against Big Jim."

"Honey, you stand just fine against him. I've seen you."

I finish drying and slide on my robe. "For myself, he doesn't scare me. But for Barry? My sweet boy would hate the man he's become. I try to shield him from it. A boy should be able to look up to his grandfather." Not to mention how horrified my Jimmy would have been at the way his daddy is treating me.

Duchess nods and helps dump the water from the tub into the garden. Then we go upstairs for story time. After I slip into my pajamas and put my robe back over them, I head to the davenport. Sister and Barry are on the floor, waiting.

Duchess rubs Barry's head. "I love our story time. What's tonight's?"

I open my Bible. "It's the story of the Good Samaritan."

Barry frowns. "Have I heard that one, Mama? If I did, I don't remember it."

"No, sugar. I haven't read this one before."

I read the parable, and as I do, I catch glimpses of my son concentrating on it. What's going on inside that head of his? When we finish, I ask, "Do you have any questions, son?"

He shakes his head. "I don't think so. Jesus told them who the man's neighbor really was. It's the same for us, right? The people in the shanties are as much our neighbors as Mr. Wade and Ozzie."

My sister ruffles his hair. "My nephew"—her voice is tender—"has a big heart."

Sometimes I worry about it being too big.

CHAPTER 10

I push down the button on my alarm before it goes off. It's three-fifty-nine. I'm used to getting up early, but restlessness kept me awake long after I should have been sleeping. Stifling a groan, I rise as my back muscles remind me of what lies ahead today. Still, it's worth it. Families will be fed, and the grocery will make some money. In the dark, I tiptoe out of the bedroom so I won't wake Duchess. Last night, I left my overalls down in the kitchen, so I throw on my robe and go out the door to the stairs.

Doc is in the yard, stoking the fires beneath large tubs for fat rendering. The first fat from the hog's belly is prized for shortening, and Barry will hurry home today because he loves the cracklings, fresh from the pot. I'll have to watch him and Ozzie, or they'll eat their weight in cracklings. I need to scavenge a bowl full to grind up for seasoning.

Light trickles from the kitchen. I open the door. Sister is pouring coffee that smells heavenly. I take the cup she hands me with a smile.

"I thought you were still sleeping. I didn't hear you get up."

Duchess waits until I take a sip of coffee, but I glance down at my cup in surprise. It smells wonderful! Oh my. I take that first sip. "It tastes as good as it smells, Sister. You're a fast learner."

She practically glows as she places the pot back on the stove. "You tossed around so much last night, I went to the davenport to sleep." She turns toward me. "It's quite comfortable."

"I'm sorry I kept you awake. I was overly tired but couldn't relax." I pull out a chair and sit for a moment. "However, today the butchering will be completed for another year." I take another sip. "Pour a cup for me to take to Doc, will you?" I push myself up from the table, arm muscles complaining, and don my shirt and overalls.

Duchess helps me with the straps, her nimble fingers playing lightly across my shoulders. "Are you going to need me to help make dinner again?"

Her willingness warms my heart. "Yes, sugar, and thank you."

"Will it be all right if I do fried chicken again? It's really the only thing I know, so far." Her wry chuckle makes me smile. Duchess is changing in ways she never expected in this lifetime.

"I'd say by the way everyone gobbled it up, it's the perfect thing. Do me a favor, please, and wake Barry at six. Make him take a bath too. He'll try to weasel out of it, and sometimes does before you're aware of what he's done."

Sister holds out another steaming cup.

"He won't get past me," she assures me as I take Doc's cup of coffee with me, after refilling my own.

In the yard, I hand Doc the coffee, which he savors. The fires he's tending warm the air. It's unusual to get weather this cold in early December. Usually, the hog slaughtering is in late December or January, but we aren't complaining. It will be a good Christmas. This year's tax money has been delivered to the state of Georgia, and the smokehouse will be filled with pork butts. As Barry would say, "We're in high cotton."

The day passes with hard work and the blessing of giving out meat to families in need. The rest goes into the smokehouse and the grocery cooler. Barry and Ozzie run into the yard after school's out, bringing with them several friends.

"All y'all sit here." I point to one of the tables. "I've got a nice big bowl of cracklin's for you."

Like ants at a picnic, they scramble to the table and attack the bowl, leaving us adults laughing. I walk away to help finish up the last of the slaughtering and divvying up. A few minutes later, Bessie Mae comes by for some of the meat.

"I was going to bring this up to you, Bessie Mae. You didn't have to come down here."

"I was at the Feed 'n' Seed for some horse liniment for my arthuritis." She shrugs. "Made sense to come on and pick some up myself."

I give her a burlap bag with some pork belly for cutting into bacon, a portion of butt, and some fat. "I'll save the rest in the grocery's cooler for you." That cooler put me in a financial bind for a couple of years after Jimmy died, but now it repays me in unspoiled food.

"Is everything all right with Mama Faylene?" I want ample warning if Big Jim is back in town.

Bessie Mae's smile is wide, revealing her beautiful pearly whites. "Everything is peaceful-like, Miss Maggie."

"Mama, Mama! Come quick!" Barry pounds into the grocery after school the next day, hollering at the top of his lungs. I'm in the middle of helping Nellie Taggart, who frowns at his interruption.

"Young man, can't you see your mother is helping me? Where are your manners?" She turns back to me. "You need to teach him better."

Immediately, my ire is irked. "He knows his manners. This means something bad has happened." I turn my back on her and squat in front of Barry. "What is it?"

He tugs on my hand. "Come see, Mama. She's hurt and all swolled up."

She? My heart begins to pound. "Who is, sugar?" Before he pulls me over, I get to my feet and follow him. Duchess waves at me to go and takes over helping Nellie.

"Where are we going, son?"

Running, Barry pulls me into the late afternoon chill. "Out behind the station. She's under your favorite sweet gum tree. I was comin' back from fishin' with Ozzie. He stayed with her. We're like the Good Samaritans, Mama. We have to take her home and care for her."

None of this makes a lick of sense, but our story time from last night moves my feet. I know my boy, and he doesn't make this kind of fuss over nothing. We scurry around the side of the station, across the field thick with chickweed, brome, and fleabane, and back by the line of sweet gum and Georgia pines. Ozzie hops from one foot to the other beside a form on the ground I can't yet make out.

Barry points toward them. "There she is, Mama."

Hurrying closer, I discover a young woman lying on a bed of pine needles. She's hardly more than a child and has the whitest hair I've ever seen. Even her eyebrows and eyelashes are white. Her skin is so fair, she must sunburn easily. I've never seen anyone with albinism in person, but I've read about it. And Barry is right. Her belly is swollen—with child. I hadn't put two and two together when he said she was "swolled up." I gauge her about six months along. Then again, she's a slight thing, so she'd show early. She might be more or less. We can't know until she's conscious.

I kneel next to her. "You did the right thing, Barry." I lift her wrist and feel for a pulse. It's strong, thank the good Lord. Her baby's should be, too, but I want Doc to examine her. The skin above one eye is split and caked with dry blood. She has a lump on her forehead and bruises on her neck. Oh my. What monster would take fists to a pregnant woman?

I draw a sharp breath through my nose and force my hands to still. "Ozzie, go get your daddy. Tell him I need him and to bring a blanket." He leaves in a scurry of bare feet. I turn to my son. "Barry, go tell Auntie Duchess to …" I stop. Tell her to what?

"Mama, we have to take her home and make her better. That's what Jesus taught in the Bible. You read it."

I look heavenward. *Lord, is this why You had me read that story the other night?* I sigh. Another mouth to feed and a hurt one at that. Well, the Lord provides. I hope. No, He does. He will.

"You're right, sugar. Jesus brought her here for you to find. I'm proud of you, son." And I am.

Wade comes flying around the corner of the station. I wave so he can see where we are. Ozzie is trailing him, puffing and trying to keep up.

Wade kneels beside me, a rare frown drawing his brow downward. "Do you know who she is?"

"No idea. She hasn't regained consciousness. From what I can see, nothing *appears* to be broken. Should I examine her, or should we get Doc first?"

Barry shakes his head. "She's *ours*, Mama. Let Doc come see her at our place, not his. He'll keep her. And God brought her to me to be a Good Samaritan." His voice rises to a squeak.

Bless his sweet, tender heart. I firm my jaw and nod. "All right. Once we have her settled, you can go get Doc. Wade, will you help me get her to my apartment? She's a slight thing. I think we can both carry her fine. But let's use the blanket, just in case she has anything broken."

We gently roll her to one side and tuck the blanket beneath her, then roll her the other way and pull it under. After a couple of maneuvers, we can lift her. Why, she doesn't weigh more than Barry and Ozzie combined. Wade and I carry her easily up to my place. Barry holds the door open.

Once inside, I need to make a quick decision. I can share Barry's room with him, so ... "Son, open my bedroom door. We'll put her in my bed."

As we settle her, she groans, and her eyes flutter open. She cries out.

"Easy, sugar. You're safe now. You're going to be all right."

At the sound of my voice, she calms and looks at me. *Thank You, Lord.* Her eyes stray to Wade. Her chin trembles, and she grabs my hand, clutching it.

"He's not going to hurt you. He's my good friend and helped me get you here. Can you tell me your name?"

She glances at Wade, biting her lip. For now, I ask Wade to leave and point Barry toward a chair. "Barry, sit with her, please. I'll be right back." Wade and I go to the living room. "She's been beaten by a man, for sure. That's why she's wary of you. Once she knows you, she'll be fine."

"It's understandable." Wade has a strange look on his face that I can't put a name to. "I'll see you later, Maggie."

He doesn't mention her unusual looks. Interesting. I'll have to ask him about that later. I also want his opinion about her being pregnant. I didn't see any condemnation in his eyes. I hurry back to my bedroom. Barry has put a pillow behind her back, and she's sitting up. I cross to the bedside. "Are you sure you should be sitting up?"

She nods, shyly. "I hurt, but not that bad."

"Can you tell me your name?"

"I'm Pinkie Y—Pinkie. I won't go back." She reaches for my arm. "Please, don't make me go back. My daddy beat me, and he'll do it again." Her hand clutches tight to my wrist.

My guess is she's about fifteen or sixteen. Old enough. "No, I won't send you back. Not to a man who beats you. But I'd like to have Doc come look you over. Especially with some of those bruises you have." When we put her in the bed, I saw marks on her stomach. It looks as if she's been kicked. I want to be sure her baby's all right.

She nods and glances at Barry.

"Sweetie, why don't you go get Doc now, while I get Miss Pinkie into one of my nighties?"

"Okay." He grins at our guest. "Don't you leave. I'm gonna take care of you until you're better." He races out. Our Miss Pinkie exhales and relaxes for the first time since we found her.

While I help her into a nightie, I tell her about Barry being the Good Samaritan. "He's sure God brought you here so he could practice."

"I believe it." She looks deep into my eyes. "If you'll let me stay,

I'll work for you. I'm a good worker. But—"

I think I know what she's trying to tell me, but I want her to be open, so I say, "But what, dear?"

She bites her lip. Her words are whispers. "What about me being pregnant?" She lowers her eyes. "I'm not married."

I appreciate her honesty. I settle gently onto the side of the bed, careful not to jostle her overmuch. "Do you want to tell me about it?"

She nods and raises her eyes. "My daddy has always beaten me." She pulls at her white hair. "Because I'm different. A freak. People have always said I was the result of Daddy's sins. When I was nine, he sold me to a circus, but I ran away. The sheriff found me and made me go home." She takes a stuttering breath. "A few months ago, a man came asking to work for food. He didn't think I was a freak. He was really nice to me when I brought him food. After a couple of days, I thought maybe he was my way out. I thought I could make him love me and marry me."

Her sad eyes break my heart. "I can guess what happened."

She nods. "Do you want me to leave?"

The door bangs loudly as it hits the wall, and Barry comes skidding into the bedroom. "I've brought Doc!"

CHAPTER 11

Thank the good Lord, Parker's is busy this morning. Guarding the entrance are a crate of potatoes and baskets of turnips, flanked by a bushel of corn ready for shucking. I know, I know—farmers have corn to eat. But those of us who live in town don't, and it's a mandatory item for a crayfish boil. That and little red potatoes. Besides, I didn't have the heart to turn down Florence Gage when she brought in the corn to barter down her bill.

I nod at customers while I count canned goods standing in military precision on the shelves. Not a single one dares to stray from General Pinkie's lineup. I'd let her recover for several days, allowing the bruises to fade some, then I brought her into the grocery yesterday to work.

There's something about Pinkie I can't explain. I guess it's God telling me it's okay to let her stay since I'm at peace. I know she belongs with us. She asked what Barry would think of her being in the family way, I told him his daddy died before he was born, so a mama without a husband isn't unusual for him. He doesn't need to know anything else. As for the women in town, and a few of the men, it might not be so easy.

True to her words, on her first day in the grocery, she immediately took over the shelves, marshaling each can to stand in line. That's when I noticed her eyesight isn't so good. She holds the cans close, no more than two inches from her eyes, to read the labels. I need to ask Doc about that. He thinks she's maybe six months along. With her being so thin, she could be less. Anyway, he says if he's right, we can expect the baby in late February or early March—if he's wrong, closer to April.

I'm not rightly sure what we'll do with a baby in the house, but Barry won't hear of her leaving. He's still playing Good Samaritan, and to be honest, I don't know where she could go if not here. Her mama died when she was four years old. There's no one but her daddy, and I refuse to send her back for another beating. I swallow hard as I flip the page on my inventory list. No, we'll manage … somehow.

I must say, the results of her handiwork bring a smile to my lips. There's not a wrinkle in a flour sack, and nary a grain of sugar dares escape its bag. Duchess and I were astonished how fast and thoroughly Pinkie wielded the broom and dustpan. And I know my sister is delighted to turn over that task.

This place is home—as if I were made to own the grocery. And as long as I have Parker's, I can feed my little family. Walking past the potatoes, their earthy aroma reminds me of working with Daddy on the farm. How I wish Barry had that opportunity. He loves animals. But that's neither here nor there, and if I want to keep my livelihood, I have a job ahead of me. An unpleasant one.

When I join my sister in the office, she's poring over the books. In contrast to the grocery, the office smells like paper and ink. And bills. And unpaid accounts.

I quietly close the door. Duchess looks up, a slight frown marring her beauty at my approach.

I perch on the corner of the desk. "I sent the tax payment to the state. We made it this year, but only because you were able to sell my jewelry for me before the crash."

She nods and lowers her eyes to the books again. "You're welcome."

My legs won't be still. Slipping off the desk, I begin to pace. "But next year, what with Pinkie now part of our household, we might not make it. I've got to put a stop to Cal's skimming. Immediately."

I glance through the office window. The object of our discussion is behind the butcher counter, grinding pork and beef for meatloaf for Alice Wiggins—when he isn't giving Pinkie the evil eye. Alice's husband, Joe Bob, who owns Wiggins Feed & Seed, is partial to meatloaf. She makes it every Wednesday night for him. She's also one of the few who pays her bill each week.

As if she reads my thoughts, Duchess turns in the book to the credit page. "We've got do something about this, too, Maggie. Otherwise, you'll be out of business in less than six months."

I gasp at the long list of customers who have nothing in the *paid* column. "When was the last time any of these folks have paid?"

She turns back to the previous page. "April. And a few haven't for over a year." Pointing to Nellie Taggart's name, my sister's mouth pinches. "What irks me is she evicts any boarders who go beyond one week without paying. Sadie told me."

A slow burn rises from my stomach. I open a drawer and pull out an envelope of Eno's antacid power. I need it before confronting Cal. I won't allow him to prove Big Jim right. If I sink, it will be on my *own* merits or lack thereof.

"I'll be right back. I need to take this." I grab a tin cup and walk out back to the pump. After my cup is filled with water, I empty the packet in it, letting it fizz some before drinking. I know I'm avoiding the coming conflict. It won't be pleasant.

The Eno's stops the heartburn … for now. I take a deep breath. It's time. Back inside the office, I stand at the door watching the scene before me. When Cal looks up—it makes me wonder what he was about to do if I hadn't caught his eye—I motion for him to come into the office.

A moment later, he enters. "You wanted something?" His stained apron smells like raw meat and blood.

"Yes, Cal. Sit down, please." My stomach can't decide whether to boil in anger or to quiver with fear. Eno has let me down.

He sits but scowls at Duchess, who hands me the accounts book. "What's she doing playing with my books?"

"First, they aren't your books. They're mine, and she's my sister. She's also a whiz at accounting, Cal. Can you guess what she's found?"

He blanches, confirming my suspicions.

"And then there's the problem with the credit extended beyo—"

He jumps to his feet. "Now just a minute—"

I hold up my hand. "No, you wait a minute. And sit down." I wait, silent until he sits. "You had no right to extend credit beyond three months. That's always been Parker's policy. What I can't understand is how you thought we could stay in business between drying up our income and skimming the books." His eyes open wide, and his face drains of color, leaving him pasty white. "Duchess has totaled what you stole. It covers more than a year's salary. You can thank the good Lord I don't prosecute you. But you are fired. You may leave now."

He's slow to stand, as if he's calculating what to do, his fists balled at his sides. Duchess rises with so much grace, I'm in awe of her. She opens the door for him. His face is an ugly mask of hatred.

"You'll be sorry for this. You won't get away with firing me. I've worked for—" He clamps his mouth shut, storms out of the office, and through the grocery toward the front door. He stops and looks back at us, a nasty smile on his face. He takes a step to the side and shoves over the display of pork and beans on his way out.

Behind the register, Pinkie's mouth gapes along with the three customers waiting in line to have their groceries tallied. I'm not sure whether to be thankful for the witnesses or be embarrassed. I choose thankfulness.

Duchess steps out the office door. "If that's the worst he does, we'll be all right. But I wonder what he meant by 'he's worked for'? For whom, if not you?"

For whom, indeed. "Big Jim. You know, now that I think of it, he used to ask me for money every couple of months. Being my Jimmy's daddy, I obliged him. It wasn't a lot, and the store had been his livelihood. He hasn't asked for anything lately, though. I wonder if Cal was giving the money to him."

Duchess squats and puts the first can back into its place in the display. "That could be, but it's still stealing. You can bet he kept some for himself too."

I crouch opposite her to replace the cans on the other side of the tower. I keep my voice low. I don't want the customers to hear me and start gossiping. "I have no proof either way, other than the books are altered, and the money isn't adding up." I grit my teeth. "What burns me is he thought I was a Dumb Dora and wouldn't find out—"

I fall back onto my rump. He's right. If not for my sister, I would have been bled dry.

"Duchess, when we finish here, go back and make a list of the names of those more than three months in arrears on their accounts. If they're farmers, we can barter. I'm not without compassion."

"No, you're not." She reaches across the tower and pats my hand, but her motion knocks all the cans to the floor once more. We stare at each other, mouths open, then begin to giggle.

Together, Sister and I can be strong. I just hope it's enough.

There are drawbacks to living in a small town like Rivers End. News spreads faster than butter on a hot biscuit. That can be good or bad, depending on the news and a body's perspective. The subdued way people are acting today, word is out about me firing Cal and cutting off the overdue accounts.

I'm guessing there's plenty of speculation about Pinkie as well, gauging from the disapproving looks aimed her way—and mine, for that matter. I blame Cal for that too. The first day she came into the store with Sister and me, he gave me an earful, calling her a daughter of evil, a brazen hussy, and more. He even called her "bad luck" because of her being albino. Most prejudices come from ignorance, and Cal has an abundance of it. Said I should throw her back into the gutter where she came from. Why, Barry would pitch a fit. Not to mention my own conscience branding me a hypocrite.

Sadie passes the grocery window, her head bent to the wind as if she's pushing it out of her way. When she opens the door, the bell jangles, and everyone turns to see who it is. Cora Cook sniffs in disdain and puts her mouth close to Nellie Taggart's ear. Cora has known Sadie all her life, but she still can't get over her blind biases. Well, she's in for a surprise when she tries to put that bag of cornmeal she's holding on her tab. She's on the "no more credit" list since her bill hasn't been paid in close to eight months. Helen Ivey at least paid a dollar last month and brought eggs in to barter this week.

Sadie ignores the women and takes my elbow, gently steering me to the office. Over my shoulder, I motion to my sister to help Pinkie. Sadie closes the door behind us. This morning, she's wearing wide-legged trousers and a short jacket.

"You did the right thing firing Cal, but he's spreading the word about you cutting off credit accounts without telling all the facts. Some folks are getting riled up. The others have enough brains to see you can't keep the doors open with nothing coming in."

"Doesn't surprise me one bit. Cal's pride is stung. If Big Jim had fired him, he'd be mad, but he'd have his pride. Since a woman caught him in his sins, he's bitter." I try to gauge Sadie's concern. "Do you think we can expect trouble?"

"I'm not sure. I'll be keeping my ears and eyes open. You do the same. I'll see you tonight."

I nearly forgot it's our weekly game night. While we play bridge with a number of folks once a month, after my sister joined our household, she instituted the weekly game night. Now, it's Sadie, Pinkie, Sister, and me. Tonight it's my night to choose the game. Spades is easier than bridge. The bidding is straightforward and not loaded with hidden meaning. Bridge is so silly—since everyone else knows what you're saying, why don't we just say it? Besides, my mind is preoccupied with the grocery's accounts and all the folks I have to insist start paying their bills.

While Sadie stops to chat with Pinkie, I go back to the register. Soon, Nellie Taggart, who'd been eyeing me and Sadie—more like trying to overhear us—approaches the counter, pulling her son's wagon, piled high with groceries.

I almost feel sorry for her. She doesn't have an auto to go to another town, so she's dependent on my goodwill to feed her boarders. But my goodwill ends with her prejudices. Without Pinkie helping Duchess and me, we'd be in a sorry state. And Sadie. Since I fired Cal, she's been volunteering in the store. She won't let me pay her—says she doesn't have anything else to do, anyway. She stopped working in the bank a few months before the crash. I don't know her financial health, but she seems to manage. I know she's a Godsend to me.

I take a deep breath. "I'm sorry, Nellie, your account is seven months in arrears. No more credit until you bring it up-to-date. You don't allow your boarders to stay for long when they don't pay."

She pulls herself up like a toad, ready to croak. "I've been a customer here since before *you* came along, missy. You and your no 'count ways, consorting with sinners. Why, I've a mind to go talk to Big Jim."

I cross my arms. "I own this store, Nellie. Not Big Jim. He has no say here."

Her eyes narrow, and her mouth pinches. "We'll see about that." She tips her wagon, spilling the groceries onto the floor. With a final toss of her head, she turns to leave. As she reaches the door, a tomato smacks her in the back of the head, splattering juice and seeds in her hair and down her neck.

I bite my lip to keep from laughing. Sadie's aim is still as true as ever. Nellie flees, not bothering to shut the door, her wagon jumping and bumping behind her. I turn to see Sadie and Pinkie gaping at my sister, who's wearing a smug expression.

Duchess? "You didn't!"

Sadie barks a laugh. "Oh, but she did."

"I kind of know how she feels, though." Pinkie looks toward the door where Nellie has fled. "I've had a lot of tomatoes thrown at me. Usually rotten ones, though."

Sadie puts her arm around Pinkie's shoulders. "We have a lot in common, you and me. But Nellie has been asking for that for quite some time. Long before you arrived. Now let's all get back to work."

Sadie returns to unloading a crate of Oxydol washing powder. Boxes of Lux and brown bottles of Pure sit open and ready to shelve.

Pinkie approaches my sister. "Thank you. No one has ever stood up for me like that before."

Duchess gives her a one-armed hug and a huge, self-satisfied grin. "Our merry little band of women is stronger than the likes of her."

"I'm proud of you for holding your ground, Maggie." Sadie nods toward the door Nellie fled through, while Pinkie closes it. "I wonder what she'll feed us tonight for supper."

I nudge Sadie's shoulder. "You will be having Macaroni Papoose with us."

"Wonderful. And Nellie can eat crow."

CHAPTER 12

Christmas is just two days away, and I am determined to make it festive, despite money being tight. No, tight is being generous. Non-existent is closer to the truth. Presents are handmade, but love and giggles and secrets are flying about the apartment.

I lift the final pot from the dishpan and hand it to Duchess to dry. "As soon as these are put away, we'll go get our Christmas tree." At least we can do that. Trees are plentiful in the woods. And they're free.

"Are Mr. Wade and Ozzie coming with us?" Barry turns to Pinkie and Duchess. "They always come with us. Mr. Wade chops down the trees, and Ozzie and me, we drags 'em home."

"Ozzie and I," Duchess gently admonishes.

"You can't drag a tree, Auntie Duchess. It's me and Ozzie who brings 'em home."

Pinkie sets the dried pot on the shelf. "Whoever. Let's get a wiggle on."

We wiggle back up the stairs and grab our sweaters. The weather warmed back up after the Thanksgiving cold snap, but it's in the low sixties, and we'll want our wraps once we're in the woods and out of the sunshine.

A knock sounds on the door. "Come on in, Ozzie," I call over my shoulder as I fold my sweater.

The door opens, but it isn't Ozzie. Or Wade. It's Big Jim, and he's wearing a scowl. I grab his elbow and push him out the door. I'm not about to let him ruin our day.

"What do you think you're doing?" He pulls his arm from my grasp. What's he doing with a new tweed jacket when his grandson's is too small?"

"I can tell you're not here to join our tree cutting party. I won't have you upsetting Barry."

He glances back at the closed door. "Then you should consider your behavior. What were you thinking, firing Cal? He's been my manager for over twenty years."

"Good for him. He's been *my* manager for over seven years. I fired him for cooking the books, not to mention letting several accounts go unpaid for over six months. A few over a year."

"If you didn't have that aberration or your sister under your roof draining food and money from my grandson, you'd be okay."

With my hands on my hips, I square off with him. "You're saying I should toss Pinkie and my sister into the street and let Cal continue to flimflam me? You've lost your ever-lovin' mind if you think I'll do that."

Big Jim shakes his finger under my nose, and only my strength of character keeps me from biting it.

"Maggie, if you don't listen to me, I'll have my lawyer call that new child protection thing, and I'll take custody of Barry. You're exposing him to sinful ways."

I'm not about to let him see how much I fear the word *lawyer*. I point down the stairs. "Out. Go on. You know nothing about Pinkie or what happened to her. Even Preacher Gordon says I did the right thing by taking her in."

Uncertainty passes over his hateful mug, but it doesn't set. The ugly scowl returns. "You're asking for trouble, girlie. I'm going to exercise that loophole my lawyer found." He jams his hat back on his bean and stomps down the stairs.

What loophole?

Turn the other cheek.

I don't know if that's God talking to me or my own conscience, but it's not a bad idea. It's disarming the enemy. Besides, asking a question isn't caving.

"By the way," I call after him. "Will you be spending Christmas

Day at home?"

He stops and turns back to me with the strangest look of bewilderment. Then the expression leaves, replaced by his anger. He snarls and disappears into the afternoon.

I swanny, that man is a bagful of ornery. What I don't understand is first he's mad, then he's bewildered, then he's mad again. Which makes me think he's hiding something. If I can find out what, maybe I can stop his threats.

Barry opens the door. "Mama?" I turn, and he snuggles in close. I cling to him. "Why does granddaddy hate everyone?"

"Oh, baby." I squat and look him in the eye. "He doesn't hate everyone. He's just … confused, I think."

"Hey, are all y'all ready to go?" Thankfully, Ozzie interrupts, and Barry forgets about his grandfather. For the moment. "Come on, Duchess. Pinkie. We've got a tree to cut down."

We make a merry party crossing the street to the station, where we join up with Sadie, the Mobleys, and the Wiggins. Joe Bob Wiggins has his delivery wagon filled with hay and his two horses harnessed, ready to go. Barry and Ozzie scurry to feed the horses the carrots they brought, and then we all climb up into the wagon.

Wade and Joe Bob help get Pinkie inside and onto the hay. Wade lingers with his hand on hers. My, my. I settle and watch Pinkie watching Wade. I've always said he is a true Christian man, never judging, always looking for the best in people. And apparently, he sees a lot of good in her—he's definitely solicitous. She brings out the protector in him.

I turn my attention back to the boys, who are in high spirits. Bells on the horses' harnesses jingle merrily, enticing us to sing "Jingle Bells." We may lack the snow part but none of the spirit. The boys rival each other with who can sing the loudest. The wagon takes us out of town past Faylene's. She and Bessie Mae are sitting on the front porch and wave at us as we drive by.

"Mama?" Barry asks. "Are we getting Meemaw a tree?"

"We most certainly are. We'll spend Christmas Day with her

as always."

"Then why are we getting a tree for our apartment?"

I brace one hand on the side of the wagon and tug his ear with the other, making him giggle. "Because Santa will need a tree to put your present under, now, won't he?" I managed to scrounge two dollars to spend on his present. It's not the model airplane he wants, but he'll like a toy automobile.

"At home? Really?" The realization of two Christmases dawns. "Yes, ma'am! I love Christmas." He tosses some hay into the air and grins at Ozzie. "You and Mr. Wade are coming over Christmas Eve, aren't you?"

"We always do. Why wouldn't we this year?"

Ozzie is logical if nothing else. I think he's going to be an engineer or a lawyer. *Lawyer.* The word sends a shiver of fear through my stomach, but I refuse to let Big Jim destroy our holiday. I start singing "Over the River and Through the Woods." Everyone quickly joins in. We wave at friends as we pass their homes on our way out of town, and soon we are in the woods.

"Last year," Wade says, "Joe Bob and I found some scrub sand pines. We trimmed them and shaped them. I'm hoping they're still here. If so, we'll have fine Christmas trees. Better even than those ones they sell over in Jesup."

"Where are they, Mr. Wade?" Barry bounces near his best pal's daddy.

It's times like this I wish Jimmy were here for Barry.

"You keep your eyes trained over yonder." Wade points to the northwest. "You should see them directly."

I'm just thankful Wade takes so much time with my boy.

"I see one!" Ozzie hollers after a minute. "There, see it, Barry?"

"Whoa." Joe Bob stops the horses, and the boys jump out the back of the wagon.

The men help all of us down, and soon we're tramping through the pine needle floor to the trees. With each step, the forest gives up its rich scent of pine mulch. I inhale with appreciation for where

I live. My cousins may have an easier life in the city, but mine is richer in so many other ways.

The trees Joe Bob and Wade trimmed are indeed nicer and fuller than store-bought ones. And they're fresh. I almost hate to cut them down, but they won't remain so pretty if left in the forest. I lean into the boughs and sniff their sweetness. The scent of pine is strong. The apartment will smell wonderful.

The men grab their axes and chop down a tree for each family. Sadie will share ours since Nellie won't allow them in her boarders' rooms.

Pinkie has her hands clasped beneath her chin. Her delight, rivaling Barry and Ozzie's, prompts me to ask, "Sugar, have you never cut down a Christmas tree?"

"We never had one. My daddy didn't believe in celebrating anything but the output of his still."

"What about when your mama was alive?"

She shakes her head. "If Mama spent money on anything but food, he'd beat her. She couldn't even make presents. She tried once. She took an old dress of hers and remade it into a new one for me." Pinkie's face pinches. "He threw it in the fire out of pure meanness."

Why are some men so nice like Wade and Joe Bob, while others are like her daddy and Big Jim?

I put my arm around her. "You're going to have yourself some fun this Christmas, sugar. We know how to celebrate the Savior's birthday."

Inside our little apartment, we're all whispering and keeping secrets. Home may have shrunk in places to get alone, but it's filled with love and laughter. Pinkie and Barry are downstairs in the kitchen, concocting something in secret. Sister and I are not allowed to go in there. I'm writing a story for Barry in which he's the hero. Duchess has been sewing a lot lately. She pulled out several of her dresses and a few coats from her trunk in the storeroom, then began tearing them apart.

Barry and Pinkie couldn't wait, so we decorated the tree as soon as it was set up inside. I still have two of our great-great-great-grandmother's blown glass ornaments, which are near the top of the tree. The lamplight makes them sparkle. The rest of the ornaments are paper ones. My favorite is the little lopsided heart Barry cut out and decorated for me two years ago. The final touch is popcorn and cranberry strands wrapped around the branches. When we finished, Barry pronounced it a fine Christmas tree.

"Maggie." Duchess lays aside her sewing. "I hear Mr. Bud whistling. I'll go get the mail. I'm hoping for a letter or Christmas card from one of my Atlanta friends." Her sigh goes straight to my heart.

I lay down my pen, careful not to smudge the ink. "They may be embarrassed over their losses, sugar. Very few but the extremely wealthy were left with anything." The afternoon sun is dipping behind the trees, so I cross the room to close the blinds. "And Mr. Alden might not have been the only one to … to …"

Sister shakes her head and sends me a sad little smile. "I've heard of others. It makes me so grateful to have you and Barry, Magnolia. Being here with y'all has taken the self-pity out of this. I grieve my husband, but not my former life." Her smile grows warm. "I like the person I'm becoming."

That deserves a hug, and I give her one. "I do, too, Duchess. You're helping me more than you realize. Cal would have bled me dry if not for you. Now go get the mail."

The apartment is quiet for a few moments. I'm alone and realize how much I've grown used to the presence of my sister and Pinkie. In the few weeks they've been here, each has woven herself into the fabric of my life. I can't imagine being without them. They spark my creativity. They're my muse.

The door flies open, and Duchess is waving an envelope. "Sister! It's from Lawrenceville. The *News Standard*. Hurry, open it." She thrusts it into my hands. With my heart in my throat—*please don't let it be a rejection*—I tear the flap from the envelope. I pull out the single page, and as I unfold it, a bank draft falls to the floor.

"Money!" Duchess grabs it up. Her eyes open wide as she stares at it. "Maggie, it's for twenty-six dollars." She waves the check under my nose. "Look!"

While Duchess dances around the living room, I stare it. Twenty-six dollars is for a year's worth of stories. One per week. For fifty-two weeks. He only promised to buy six months' worth. I pick up the letter from the floor where it fell when Duchess said "twenty-six dollars" and scan it.

"Read it to me. What does he say?"

"His readers loved my bedtime story and are clamoring for more. The check is pre-payment for one per week for six months." I frown and look at my sister. "That can't be right. I told him fifty cents per story."

She peers over my shoulder. "There's more. Read that." She points to the last paragraph.

"I'm paying you one dollar per story so the *News Standard* has exclusive rights to them. We can renegotiate in six months. Welcome aboard, Maggie. We plan to syndicate your Helpful Home Hints column, as well. Merry Christmas."

Duchess pulls me to my feet. "Merry Christmas indeed, Sister."

Footsteps pound on the stairs outside. Barry and Pinkie burst in the door.

My sweet boy is wide-eyed and frightened. "We heard Auntie Duchess screaming. What's wrong?"

I pat the cushion next to me on the davenport, and he hops up. "Nothing is wrong, my darling. Mama just sold a whole lot of stories to the newspaper in Lawrenceville. And they sent me a real bank draft for them."

"Your mama is going to be a famous writer, Barry. All over Georgia." Duchess grabs his hands and pulls him up to dance with her.

Pinkie turns on the radio and finds a music station while Duchess and Barry roll up the rug. Pinkie's quite a sight, doing the Charleston. With her large belly, she can't quite reach her knees. Sweet laughter fills the apartment.

God is good to send this blessing just in time. I can get Barry that model airplane. And now I can get Duchess and Pinkie each a small bottle of toilet water. Or—Ida Clare said she got some new felt cloche hats in. If they aren't too expensive, maybe I could get one for Pinkie. She doesn't have a hat. And Sadie. I want to get something for her. She's been my best friend for so long. I already have a gift for Mama Faylene and Bessie Mae. And Barry has one I helped him buy for his grandfather.

The song ends, and Barry jumps around the room, giggling. "We're in high cotton now, Mama."

I don't want to dampen his enthusiasm, or anyone else's, but while this money is very helpful, the next tax bill weighs on me. And the fate of Parker's Grocery. The fingers of this stock market crash and banks closing have everyone in a vice grip. And they're squeezing tighter every day.

As soon as the doors open, I'm in line to cash this bank draft. Who knows how long or even if our bank will remain open? This morning, five people are in line in front of me. Nellie Taggart's husband, Harry, and Oscar Saddler are behind Karl from the *Farm Whistler*. Nellie chats with Minnie Saddler while they wait for their husbands. Lovely. Two women who dislike me intensely.

Oh no. Cal Llewellyn is in front of Harry. Lord have mercy, he's talking to Doyle Cook—one of Rivers End's good ole boys. Doyle and Harry Taggart continue to operate their still in the woods. It's amazing how every time the Feds come, it's not where it's supposed to be. The good ole boy network at its worst. I wish Rosa would hurry with their transactions before they see me. Maybe I should come back later.

I'm about to turn around and go when Karl Fiedler leaves. He tips his hat to me. I smile and decide to stay. Doyle finishes and turns. Applesauce, he sees me.

"Well, well, well. If it isn't little Maggie Parker. Now, I know for a fact you don't have a bank account, Maggie. What are you doing here?" His hand snakes out and snatches the check from me. He holds the draft up for everyone to see. "'Pay to the order of Magnolia Parker. Twenty-six dollars and no cents.' What's this for, Mag-knolll-ya?"

"Give me that back."

Cal barks a laugh and plucks the bank draft from Doyle. "It's from a newspaper. What did you sell him, Maggie?"

My heart is racing. "It's none of your business, Cal."

Doyle giggles behind me. "I'll bet it was her services, and I don't mean the writin' kind." He cackles like a hyena.

Nellie and Minnie gasp.

I whip my head around. "I sold him stories."

Cal rocks back on his heels, looking down his nose. "Bolshevik ones, no doubt. You know, Doyle, Maggie never gave me any severance pay. I think this should be mine. What do you think?"

"Oh, I agree. Yours, definitely."

I make a grab for it, but Cal holds it up high.

Minnie and Nellie snicker. They wouldn't laugh if it were one of them.

"You stole more than a year's wages from me, Cal. I owe you nothing." I reach for the check. "And it's my name on it. Not yours. You can't cash it."

Rosa looks up from her work, her eyes open wide and her jaw slack.

Cal dons an evil leer. "Neither can you."

He tears the check in two. I lunge for him. I manage to grab one half, but he drops the other on the floor and grinds it under his heel.

"She's got half of nothin'." Cal laughs and walks to the door with Doyle as I scramble for the crumpled and torn piece of check. "That's probably all her services are worth. She ain't got much meat on those bones o' hers."

As I straighten, Minnie sniffs, looks down her nose, and turns her back on me, muttering loudly. "Apparently, the hussy she took in to live with her isn't the only one in that household."

Nellie picks up the diatribe. "Next thing you know, they'll hang out a shingle and a red light." She tosses her head and walks out behind Minnie.

The good ole boy network has fired a direct hit. I'm standing alone in front of Rosa, my reputation in tatters, holding an equally tattered bank draft I desperately need to cash.

CHAPTER 13

The window blinds crack open, spilling weak light into my eyes. Small feet tiptoe across the floor. I'm ready for him. The moment Barry reaches the side of my bed, I flip back the covers and grab him, smothering him with kisses.

Barry's shrieks and giggles will wake everyone. I shush him then look him straight in the eyes. In an attempt to hurry to the presents, his hair is hand-slicked, and a drop of water trickles down to his chin. It's hard to keep a straight face. He grins and swipes the drip away.

"You've been up peeking, haven't you, sweet pea?"

"No, ma'am. Honest. I heard Auntie Duchess and Miss Pinkie giggling."

I climb out of bed and stick my head out the bedroom door. Theirs stands wide open like a yawning tiger with wrinkled bedclothes on its tongue. "I guess we didn't wake them. Where can they be?" I tousle my boy's hair, relishing the feel. Who knows how long he'll let me get away with such liberties.

"They're in the kitchen, Mama. Auntie Duchess is making coffee, and Miss Pinkie is fixing up flapjacks."

I open my eyes wide. "Do you think your auntie remembered to put the grounds in the basket, or is it cowboy coffee for Christmas?"

His giggles are the best present I can receive. "You're silly, Mama. She knows how."

He has no concept of our money struggles. But then, why should he? His friends' families are in the same mess. I pray I can shelter him for a few more years. I grab my robe and slip it on.

"Come on. Let's go see if they're ready."

He doesn't wait to be told twice but races out the door and thunders down the stairs. After breakfast, I'll let him get his present from Santa. I thank the good Lord for Rosa at the bank, who managed to tape the check back together and cash it. I'm saving the model airplane to give him at Faylene's. If it weren't for my sweet mother-in-law, I wouldn't go up there. But I can't deny her Christmas with her only grandchild. While we don't have a great deal of packages to take, we'll use Barry's little wagon, a gift from his meemaw last year, to deliver them.

Breakfast is a hurried affair with Barry unable to sit still. We give up and carry our coffee back to the living room so he can find his presents from Santa. The toy automobile is a big hit, but when he sees the black, high-topped, canvas athletic shoes, his eyes open wide. "Mama? Did you tell Santa I wanted these?"

I cross my fingers behind my back. I'm sure the Lord will forgive me. "I never said a word to Santa." At least that part is true. "He just knows what boys like, sugar."

Barry promptly sits on the floor and slides his feet inside them. "Can I wear them today?"

"You may, with socks, and let's get a wiggle on. Your meemaw is waiting."

We stop at the boarding house to collect Sadie, who is on the front porch, waiting for us with packages at her feet. What a merry cohort we make, pulling that wagon piled—if not high at least gaily—with food and colorful packages. Barry dances ahead of us with his toy auto in hand.

I have another special gift waiting for him. I had his daddy's pocket watch cleaned and put a picture of him inside it for Barry. It's a bit grown-up for him, but he's such a responsible boy, and I want him to have it while he's young. He's been asking a lot of questions about Jimmy lately.

We round the corner, and Faylene's house comes into view. Just as Sadie was, she's out on the porch waiting for us.

"Meemaw!" Barry calls and runs ahead. "Merry Christmas! See

what Santa brought me?" He waves the toy auto over his head and hops on one foot, sticking out the other for her to see.

While she exclaims over his shoes and toy, Pinkie and I go inside to take the food to Bessie Mae. Duchess sets the presents under the Christmas tree, which has many of my Jimmy's childhood decorations on it. On my way to the kitchen, I peek up the stairs, but I don't see any sign of Big Jim. Where can he be on Christmas morning? Surely, he's here.

Bessie Mae is bending over the oven, basting a goose. It smells divine. "Merry Christmas, Bessie Mae." I set the box of food we brought on the kitchen worktable.

"Merry Christmas, Miss Maggie. Where's that boy?" She closes the oven door and wipes her hands on her apron.

"Still on the porch with Mama Faylene." I hand her the bowl of salad. It's a new recipe I found in the newspaper called Hardscrabble Salad. Bessie Mae sniffs it and picks up a fork. She takes a small taste and nods her approval.

"What can I do to help you?"

"Now, Miss Maggie, you knows I got it all in hand." She shoos me out the door.

Duchess has wheeled Faylene into the front room, and they're watching Barry inspect the wrapped packages under the tree. I hope she likes the lap robe I knitted for her. She turns her head at my approach.

"Dear, I believe my grandson has waited as long as he can. Shall we open presents?"

"What about Big Jim? Where is he?" I keep my voice low for Barry's sake.

"I haven't seen hide nor hair of him in a couple of weeks now."

She doesn't appear to be concerned by that, but I am. It's a conundrum for certain. While life is more peaceful without his bluster, his place is home with his wife. Where can he be, and worse, what is he up to?

"Do you have any idea where he is?"

She waves away my concern. "Barry, sugar, do you see that green ribbon on the big red box?"

Barry scrambles toward the other side of the tree. "This one, Meemaw?"

"Yes. It's the one from all of us. Let's have your mama open it first."

From all of them? Barry struggles to drag it over. Duchess lends him a hand with a twinkle in her eye. She must have helped them buy it. But how did they get whatever it is here?

"Y'all have really been keeping secrets. Want to help me, son?"

Together, we remove the ribbon, and he rips the paper with glee. My eyes widen as a wooden box appears with a sloped lid. "It's a portable writing desk." I run my hand over the finish. "Where—?"

"Mr. Wade made it." Barry wiggles beside me. "Open it, Mama."

"I knew Wade's hobby was woodworking, but he outdid himself." I reverently lift the lid. Inside is a neat stack of paper and a fountain pen. An expensive one, I can tell. I pick up the pen and turn to my sister. "How—?"

"It was Mr. Alden's. I hid it from the creditors. I want you to have it. My dear husband loved your stories. He was so proud of you and planned to give you one of your own, but ..." She pulls a hankie from her pocket and dabs her eyes. "He ... he said he was going to bring me here for Christmas and had such plans—" Her face crumples and tears stream.

My heart breaks for her. I close the lid on my beautiful writing desk and go to where she sits. Pinkie joins me, and we hold her as she cries. Barry pats her head.

"Don't cry, Auntie Duchess. Uncle Will wouldn't want you to be so sad. He's celebrating Jesus' birthday with Him in heaven."

Out of the mouths of babes. Barry's simple logic makes Sister smile through her tears, and she hiccups. I squeeze her shoulder and whisper in her ear, "I'll treasure it always, as I do you."

"Bessie Mae?" Faylene calls toward the kitchen.

"Yes'm?"

"Please come in here. Barry, get Bessie Mae's present."

When she joins us, Barry carries the package to her. She carefully opens the lid, and her eyes light up at the new apron. She runs her fingers over her name in pink and gray thread.

"Auntie Duchess did that." Barry points to the embroidery.

"It's mighty fine, Mistah Barry."

"What is the meaning of this?" Big Jim's voice booms. He stands in the doorway glowering, his fists on his hips, his feet planted wide. The sunlight from the window opposite the parlor is blocked by his presence, and the room darkens perceivably. Barry dives into my arms, Pinkie clings to Sadie, and the only one who doesn't screech is Faylene.

"It's Christmas, James. The usual occupation is exchanging presents."

His scowl deepens. "I know what the day is, Faylene. What I want to know is why Bessie Mae isn't in the kitchen where she belongs and who invited that ... that ... oddity into my house? Not to mention the half-breed." His hand shakes with anger as he points to Pinkie and Sadie. I'm about to jump up, but Faylene turns and fixes him with a gaze that stops me. She crooks her finger and beckons him closer. She whispers, but I overhear her.

"I invited them. It's *my* house. I can invite whomever *I* please."

What does she mean it's *her* house? Even stranger, I've never seen her stand up to Big Jim. For anything. But then again, he's never attacked Bessie Mae before.

Big Jim flinches at her words and straightens. Blustering, he sits on the divan, and his glowers dampen the festivity of our holiday. Pinkie and Sadie cross the room to sit on a bench near the bookcase. Pinkie selects a book but doesn't open it. It lies closed in her lap. Bessie Mae takes her apron and retreats to the kitchen, mumbling under her breath. Something about an old goat. A snicker begs release, but I subdue it. No use throwing kindling on that fire.

"What have you got there, boy?" Big Jim asks Barry, who takes a step toward his grandfather.

"It's a toy automobile, sir." I'm glad he's remembering his manners. That should put the old curmudgeon in a better mood. Barry hands over the toy for Big Jim to look at.

"Mama? There's more presents. May I look?"

"Yes. I believe you'll find the one from you to your granddaddy in that blue box."

Big Jim whips his gaze toward me, his expression unreadable. Barry finds and hands him the small box. When he opens it and pulls out the penknife that Barry saved up for, he nods at his grandson and slides it into his pocket. Not a "thank you" passes his lips. Are good manners only for the young? Sadie nods at something Pinkie whispers, but her eyes never leave Big Jim. She's tense—coiled and ready to strike should his temper get out of control.

Arms folded, Barry taps his foot, standing in front of his grandfather. After a moment, his small fists thump against his hips. "Well? Do you like it?"

"Of course, I like it." He offers Barry an obligatory grimace.

I've had enough. "Sugar." I drop to the floor next to the tree and pull out two boxes from beneath its branches. "This is for you." I hand him the larger one, cradling the small one in my lap for now.

Barry rips the paper off to reveal his long-awaited model airplane. He squeals and jumps up, throwing his arms around my neck.

"Thank you, Mama. I've wanted this for my whole life!" He pries at the lid.

"Wait until we get home to start putting it together." I hold out the little box to him. "This is something very special for you from me—and your daddy."

Big Jim's head snaps up. Barry stills, and his eyes grow large. "From my daddy?" His small hand opens for me to lay the box in it.

"He talked about when you'd be old enough, that he wanted you to have this." I glance at Faylene, who smiles her approval. "I think this is the right time."

Big Jim scowls and slides forward in his seat, watching Barry like a bird of prey, ready to swoop in. I slip my arm around my son's small shoulders and draw him closer as he opens the box.

"Oh, Mama." He lifts out the pocket watch. "Was this Daddy's?"

"Open it up and see."

With care and more than a little reverence, he pushes the stem down, and the watch face pops open. He stares at the small image of his daddy's face. "He looks like me, Mama."

Big Jim growls and pounces, making a grab for the watch. I cover Barry's hands with mine before his grandfather can snatch it away. Duchess gasps, and Sadie is off the bench, taking a step toward us.

He stops, glares at them, then looks down at us. "That should have come back to me, not given to a child. It's too valuable." He thrusts out his hand. "Give it to me, boy."

Barry's chin trembles. "It's for me. From my daddy." He scoots behind me.

"He is very responsible, and it's my decision."

Big Jim's face grows red. "You can't make a decent decision about anything. You fill this boy with unfit ideas and surround him with people of loose morals." He glares at Pinkie and snorts. "Between having the cook at the family table and this"—he waves his hand at Pinkie and Sadie, who have locked arms—"this misfit and the half-breed, you don't even know what a decent family is."

Barry jumps up and faces his grandfather. "I know they're nicer than you are. You're a mean man, and I don't care if you like the present I gave you or not." He drops back into my lap and buries his face in my shoulder, crying.

"And there's a good example. The boy doesn't respect his elders."

"To be respected"—Faylene's soft voice demands attention— "one must act worthy of respect. It's time for our Christmas dinner. Everyone here is welcome at my table." She sets her gaze on Big

Jim. "Even you."

In two strides, he's at the front door. "I won't eat with the sinners." He grabs his hat off the hall tree and storms out.

For a moment, nobody moves. Then Sadie snorts, breaking the tension. Barry climbs off my lap and crosses to his grandmother's side. He lays his head on her shoulder and puts his arm around her neck. "I love you, Meemaw. I'm sorry I made Granddaddy angry."

Faylene pulls him onto her lap. "Sugar, you didn't make him angry. He's got a mad hornet living inside him, and it starts buzzing any time somebody doesn't agree with his thinking." She pushes his mussed curls off his forehead. "Now, if you straddle my legs, let's see if you can wheel this chair with both of us sitting in it." She grins and wiggles her eyebrows at him. "Do you think we can?"

Barry grins and nods. He turns face forward on her lap. Putting his little hands on the metal rings that turn the wheels, he grunts and pushes them forward a few inches. Duchess sneaks up behind them and gently helps.

Our festive mood restored, we parade into the dining room. We're just about to sit when the doorbell rings. I exchange glances with Faylene. *Big Jim?* She shakes her head.

She has a gleam in her eye. "That will be Louella with Wade and Ozzie. I invited them."

Pinkie blushes and I share a surprised "oh" with Barry. "Go let them in, then, son."

He runs to the door. "Ozzie! What did Santa bring you?"

"Bring them on in here, Barry," Faylene calls to him. "After all, Wade provided this goose."

Louella carries a large, cloth-covered bowl into the kitchen. By the aroma, I believe we are about to be treated to her special stuffing, which means she hunted for wild mushrooms for hours. I never know which ones are edible, but Louella knows. She says she learned from her Gullah granny.

We retake our seats, waiting for Bessie Mae and Louella to join us. As I look around this table, I'm proud of my family. We may be ahead of our time, but I can't help but think this is what heaven will be like. All colors of people sitting together in fellowship, sharing a meal.

While Wade carves the goose and Ozzie regales us with the story of how he and his daddy shot it, my mind turns to Big Jim. Somehow, I think today may come back to bite.

CHAPTER 14

In Rivers End, life returns to normal the day after Christmas. We're a farm community, and those of us who depend on the farmers' trade adhere to their schedules, no matter how late we celebrated the night before. Farmers don't have long, lazy holidays. Animals need feeding or milking. Their crops need seeing to, even if they don't have much beyond an acre or two of corn and a few vegetables. It's sad how many men have gone to the cities trying to find work. Every week, I see their wives and children who have been left here to eke out a living from the depleted soil. The 1925 drought was so bad, we could walk across riverbeds that normally flowed deep and fast. Georgia crashed long before the stock market, and that's a fact.

It's after nine in the morning, but only three women are in the grocery. Just two months ago, I would have seen a dozen by now. On my way to the office, I slide a box of soap powder, sitting too close to the edge of its shelf, back into place beside its companion. I shake my head. It's downright sorry, only offering my customers two brands of soap powder. I cut back on my inventory when some of our customers left us—instigated by Nellie, who needed the ride—to shop in Uvalda, the closet town to Rivers End. Uvalda is no great metropolis, and the grocery store is smaller than Parker's. But apparently, Nellie and her cronies hold their self-righteous indignation over Pinkie in higher esteem than their convenience.

Duchess is already in the office when I open the door. I stop, confused. "I thought you and Pinkie were going to reorganize the store today."

"We are, but I wanted to get these bills ready for you to pay."

My sister glances up, and her eyes search mine. "Some are past due."

Fear gnaws at my stomach. "The money left from the *Farm Whistler* will cover those, won't it?"

"Only the past due ones. There are a few others that are due later this week. Today's sales will help some, but we need to draw customers back in." Duchess turns and drapes one arm over the back of her chair. "I used to shop in some nice stores in Atlanta. Oh, not grocery stores. Cook did that. But still, there are things they did that made going there a pleasure."

"Like what?" I'm willing to try almost anything to get more customers. Maybe even a few from Uvalda.

"Music, for one. We have electricity here. Let's carry the radio down with us in the mornings. Music playing in the background makes one forget their problems."

I don't think I've ever heard music playing while I shop anywhere. How fun. "That's easy to do. What else?"

"Some of the stores would spray toilet water in the air. That wouldn't be right for Parker's. However …" Her smile lights up the office. "I'm thinking if we could bake something and leave the door open between our kitchen and the storeroom, that aroma should drift in here. It makes one hungry, just smelling bread or a cake baking. And hungry people buy more groceries." She pulls out a piece of paper. "I'm also thinking about us doing demonstrations of new recipes." She draws what she's envisioning. A moment later, she holds it up for me to see.

My sister is amazing. "Duchess, that's brilliant. You should be an advisor to the president or someone." My mind begins to whirl. "Why, we could show women how to make some meatless dishes and other inexpensive meals that would really help them stretch their budgets."

Her eyes crinkle with laughter. "Now you're on the trolley."

We leave the office and go find Pinkie, who is on her knees moving cans around near the front door. She rises, dusts off her hands, and takes the drawing Duchess shows her, while Sister explains about demonstrating recipes and our other ideas.

Holding the drawing, Pinkie turns in a circle. "I can see it. How about the demonstration table back there?" She squints and points to a nook close to the office. "That way, it's in a straight line with the door, easily seen by anyone entering the store, but won't interfere with other shoppers."

My gaze follows her pointing. She's right, customers will see it the minute they open the door. Pinkie and my sister are born businesswomen. "I love it, and I've got a table in the storeroom that will fit perfectly." Her squinting reminds me about Doc. "You went downstairs before Doc came over this morning. He gave me the name of an optometrist in Baxley who might be able to help with your eyesight."

Her pretty white brows draw together. "I don't have enough money saved up, Maggie."

"Saved up for what?" Sadie joins our little circle.

"For glasses." I lower my voice. No need to tell the world. "Doc has been researching albinism and found a doctor over in Baxley who can help."

Sadie nods and slips a clove in her mouth. She chews for a moment. "I'll pay what you don't have, Pinkie. Don't say *no*. It helps us all for you to see better. Now, let me look over the plans you drew for the store reorganization."

That's the end of that discussion and so like Sadie. When she makes up her mind, there's no use arguing. And I'm glad she's going to help Pinkie.

I leave them pointing to various spots in the store and referring to the drawing.

In the office, I lay out the cash for the bills. With the banks failing and so many closing, most of my suppliers prefer to pick up their money. I dole it out according to the vendor. Whoa, my sister is right. The cash left from the sale of my stories isn't going far. When I finish, two envelopes remain empty.

What am I going to do? I have no money to fill them. If I can't fill them, I can't get any more supplies. Without the groceries, I have nothing to sell. It's a vicious circle, and like the vortex in the river, it's pulling me under.

I open the drawer and withdraw my manuscript. I need to write. Soon I'm lost in the low country marshes, pouring my heart and soul into the pages. My pen flies of its own accord. My heroine is at the worst moment of her life when the office door opens.

"Maggie?"

My head snaps up, and my gaze stops on the wall clock. Three hours have passed? Preacher Gordon's wife stands in my doorway, wearing a bewildered smile. "Emma? How can I help you?" People rarely come to the grocery's office.

In her hand, she holds an envelope. "Duchess said I could find you here. This was in my mailbox today. I don't know who it's from, but the dear Lord knew I needed it. It's exactly enough to cover my debt to you and to Mobley's. God is so good."

Forgive me for worrying.

"Thank you, Emma." I take the money she counts out. "It seems the good Lord has us both in His sights. This is exactly what I needed to pay *my* debt to my suppliers."

"Well, hallelujah and amen." Emma's grin is contagious. After she leaves, I straighten my manuscript papers and slide them into their folder. I'm anxious to tell Duchess how God has provided. And to see what the girls have done to the store.

I find my sister and take her into the storeroom to tell her in private. He eyes open wide. "That's … it's … really? The exact amount?"

"I'm ashamed for worrying."

She links arms with me. "I think God will forgive that, sugar. He knows you have a family of four now, soon to be five, to care for. That's new to you. Why"—she stops and stares at me—"just think of it, Magnolia. A mere six weeks ago, it was only you and Barry."

She's right. And I know the good Lord forgives, but I can't help feeling badly. Duchess leads me back into the grocery.

"Maggie, let us take you on a tour." Sister links her arm through mine while Pinkie leads the way. Sadie stands near the demonstration table wearing a proud smile.

Their handiwork tickles me pink. "It looks so clean and uncluttered."

"Starting from the door …" Pinkie narrates, and Duchess draws me forward. "The first items are staples. Flour, cornmeal, sugar, rice, beans, etc."

Most grocery and dry goods stores still operate the old way, with the inventory behind the counter. The proprietor picks up what the customer wants and sets it on the counter. But my Jimmy was progressive, modern. I remember him telling me, "Maggie, customers will buy more when they can pick up an item, read labels, hold in their hands what they might like to have."

So he changed Parker's. But oh, how his daddy objected. I can still hear him. "What in blue blazes did y'all do to my store?"

Jimmy quietly explained, but Big Jim said the store would go under in a year. Well, he was wrong, and Jimmy was right. I see the fruits of that decision all the time. A woman holds in her hands some item she doesn't need but wants. Something small that makes her life a little brighter, a little easier. And she gives into her desire.

And now, moving around the aisles, I see a new thoughtfulness that went into this. All the cleaning items are together. The canned goods are contained in one area, according to type. We don't carry a lot of canned goods since most people hereabouts put up their own, but we do have a few vegetables, some canned fruit, soup, and pork and beans. In Parker's heyday, we carried canned sardines too. But nobody has that kind of money anymore.

As we move around, the boxed cereals are next to the sliced bread, tin pails of peanut butter, and jars of jams. A couple of local farmers have bees, so we buy the honey from them and sell it. The tour ends by the bins of potatoes, onions, any other root vegetables, and fresh fruit if we have it.

Without knowing it, they've surpassed Jimmy's vision. I can't help smiling. "It's beautiful and very different. I hope everyone appreciates what you've done."

"It's a logical layout, Maggie." Sadie fans herself with the folded drawing. "Cal used to add new items willy-nilly wherever he had room. The store had become a hodgepodge."

"Rearranging the store will surely bring a harangue from Big Jim, but I don't care. I love this."

Sadie, Sister, and Pinkie's smiles show me they're tickled pink with my reaction.

"I think the customers will love it too." Sadie brushes off a bit of paper clinging to her pants leg. "They may resist at first since it's different. But that won't last."

I can't afford for it to. The door opens, and Martha Lenger enters with her children hiding behind her skirts. Martha is one of the poorer farm wives in the area. Her husband left nearly four years ago to find work in Savannah. No one has heard from him since. The children have no shoes on their feet nor any coats. Martha startles and looks around the store.

Duchess leaves us and heads toward her. On her way, she stops by the register and picks up a penny candy jar. What is she up to? Martha doesn't have money for candy.

"Mrs. Lenger, might I give the children a piece?"

Martha's face puckers with worry, but Sister puts her hand on the woman's shoulder.

"It would be a favor to me. Please? I don't have any children of my own, and my husband is … has … passed on." Duchess lifts a knuckle to the corner of her eye. "I dearly love to treat children now and again. Will you oblige me?"

I turn away to hide my smile. There's no way Martha can deny her. When I peek back, her four children timidly gather around Sister and accept the candies she hands them. They are wide-eyed over this bounty. My Barry can take a piece of candy any time I allow it. I know for a fact these children have never tasted store-bought candy.

As they suck on the treasures, Martha shops in peace.

I turn to Sadie. "What if maybe one day, when finances get better, I offer our customers coffee? And a place to sit? It would make grocery shopping more relaxing."

"You mean like a cafe?"

"No, just one table with a couple of folding chairs. With our new layout, ladies can shop faster and maybe have time left over to chat with a friend. It makes us a place to see their friends."

She considers that for a moment. "I think you're onto something. I've never heard of any grocery ever doing that. You're ahead of your time, Maggie. But it could work."

After the Lengers leave, Duchess stands by the window watching them. Her fingers worry her collar. Finally, she faces me.

"Something needs to be done about those poor babies." She says no more but turns and walks into the office.

At five o'clock, I turn the door sign to *closed*, and Sister, Pinkie, Sadie, and I leave, locking the door behind us. "Join us for supper, Sadie? It's nothing exciting, but something we might want to demonstrate for our customers. I'd like your opinion. Besides, I think we all could use a game night."

"I'd be obliged." Her mouth pinches as though she's sucked a persimmon. "Nellie's become downright miserly over our meals. Small portions, with no thought into being creative, and the meat reminds me of chewing hides to soften the leather for making moccasins."

Something awakens me. I lie there for a moment in the dark, listening. Out of habit, I turn my head to Barry. He's sprawled on his bed, asleep. I close my eyes and concentrate. All I hear is my son's soft snoring. What woke me? I hold my breath, listening for any sound.

Nothing.

Still, I can't shake the feeling something's wrong. My heartbeat ratchets up a notch. After a moment, I sit up and slip out of bed, then tiptoe to the window overlooking the common backyard. Maybe Doc had a late-night patient and is taking something to the burn barrel, or perhaps there's an early delivery at Mobley's. No, it's the middle of the night—too early for any delivery.

There's no moon. It's completely dark, the big oak in Doc's yard barely visible. I strain to hear … what?

There's only silence.

No, wait … there it is again. A muffled tinkling like glass breaking. Why would gla—it's downstairs. In the grocery!

I bolt to the other bedroom. "Wake up." My whisper sounds harsh and frightening in the dark. I hope Barry can't hear me.

"Is it morning?" Pinkie stretches and yawns.

"No. Shh. Someone is in the grocery." I peer out the front window, but it's too dark to see anything other than the soft light inside the train station across the street.

Duchess gasps. "Oh no!" She grabs her robe from the foot of her bed and clutches it in front of her, trembling.

Pinkie pulls the covers up to her chin. "What should we do?"

"I don't know. Yes, I do. I'm going next door to get Wade. He has a gun and can scare off whoever it is or hold them until we get Jubal, the sheriff." I forgot my bathrobe, so I snatch Pinkie's coat from a peg on the back of the door. "Stay here but keep watch. If Barry wakes up, don't let him come downstairs."

And please keep the invaders from coming through the storeroom and up here.

Duchess crawls over her bed to the window. With her fingers, she parts two of the slats in the Venetian blinds and peeks out. I slip into Pinkie's coat on my way out the door and hurry down the hallway. I restrain myself from frantically pounding on Wade's door. Ozzie doesn't need to be frightened. It takes a long moment, but when it finally it opens, Wade is tying his robe over his pajamas.

"Maggie, what's wrong?"

"Someone has broken into the grocery."

"I'll get my gun." He disappears inside. My stomach churns while I wait. The money for my suppliers sits on my desk. *Please, God, don't let them find it.* What a dumb prayer. The office is the first place a burglar would go. I can't let them take the money. I start for the stairs.

"Maggie, stop." Wade's behind me and has his pistol ready. "You stay up here."

"I'm not letting you go alone. I want to know who it is."

"Okay, but stay behind me." He knows it's futile to argue with me.

I follow him down the back stairs, carefully avoiding the one that creaks. We tiptoe through my kitchen and into the grocery's storeroom. My heart pounds so hard I can't hear anything but its beat. Wade stops before we enter the grocery proper and motions for me to stay put. The storeroom door opens without a sound, and he slips into the grocery. He moves with stealth. I can see why Jubal deputizes him.

Wade disappears from my sight. I'm more frightened staying here alone than I would be in there. I slip into the open doorway. There he is, moving down the center aisle—at least I hope it's Wade.

He stops. The click of a gun being cocked resounds in the silence. "Don't move."

Something crashes into the wall next to me, making me jump. Wood splinters.

Curses fly.

Footsteps pound.

Glass breaks.

A gun fires.

I scream Wade's name as I hit the button, flooding the grocery with light.

CHAPTER 15

hree figures race out the front door and into the darkness. But my gaze doesn't follow them. It's arrested by the carnage. The grocery lies in ruin. The front window is broken, vegetable bins splintered on the floor, potatoes and onions smashed and scattered. Those that aren't squished are contaminated with glass. Cans of fruit and beans have been opened and the contents smeared everywhere. Boxes of oatmeal and dry cereal have been torn open and the contents strewn everywhere, mixing into a slippery goo with the beans and fruit syrup. Not a corner is untouched.

Why? Gaping, I fold my arms across my stomach. It isn't just me they've hurt. It's the people of Rivers End who depend on Parker's for food. The scene blurs. Why didn't I hear anything until too late? The damage—the mess—the cost. How can I recover from this? Who did it? And why?

Wade. Where is he? "Wade? Where are you?"

There's no answer. I turn in a circle. "Are you all right?" The gunshot—it couldn't have been him. Oh, dear Lord, no!

I tiptoe through the slippery mess on the floor, making my way toward where I thought I'd last seen him, and—there he is lying next to the smashed meat case. I hurry to him, slipping and sliding.

I get close enough to see his chest rise and fall. Thank God, he's alive. But my friend is bleeding from a deep gash in his forehead. And he's out cold.

I find a hankie in the pocket of Pinkie's coat. Praying it's clean, I press it to Wade's forehead. He flinches. His eyes flutter open, and he groans.

"Stay put, Wade. Are you hurt anywhere else? Were you shot?"

"No, I'm okay." He sits up and winces. "I got beaned." He points to a large, dented can of pork and beans next to him. "Literally."

"Oh, Wade, I'm so sorry. This needs stitches. Stay here. I'll go get Doc." I put his hand over the hankie. "Keep that on there." Carefully avoiding the glass in the meat case, I grasp the metal frame and rise. "Did you see who it was?"

Holding the material to his head, he turns it in a slow shake. "No." He motions for me to help him up. "We've got to get the sheriff."

I take a step back. "Wade, look around. They're gone. There's no hurry now."

"I'm sorry, Maggie. But we do need to get Jubal. I wounded one of them."

"Oh my. All right. But I'm getting Doc first so he can stitch you up. I'll send Duchess for the sheriff."

He sits back, leaning against the meat case. My heart sinks even lower. Due to the broken glass, all the meat will all have to be thrown out. Duchess will have to start using red ink on the account books.

The front door opens, making me screech.

A deep male voice calls out. "What in tarnation happened? I heard a gunshot."

"Jubal, thank God you're here. I've been—" My money! I hurry as best I can and still remain on my feet through the mess to the office. I grab the doorjamb to steady myself. I'm starting to hyperventilate and can't stop. My desktop is empty, and the envelopes lie torn open on the floor. The money is gone.

Why, Lord? You sent that money in the nick of time. Why did You take it back?

In the middle of the mess and the loss of all that keeps Barry and me from the poorhouse, that still, small voice pierces my heart. He will always take care of me. As He sends, He takes. But as He takes, so will He also send. I can trust in Him.

"Maggie, breathe into this." Jubal sticks a paper bag over my nose and mouth, but I push it away.

"I don't need it." And I don't. Not now. "But Wade needs Doc."

I leave Jubal questioning a bleeding Wade, while I pick my way around the worst of the carnage. After summoning Doc, I hurry upstairs. I need to check Barry. In his room, his bed is empty.

"Duchess? Pinkie? Barry?" My voice rises with each name.

"We're in here." The closet door opens, and they tumble out. Duchess pushes her hair out of her face, offering a sheepish expression. "We heard a gunshot and hid."

In dawn's first light, Sadie, Pinkie, Duchess, and I stand on the sidewalk, staring at the epithets scrawled on the walls of Parker's Grocery. Louella is watching Barry and Ozzie since school is closed until next Monday. The children are the only ones with an extended holiday.

I turn to Sadie. "Why do people hate so much?" The epithets are slurs against Sadie and Pinkie—one aimed at me, but the financial loss to me is devastating. I'm not sure I can survive this.

"The sheriff wasn't much help at all." Pinkie puts her hand in mine. "He said Wade's description could fit a dozen men, and with all the hobos around, it could be anyone."

Sadie spits a chewed clove into the gutter. "Sounds to me like he isn't going to put out much effort over this. Since no one was hurt other than one of the varmints, he doesn't think he needs to."

I stare at her slack-jawed. I can't believe it. "A town business vandalized and robbed and he's not going to investigate it because—"

"Face it, Maggie." Sadie rests a hand on my shoulder. "If you were Big Jim, he'd call out the state militia to help."

"Why? Because I'm a woman? Because *we* are? Is that what you're saying? That burns my biscuits."

"I didn't say he wouldn't investigate. Just don't expect him to hand you the perpetrators. This is a matter of 'us versus them.' Why do you think I marched with the suffragettes?"

Duchess folds her arms across her chest and considers Sadie. "Hmm. The biggest opponents to women working I know of are Cal and Big Jim. They don't seem to have any problem with the other women in town who work. So, following that reasoning and Sadie's, the only two people this would have been are them. Cal has a vendetta. Maggie fired him, but why would Big Jim try to destroy Parker's?"

"Because he wants your sister out." Sadie opens a tin she's drawn from the pocket of her overalls and pops another clove into her mouth.

"But why?" I gesture to the mess in front of us. "He's too old to run the store."

Sadie nods. "I agree, and I intend to help you find out why. Something doesn't add up."

Pinkie is rolling up her sleeves. "Before we can start playing detective, we have to clean up the store. I'll grab the broom."

Duchess stops her. "No. You're too far along for that, sweet pea. How about we set you up at a table out here? You can take orders and tell people we'll deliver their groceries until Parker's is ready to reopen."

My sister, the family princess, takes the lead. Like a soldier into battle, she slogs into the mess, a broom her weapon. I've never been so proud of her.

Sadie taps my shoulder. "Maggie, look." She points down the street.

Coming down Main like an advancing army are Ida Clare Mobley, Emma and Pastor Gordon, Alice Wiggins, and Bessie Mae.

"How did—?" I glance at Pinkie, who is grinning. "Did you ask them?"

She shrugs. "I used Wade's phone to make a call. Ida Clare took care of the rest. Most of this town's residents are good Christian people, Maggie."

They are indeed. My heart fills with gratitude—for Pinkie and for the recruits. We'll get this mess cleaned up in a day with their help. But what I'll do for supplies, God only knows. I certainly don't. With an eye roll heavenward, I follow everyone into the grocery.

I'm heartbroken over the loss of the girls' beautiful rearranging. But as Daddy used to say when milking the cows, "There's no use in bawlin'. Grab a teat and a new bucket."

Alice helps Sadie, Duchess, and I attack the floors, while Emma, Bessie Mae, and Ida Clare wash the inside walls. Pastor Gordon and Wade work on painting over the epithets outside and boarding up the broken window. Too soon, Wade's eye swells shut though. He goes upstairs, but Beau Hampton replaces him.

I don't think I've ever seen our pharmacist mayor without a pipe clenched between his teeth. Yet I've never seen him light it.

Beau pulls on one of his over-large ears. "Wade told me about what happened when he came to fill the script Doc gave him. I figure anyone who wants me can see me out here working and holler for me."

I kiss Beau's cheek, which brings him to blushing, then I retreat inside. We're making progress. All the cans, ruined food, garbage, and glass have been put in the trash and taken to the burn barrel. Doc and Clara will watch over the fire. Soon, it smells like someone spoilt their dinner.

At noon, each bearing a platter, Louella brings the boys downstairs. Hers is huge and heaped with fried catfish. Ozzie and Barry bring the biscuits and collards. Wade follows with cold jugs of sweet tea and lemonade.

When Pinkie comes in to eat, she shows us her list. "I've taken more than a dozen orders, Maggie." She pauses—for dramatic effect, I'm thinking. "Even Nellie Taggart gave me an order."

Sadie and I exchange surprised looks. I can't help wondering if an apology accompanied the order. I'll have to ask Pinkie later. What doesn't surprise me is how she's making over Wade, sitting beside him and calling him a hero. And how much he's liking it. When he's around Pinkie, he stands taller. Did my Jimmy stand taller when I made over him? I can't remember. For Barry's sake, I try, but it's over seven years he's been gone.

By suppertime, the grocery is clean and ready for stocking. I'm trying to stay positive. After all, I'm counting on the good Lord to help. He provided workers, so I suppose He can—

"Maggie?" Duchess stands beside the hand truck Pastor Gordon is pushing. It's stacked with three cartons. "These are the first of several. We're fixing to start stocking the shelves. You want to help?"

"Yes, but where did you find those boxes?"

"Don't you remember? Sadie said to not add any more inventory until you approved the layout. Yesterday afternoon, when you said you liked the arrangement, it was too late to do anything. Then …" She gestures to the front window and watches me closely.

"How much is back there?" My words come out in a whisper. I'm beginning to see God's hand in this, and I'm in awe. Will I ever learn to simply trust? I'll still owe money for those supplies, but I can't sell thin air. "Can we fill the orders Pinkie took with what's in the storeroom?"

"There's some of almost everything. We don't have potatoes or onions, but I'll get a couple of farmers to bring us those. We'll be back in business in no time."

Sadie pats me on the back. "And there's meat in the cooler, both smoked and fresh. You'll make it with God's help."

"And yours. Y'all are His angels."

Sadie's smile turns to a scowl. She's staring over my shoulder. "Speaking of angels, here comes the devil."

She's right, and he's yammering a mile a minute as he storms through the front door. "Well, you finally did it, Maggie. You destroyed Parker's. I'm putting it on the auction—" Big Jim stops in his tracks and stands frozen, only his eyes moving to take in the grocery. Does he finally see more than his anger and greed? "What in the devil?"

Now that's a bit of irony. "What are you putting up for auction, Big Jim?"

His frown makes his brows meet his crooked beezer. "I heard the store was vandalized last night. It's because of your Bolshevik ways, Maggie."

"No. Don't you try to lay it on me. The store was vandalized because of hate and ignorance with a side of stupidity. And outdated prejudices. Whoever did this needs to move into modern times. With the whole nation struggling, we need to help one another, not fight amongst ourselves." Let him put that in his hat and chew on it.

"And just how are you going to open up again with empty shelves?"

He's so sure of himself. As much as I try to remember he is God's child, too, the man is getting on my last nerve. "The storeroom has enough to get us going again. Now if you'll excuse me, I have work to do." I turn away from him and head toward the office.

"Maggie Parker, you get back here." He follows me. "I'm not finished."

I'm weary of struggling, but I know this is nothing more than bluster. "What?" Swiveling to face him, I fold my arms. "Are you here to help stock the shelves?"

"Of course not. I want what I'm still owed for the store."

The word *owed* might as well have been shot from a cannon. It blows a huge hole in my confidence. Was *this* the loophole he keeps talking about? "Jimmy paid you." *Didn't he?*

"Not all. When he died of that flu you brought in the house, he still owed me four thousand dollars. I want it now."

I'm not arguing that flu business again. Jimmy caught that of his own accord. As for his money … "Sure. Help yourself."

I almost laugh as he heads for the office. He has a surprise coming if he thinks there's money in there. Why, he—wait a minute.

There is something very wrong here. I look over my shoulder. "Sadie? Do you see what I do?"

She narrows her eyes and nods.
Big Jim is limping.

CHAPTER 16

"Do you think it was him last night?" Sadie's gaze searches my eyes for an answer.

"I didn't get a good look, but if I were a betting woman, I'd lay odds on it. He's never limped before." I make a beeline for the office with Sadie right behind me.

Big Jim stands in front of the empty safe. The *open* empty safe. The one I left closed and locked. So he still remembers the combination.

He whips his head around as I step inside the door. "Where's the money?"

"In your belly. I figure the food I've provided for you and Faylene over the past seven years has eaten up a large portion." I lean against the corner of my desk and cross my arms. "Let's see, now. You've used the store truck—the one I bought—for years for your personal gallivanting who knows where. Doctor bills for Faylene have taken a good amount more of what you say I owe you. And now it appears I may have to pay for another one."

He doesn't say anything but scowls at me.

"What happened to your leg, Big Jim? Shall I call Doc to come look at it for you?"

"Don't need a doctor for a twisted ankle."

"How'd you do that?" Sadie asks. I'm glad she's here to lend me a bit of her iron.

His gaze bounces between us. "What is this? An interrogation? I come in for the money you own me before you run Parker's into the ground, and you question me?" He pulls himself up like an overblown toad. "I'm warning you, Maggie. You find a way to get the money you owe me. Or else." His attempt to minimize the limp as he leaves is ineffectual. It's more pronounced.

Sadie and I stand in the doorway, watching his retreating back. Outside, the sky is growing dark. Another storm is moving in from the west. I need to know Big Jim's gone. Sadie follows me to the front door.

"Do you believe him?" She pulls out her tin, opens it, and selects a clove. "About the twisted ankle, I mean."

"No. Maybe." I shake my head, my gaze refusing to leave the street as if he might come back. "No, definitely not. What bothers me are his repeated demands for money. I know he has savings—or had them when he retired. Jimmy made sure. After he died, I continued to provide their food. I also pay Bessie Mae's wages. Big Jim wanted to let her go a couple of years ago, but Faylene needs her. And now—" I turn to Sadie. "Now he's gone all the time. It has to tie into his demands. But how?"

Sadie shoves the clove tin back into her trouser pocket. "I don't know. What I do know is we aren't going to leave the store unguarded tonight. I'm going home to get my shotgun. I plan to camp out in front of Parker's all night. I have a feeling we'll be getting another visit." Bending her head to the wind that's now kicked up in the oncoming storm, she leaves.

I go back into the grocery. I've got to replace the front window, though where the money will come from, I don't know. I send up a quick prayer and go help Sister and Pinkie, who are restocking the shelves.

Sister pushes a carton toward me, pointing. "Third shelf down. Why did Sadie leave? I thought she was going to stay and help."

I glance out the front door before squatting to pull a can from the box. I keep my voice low. "To get her shotgun. Apparently, we're staking out the front of the store tonight. She says to keep watch. I need to get Jimmy's old hunting rifle out. Not that I could shoot it, but nobody has to know that, other than us." I grin at my sister's horrified expression. "It'll be fine. Like camping. I don't expect anyone to actually come along."

"Don't count on that." Pinkie eyes the soup cans she shelved and moves one. "I remember when some do-gooders came and broke up Daddy's still. He and his partner figured they wouldn't come back and rebuilt it. Those same men did come back the next night. And they brought the Feds with 'em."

"More the reason for me to sit with Sadie tonight."

"I'll be joining you."

I gape at Duchess. I can't help it. A snicker pops out from between my lips. My sister is the most ladylike woman I know. Plus, a big 'fraidy cat. Why, she ran from the chickens when we were kids. The idea of her sitting with a gun across her knees, waiting on the bad guys to show up, sends me into gales of laughter.

She tosses her head. "I'm delighted I could afford you some mirth, Sister." Then her eyes grow mischievous. She wags her finger at me. "I'm not letting you and Sadie have all the fun." She nudges Pinkie. "Right? You with us?"

Pinkie shrugs. "Sure, why not. I'm not scared."

I wipe my hands on a dishtowel, then lay it on the counter. "Don't y'all forget to bring a chair when you come out," I call over my shoulder to Duchess, who's putting away the dishes with Pinkie. "I'll take Barry to stay with Ozzie. Louella will watch them until Wade gets home."

Pinkie lifts a stack of plates to set in the cabinet.

My sister takes them out of her hands. "You know you're not supposed to lift those over your head. You could bring the baby on."

Our little mother-to-be relinquishes them. She picks up a dish cloth and begins to wipe the counter dry. "Do you think Wade will come out and sit with us later?"

From her failed attempt at nonchalance, I cotton the infatuation has been percolating. At least, on Pinkie's side. I need to ask Wade how he feels, especially given her condition. It's hard to tell since Wade's always the perfect gentleman.

"I don't know. The boys would be upstairs alone if he does. Don't forget, Louella doesn't live in."

"But maybe after they're asleep?"

Wade is solicitous of Pinkie. And he tries to protect her. She's wonderful with Barry and Ozzie and will definitely make a good mama. But I need to hear it from Wade. Otherwise, I need to squash it. I don't want her hurt. Her mama died when she was six years old. She's not had any guidance, obviously. But she's a good girl.

"Sugar, when y'all come downstairs, pull your chair up to mine. We need to have a little chat."

The old fear enters her eyes. "Did I do something wrong, Maggie?"

"No, darlin'. I want to talk with you like I believe your mama would have."

Her expression changes to relief. I haven't seen that fear since Christmas. I hope we never see it in her again, poor girl. Ignorance is what causes superstition. It makes me glad Georgia declared education mandatory in 1916. Unfortunately, there are still generations of uneducated people around, like her daddy. And Big Jim. And therein lies my troubles and why I'm going to sit up all night.

I push a strand of hair out of her face, then call Barry. "You ready, son? I need to get you settled with Ozzie."

"Coming, Mama." He drags a suitcase, no doubt filled with books and toys, into the living room. I shake my head. "You planning on staying a week?"

He turns that heartbreaking grin of his on me. I swanny, he's going to have all the girls in the county chasing him one day.

"You're silly, Mama. But I have to take my school clothes and my books and some toys. Teddy has to come too. He doesn't want to stay home without me."

Ever since Duchess sent him that stuffed bear two years ago, it's been his constant companion. "Okay, get Teddy, and let's move this train." I lift his suitcase and take him over to Ozzie's. Louella greets us at the door. Barry gives me a hug then scoots inside.

I hand Louella a quarter. "Thanks. I'll be out front if you need me."

"Thank you, Miss Maggie." She slips the quarter into her apron pocket.

I go out to join Sadie. The sun has gone down, and I love the twilight. But soon enough, it will be dark out. There's a new moon tonight. That won't help us see if anyone does come.

"Hey." I set my chair down by her. She's wearing overalls and a beat-up old hat. The brim looks like mice have been chewing on it. "Love your get-up."

She grins at me. "From a distance, I want 'em to think there's a man sitting out here. Then when they get up close and see me, they're going to realize it's much worse than that." Her soft chuckle belies an undertone of menace. I almost feel sorry for any man who comes up against her. Then again, they deserve whatever they get.

"I found Jimmy's old rifle." I lay it across my thighs. "I haven't tried to shoot it since he took me hunting right after we first got married. I cleaned it, but there wasn't time to try it out."

"Don't worry. Just aim it, but make sure you take aim at their nether regions."

"Sadie, I was never that good a shot."

"No need. It's the aim that'll scare them. I'll handle the shooting if it comes to that."

I'm so glad I've got my friend beside me. Her shotgun should hit enough to send 'em skedaddling. I wonder if she has it loaded with buckshot or rock salt. Either way, I wouldn't want to be on the receiving end.

We sit in silence for a few minutes, just enjoying the evening and each other's company. The tree frogs tune up for their nightly concert. A door opens and closes with a bang at one of the shanties, momentarily stopping the prelude. The frogs don't stay silent long. They've heard doors banging before and know they mean no harm for frogs. Out at the Worley farm, a couple of barn cats get to fighting and a dog barks, whether at the cats or something else remains unknown. It's all part of a country symphony. When you're raised on it, you can recognize each sound and know what they mean. Right now, all is well.

Sadie pulls a clove from its tin box and slips it into her mouth. The door upstairs opens. Duchess and Pinkie clatter down, giggles and bumps from the chairs accompanying them. They join us, pulling up close with Duchess on Sadie's other side and Pinkie by me.

Sister settles herself. "I hope we really don't have to use those." She leans forward and points to my gun.

"I doubt it, but Sadie's a crack shot, and folks around here know it."

"How'd you get to be so good at it, Sadie?"

She and I share a glance. "Pinkie and Sister don't know your story, Sadie. It's a good one for sitting out on a night like this." It will also be of help to Pinkie, I'm thinking.

"Well, it's like this." Sadie leans forward and spits the chewed clove into the gutter. "When my mama was around four years old, her parents died. No one ever knew of what. Anyways, she wandered from the cabin, looking for food. A band of Yamasee found her. They took her, and when she was thirteen, they married her to a brave. I was born barely a year later. My father was killed on a hunting trip, and Mama was taken by another brave. I was barely three years old." Her brows draw down into a fierce scowl. "Her new *husband* didn't want another brave's half-breed. I can still remember the beating he gave me. And because of it, the younger braves thought I was fair game. I was beaten and worse. I didn't stick around for another go."

Pinkie's mouth slowly drops open. "What did you do?"

With a shrug, Sadie rubs one hand over the barrel of her

shotgun. "I stole his shotgun that night and left. I walked as far as I could, that gun being bigger than me. Dragging it and a branch to erase my trail wasn't easy."

Pinkie and Duchess both gaping at her make me chuckle. I did the same thing the first time Sadie told me.

"Before daylight, I hid among the tree roots in the forest and covered myself with leaves." She grins and laughs. "They came looking for me, at least a couple of them did. They walked right past me."

Her derisive snort makes me smile. She's beyond the part of the story that always makes her sad. Sadie never saw her mother again.

"But how did you eat? You couldn't have shot that gun. Could you?" Pinkie's wide eyes never leave Sadie's face.

"There was one shell left in it. I tried a couple of days later, but it knocked me flat and durn near broke my shoulder. I was so mad." Sadie laughs. "I buried it deep in the woods. Probably still there, rusting away."

Pinkie turns sideways in her chair to look past me. "So how did you end up here in Rivers End?"

"I stayed to the edges of towns, scavenging what food I could. One time—I was about four, maybe five—a missionary found me and took me to an orphanage, but I ran away after the first month. The priest … well, he did what he shouldn't have to the children. I moved on and made sure I stayed out of sight. Food was easy enough to find at night. Then, a few years later—I reckon I was around seven—a man came through the area. He smiled at me but didn't throw rocks like everyone else did." She pauses and looks at Pinkie. "There are some good men out there, girl. This one didn't chase me away, nor did he try to touch me. I was still wary, but I followed him. One night, I hid in his wagon. When he found me the next morning, he was sympathetic. He never came too near me but left food and a blanket for me."

My sister's brows knit as she tilts her head. "What I don't understand is how you managed to stay alive all by yourself."

"By the time we can toddle, Yamasee children are taught how to survive. I knew how to fish with a sharpened stick as a three-year-old. We all did."

"My word, I can't imagine," Duchess says. "At three, I didn't know how to do anything but pout."

"Sam Hardee—that was the man's name—took me home to his wife. I'd learned some English from my mama, so I understood him when he said I could work for her. Since he was good to me, I was hopeful and said yes. Mrs. Sam was an angel, pure and simple. She never treated me like a half-breed. She and Mr. Sam educated me, and later after his wife died, he hired me at the bank." Her eyes soften. "He was the only *father* I ever knew."

"But," I say to my sister and Pinkie, "you should have seen the stir that caused in town."

Sadie barks a laugh. "Some people took their money out of the bank."

Duchess snorts in a very unladylike manner. "That's acting dumber than a box of rocks. But you still haven't told us how you got to be such a good shot."

"Ah, well, that would be Mr. Sam. He knew how people felt, and it would be a long time before they got over their closed-minded hatred." She eyes Pinkie. "Some never do, but most are more intelligent than that. Anyway, he bought me a pistol and taught me to use it. Every night, we'd go out behind the bank and practice. It didn't take me long to become proficient. And just knowing I was a good shot kept the boys away from me."

"Maybe that's what I need." Pinkie's wry sarcasm makes us all chuckle.

But I agree. It certainly can't hurt. Which reminds me ... "Pinkie, I've seen your interest in Wade." She dips her chin, smiling. "He's a good man, worthy of your interest. But until I know his intentions, I want you to—"

The tree frogs stop their symphony as abruptly as if a conductor has directed its end. Someone is coming.

CHAPTER 17

I squint into the darkness. The silhouettes are unrecognizable walking down the middle of the street, like in the Wild West, ready for a showdown. And it is a showdown of sorts. There's four of them. At least we're an even match. No. We're more than even, because across the street in the train station window, a light goes out—Wade's signal that he's seen them coming. It also means he's got his shotgun trained on their backs should the need arise for varmint shootin'.

When they get close enough, I can see they're wearing white hoods, and three are toting guns. One holds a torch. It bobs and flares with each step he takes. My thoughts fly upstairs to my boy. If they throw that torch … My heart leaps, and I start to get up.

Sadie's hand stops me. "Don't move," she whispers. "And don't let them know you're frightened. That'll throw them off. Be strong."

How can I, when I'm shaking?

The men draw closer. One is tall and as skinny as a skeleton with skin. Two are of medium build. The hoods hide most identifying features. The fourth is the tallest and has broad shoulders and narrow hips. I don't know anyone around here with a build like that. Who is he? When they reach the grocery, they stop in front of us, feet planted apart. There's no more than ten feet between us. I've heard of the Ku Klux Klan, but I've never seen them. Not in Rivers End. Until now. My heart beats loud in my ears.

The muscular one moves his head, peering at each one of us through holes cut in his hood. He pauses a long time on Duchess. A boulder takes up residence in my stomach. What will he try to do to her? This is a bad idea. I attempt to see Sadie without moving my eyes. They don't say anything, they just stand and stare. If they're trying to intimidate me, it's working. I need to swallow, but my throat is as dry as dirt.

After what feels like forever, the one staring at us jerks his head. The skinny one steps forward.

"You didn't learn from our little message yesterday." He tugs his hood away from his face a bit and spits. "Since you're still consorting with half-breeds and sluts, we're gonna have to make a stronger statement."

Sadie leans forward and spits the clove, obliterating his spittle. She slouches back in her chair with nonchalance. How can she be so—

"Cal Llewellyn, you are a fool."

Cal? How does Sadie know it's Cal?

"Do you really think that silly hood hides your identity?"

I lean forward and stare hard at the man. Sure, he's skinny like Cal, but—his shoes. They're enormous. Everyone knows Cal has the largest feet in three counties, maybe all of Georgia. His shoes have to be special ordered from the Bona Allen factory up in Buford. He always shows off when he gets a new pair.

Anger boils up in my belly, chasing all fear away. And maybe good sense, but I rise with all the dignity I can muster, calling on what I remember Mama teaching Duchess.

"Cal, you are a blight on Southern gentility." I raise Jimmy's rifle and aim at his nether regions like Sadie told me.

The others take a hesitant step back. Sadie always says a woman with a gun sets a man's heart to pounding and not with love.

"How many years did I keep you on my payroll when you were stealing from me?"

He shifts his feet but doesn't say anything. The tallest one startles.

"You don't remember? Well, I can tell you. It started right after my husband died. When my sister found the discrepancies in the books, I didn't prosecute you. But I could have. Look at you now. Big man, hiding inside a pillowcase. Go on home, or I'll tell the sheriff and everyone else how you stole from a widow and a fatherless, little boy."

I pull back the hammer on the rifle.

Cal flinches.

Muscle-man turns on him. "You didn't tell us you were stealing from her. You said she fired you unjustly."

"I … I …"

The one on Cal's left steps back. "You also forgot to tell us she's a widow woman with a small boy. They ain't fair game."

The South has the strangest code of ethics. Single, I was fair game? Who are these men? They're not from Rivers End.

"If you'll turn around and leave now"—Sadie raises her shotgun—"I won't need to use this. If I don't, the sheriff doesn't hear a gunshot and come running. And since you others seem to be gentlemen, I'll not bother to find out your identities. Mistah Llewellyn, on the other hand, will stay put." She raises her voice a notch so it'll carry across the street. "Wade? I'd be obliged if you get the sheriff."

Cal's companions leave without a backward glance. Cal shifts his feet nervously.

"Pinkie." Wade's shadowy form appears in the doorway of the train station. "I think it best for me to stay here with my gun aimed at Cal's back. Will you and Duchess go roust out Jubal?"

Duchess hops up. Methinks my sister delights in this role. Pinkie titters at being singled out by Wade. They scurry off down the street toward Jubal's house. Well, Duchess scurries. Pinkie waddles. My heartbeat returns to normal. Another disaster has been averted with the help of my dear friends.

Thank you, Lord.

Now, we have to see what the sheriff will do with Cal. I almost feel sorry for him, standing there, facing us with Sadie's gun aimed at his heart, Wade's at his back, and mine at the family jewels. But

I can't help but wonder where Big Jim plays into all of this.

It doesn't take long for the sheriff to arrive. "What's this all about?"

I move in front of my former manager. I want him to see me as I accuse him. "Cal is into intimidation. He was the one who instigated and perpetrated last night's break-in. What I didn't tell you is he's been stealing from me for years. And yes, I have the evidence. My sister found it."

Jubal raises an eyebrow as he looks at Sister. Then he takes Cal by the arm.

"All right, Llewellyn. Put your hands behind your back."

"Aw, Jubal. You gonna believe a bunch of women over me?"

"You forget me, Cal." Wade taps his gun barrel into Cal's back.

"Why you—I oughta—"

"Shut it." Jubal closes the handcuffs over Cal's wrists. "Maggie, you bring me that evidence tomorrow, or I'll turn him loose."

"I'll have it to you by afternoon."

Cal smirks just before Jubal leads him down the street to the jail. Does he think this is funny? Or does he know something I don't?

Whatever, I'm just glad it's over. "Wade, thanks for having our backs." I give Sadie a hug. "Sadie, you were magnificent. I didn't spy Cal's shoes until after you said his name. Is that what made you recognize him?"

"Nope. It was his voice. I knew it right off. Never look down. Always keep your eyes on your enemy's. Once you look away, they've got the upper hand."

There's a lesson in there for me. I pick up my chair. "Let's go to bed." An idea makes me pause. "Wade, do you know anyone who might want a job cleaning the grocery at night? I can't pay a lot, but someone inside with a light on might stop any more break-ins."

"I think there should be any number of people who would love the opportunity to make an extra two or three dollars each week.

I'll pass the word."

"Thanks." I think. Two or three dollars out of my already stretched-to-the-limit budget?

The memory of the torch makes me shiver. It will be worth it.

With the store back to rights and no scheduled deliveries today, I leave Sadie and Duchess manning the store, and I'm using the grocery truck to drive Pinkie and myself into Baxley for the appointment with the eye doctor. Baxley isn't much larger than Rivers End, but it does have an optometrist. Beside me, Pinkie twists her hankie into a wrinkled mess. I can't blame her. I've never needed glasses and have no idea what the doctor will do. My heart goes out to her.

"Sweetie." I reach over to stop her frantic wadding. "Don't fret. Eyeglasses are fairly simple to get." I don't think I'm lying to her.

"I hope you're right. The lady doctor is embarrassing."

How well I remember.

We leave the paved highway and enter Baxley. Last night's rain has the road muddy and makes it difficult to steer the truck. The buildings face the railroad tracks, and it's in sorrier shape than Rivers End. We pass an old Queen Anne house with two of its shutters hanging by a single hinge. An abandoned wagon with all its wheels broken sits beside the tracks across from the general store. I believe the doctor's office is on the second floor above that.

I pull up in front and park. "Okay, take a big breath. You don't want to make your baby colicky."

We climb the outside stairs and enter the office. A middle-aged woman greets us from behind a plain desk facing the door. "Do you both have an appointment?"

"No, just Miss Yates." I wink at Pinkie, hoping she'll smile. It works.

The receptionist hands Pinkie a clipboard bearing a small card. "Fill this out and bring it back when you're done."

I read the card for Pinkie. "Name, address, and any ailments. It's pretty straightforward."

"I probably don't need to say I'm in the family way. It's not an ailment, and it's rather obvious." She smirks, making me chuckle.

The receptionist takes Pinkie's card and glances at her gloved hand. If she's checking for a wedding ring, she's out of luck.

She opens the door and ushers us into the exam room. A single chair stands in the center. A number of charts and a few odd-looking contraptions reside on shelves behind the chair. The woman places Pinkie's card on the shelf and leaves, closing the door behind her.

"Go ahead and sit down, Pinkie. Take a load off those ankles." They've been swelling if she stands too long.

Within a couple of minutes, the door opens, and the doctor appears. He's wearing a gray suit and looks to be in his fifties. He gives us a kindly smile.

"I'm Mr. Foster." He offers Pinkie his hand and studies her quietly. "Your doctor mentioned you have albinism." He peers closely at her eyes. "You do have a light pigment in your irises. Do you have any questions for me before we proceed with your exam?"

Pinkie shakes her head, and her grip on her skirts relaxes as the doctor explains every step to her.

"These spectacles have the left lens blacked out. That's so I can test each of your eyes separately." He has her read the chart, then tell him which direction some arrows are facing. He makes notes on the back of her registration card. After he changes the glasses for another pair with the right eye blacked out and checks both eyes, he put some drops in her eyes.

His relaxed and calming manner reminds me of Doc. Pinkie isn't fidgeting or wadding her hankie.

"These will dilate your pupils and allow me to look into the back of your eye."

He can see the inside of her eyes? Modern medicine is miraculous. I catch myself leaning toward her as if I could take a peek. I quickly regain my posture.

After a few moments, he pulls up a stool and puts what looks like a small magnifying glass to his eye, and as he moves his face close to Pinkie's, he explains what he's doing.

"I'm looking at your retina, Miss Yates, and it looks like I expected it to." He pulls back, moves his stool to her other side, and examines her other eye. Finally, he turns off his light and switches on a smaller desk light in the back of the room.

He hands Pinkie a pair of dark spectacles. "You'll need to wear these for a few hours. The sunlight will hurt your eyes. I should have your corrective ones ready in about ten days to two weeks. You can return these to me when you pick up yours."

"Corrective? You mean I'll actually be able to see well?"

He takes her hand between his. "Yes, my dear, you will. Your eyes aren't as bad as others I've seen with albinism."

The joy on her face is worth every penny Sadie and I are spending.

Back in the car, she turns to me. "Do you think I'll look older in those spectacles?"

"Do you want to look older?" I stick my arm out the window to signal a turn left.

"Well …" She turns in her seat to face me. "You know how I kind of like Mr. Wade, and he's *so* nice and such a gentleman—well, if I was going to look for a daddy for my baby, he's the perfect choice." Her words rush out, one on top of the next. "I worry I look too young."

Oh dear. My hands tighten on the steering wheel. I'm not sure how to answer her. Yes, I am.

"Sugar, I'm going to tell you what I think your mama might. Don't try to rush things. Pray about it, and if it's God's will for you, it will happen. In His time." I hope that's what her mama would say.

Pinkie stares at me, nodding. "Yes, I think that's exactly what my mama would have said. And I'll do that." She blushes. "I do like him. He's a real nice man. I don't think I've ever met a man like him."

"He's a good friend too. He and my late husband were the best of friends. He helped me a lot when my husband died."

I stick my hand out the window to signal another turn. Pinkie doesn't say anything. Her sudden silence surprises me, and her fingers are worrying her hankie again.

"Is something wrong?"

"Do *you* like Mr. Wade, Maggie? Because if you do, well, I won't. I mean, I'll …."

So that's it. I chuckle. "I like Wade as a good friend. But that's all. If the good Lord sees fit to have him express interest in you, I'll be all for it. He'd make a wonderful daddy for your baby. And you would be a sweet mama for Ozzie."

Pinkie's hands grow still, and she smiles. My sister and her husband come to mind. Will was much older than Duchess, but they had a wonderful marriage. Of course, Sister wasn't pregnant when they married. But then again, Joseph married a pregnant Mary.

Later in the afternoon, I call out my office door to my sister. "Duchess, can you come in here for a minute?" While I wait, I pull open another desk drawer.

"What do you need?" Duchess is in the doorway, wearing a butcher's apron.

I gawk at her. "Are you cutting meat?"

With a grin, she holds the apron wide to reveal bloodstains. "Sadie's teaching me how."

Well, shut my mouth. Duchess … the one who flinched when I whacked the chicken apart just a few weeks ago?

"So what do you need, Maggie?"

"What? Oh. Yes. Where are the account books? I need to take the ones showing Cal's thievery to the sheriff."

My sister frowns. "I had them in the bottom, right-hand drawer."

I open it again. It's empty. "Are you sure you didn't move them?"

"Yes, I'm sure." Her frown deepens. "Yesterday, no, the day before, I—oh no." She moves to the left side of the desk and yanks open the bottom drawer. It's also empty. Her face drains of color. "Did we put them in the safe?"

Swiveling in my chair, I turn the dial and open it. Account books sit on a shelf along with the cash box. Relief floods over me, making me clammy. I reach in, pull them out, and lay them on the desk. Sister turns to go back into the grocery.

"Duchess!"

She stops and looks back. "What?"

"These are from 1903 to 1919."

"I don't understand. What do you mean?"

"None of these books goes past 1919. Someone took the ones that are from 1920 on."

We stare at each other as understanding dawns. The evidence to hold and convict Cal has been stolen.

CHAPTER 18

Bud Pugh passes the grocery's front window, his postal bag bouncing on his hip with each jaunty step. He nods at Pinkie, who is supervising the workmen replacing the window glass. He's waving a fat envelope in his hand. When he pushes open the door, he calls out loud enough for everyone to hear, "I've got a registered letter here for Mrs. Duchess Alden, and it needs her signature."

Not many people in Rivers End get registered letters requiring signatures, but does he have to announce it to the whole town? With a glance at Myrtle Davis, whose attention is off her groceries and on the letter, I hold out my hand.

"I'll sign for it, Bud."

He pulls back his hand and clutches the letter up against his shoulder. "No, ma'am. It requires your sister's John Henry, not yours. It's from an attorney's office, so it's got to be legal and right."

Not one to correct my elders, I bite my lip to keep from snickering. For as long as I've known Bud, he's never called a signature a "John Hancock."

"She's in the office."

With a sharp nod of his head, Bud heads that direction. A moment later, he's back out with a satisfied smile on his face, pointing at the signed card before sliding it into his shirt pocket.

Honestly, we have some real characters living in Rivers End. I finish up with Myrtle and go into the office. There's no sign of the envelope, and Duchess is working on some numbers. She doesn't look up. Curiosity is getting the best of me, but I know if she thinks it's important for me to know, she'll tell me. I need to respect her privacy.

I walk to the desk, trailing my fingers over its varnished top. "So did you sign for the letter Bud brought you?" I want to snatch the ill-spoken words back as soon as they leave my mouth. What a Dumb Dora.

Sister glances up. "Hmm? Oh, uh-huh." She drops her gaze back to the books.

Well, she either hasn't opened the letter, or she isn't curious. Maybe she knows what's in it. She doesn't look upset.

"Is there something else you need, Maggie? I'm trying to work out where we truly are financially."

"No. Not really." If she isn't going to tell me, then there's nothing I can do about it, but it's going to eat at—

Pinkie opens the office door and sticks her head in. "Maggie? Can you come out here?" She turns and walks toward the front of the store, where the men are still replacing the window.

With one more fruitless glance back at my sister, I go see what they need. Out front, Bobby Mobley and his helper, Tommy Lowe, are glazing the window, intent on their work as well. It seems strange to see Tommy working off his farm, but, of course, I'm seeing that more often now—men seeking work elsewhere.

"Pinkie, what did you call me out here for?"

"Mr. Mobley wants to be paid for the glass window. Do you want me to pay him from the cash register?"

My budget squeals as more dollars fly out. "How much is it?"

She looks at her feet—or would if her belly weren't in the way. "Pinkie?"

"He said four dollars and twenty cents."

"Do we have that much in the register?" I may have to take it from what I'm saving for the taxes. That makes my heart pound. If I can't take the next tax payment, I'll lose the store. *Why can't I catch a break here, Lord?*

Pinkie opens the drawer and counts the money. "There's three dollars and eighty-seven cents. And we'll need change for other customers."

There's no choice. "Give me two dollars. I'll get the rest from the cookie jar."

My feet are heavy as I pass through the storeroom to the kitchen. I pull the small cookie jar from the cupboard and take out two dollars and twenty cents. My savings are woefully slim. The remainder from the check I got from Mr. Evans and what I have totals seventeen dollars and some change. The last tax bill was $273.42. By next November, I'll need $256.00. A fortune.

Back in the grocery, the new window is in. I count out the money into Bobby's hand.

His fingers close around the cash. "Thanks, Maggie. I wish I could put it on your account, but I had to pay for the glass."

"I understand. I have to do the same. Thanks for getting it in so fast."

He shoves the money into his pocket. "Have you found someone to clean the store at night yet?"

I shake my head. "No, do you know someone who's interested?"

"Yes, Katherine Hopper."

"Asa's wife? She seems a bit timid to clean at night alone."

"Well, Asa's struggling. Hair isn't getting cut as often. I think he figures the two of them could do it together and he'd be there to keep her feeling safe."

"I'll go ask her. Thanks."

"We're all sleeping with one ear open, Maggie. I hear Cal got out this morning."

"He did, and the evidence I had that would have convicted him was stolen. I imagine while his pals had fun out here, Cal was in the office, taking my account books."

Bobby pulls his ball cap out of his back pocket and plops it on his head. "I hate to say it, but that doesn't surprise me. Cal always impressed me as sneaky. Ida Clare has told me more than once she caught him with his thumb on the meat scale. She called him out on it, knowing you wouldn't abide that."

I glance back to the meat counter, which Sadie claims as her territory now. Bobby's eyes follow my gaze.

"That was a smart move, hiring Sadie."

"I wish I'd asked her to work for me years ago. But she won't take any money. Says she's fine. She just needs to fill the hours in a day."

"Well, if she gets tired of slinging meat, send her down to see Ida Clare."

That makes me laugh. As if I'd send her away. He raises a finger in a "so long" salute and leaves.

Because it's New Year's Eve, I'd planned a special evening dinner for all of us. Sadie cut a nice pork loin for me, and I plan to cook it with apples and a coating of herbed whole grain mustard. I check my wristwatch, and it's time to go to the kitchen.

I wave to Sadie and Pinkie. "I'll see all y'all at five."

I stop at the barbershop to see Asa before I go home. He doesn't have any customers when I walk in.

"Need a haircut, Maggie?"

"No, but I wanted to ask if you or Katherine would be willing to clean the grocery at night for three dollars a week. I only need it swept and the windows cleaned. Mostly, I want a nightly presence in there."

"We'd be glad to and appreciate the extra money. How about we vary the time we go in? That way, nobody will get a set schedule in case they're watching the place."

He's got good sense. "Excellent idea. Can you start tonight?"

He nods. With that done and the grocery safe hopefully, I head home, stopping in the garden to pick some fresh vegetables. As kids, we followed the Southern tradition of having collards and black-eyed peas on New Year's Eve. Supposedly, it means good luck, but neither my sister nor I could ever stand collards. Pinkie says she used to love them, but right now she can't stand the thought of them. So no collards for us tonight.

An hour later, the roast has its herb dressing on, and the fire feels like it's the right temperature, so I slide in the pan. A door shuts upstairs. It's too early for Barry to be home from school. That means it's either Duchess or Pinkie. If it's Pinkie, she probably needs a nap. The further along she gets, the more she seems to need one. It has me concerned. By this time in my pregnancy with Barry, I was full of energy. I hope everything is all right. I tidy up the kitchen, check the roast again, and go upstairs.

In Pinkie and Duchess' bedroom, thumps and bumps resound. I throw open the door. It's Duchess, not Pinkie, making the noise. She's pulling out her trunks from the closet, working as though she's got a demon on her tail.

"Duchess, honey, what's wrong?"

"Oh, hey, Maggie. I thought you were in the kitchen."

"I was, but I heard such a racket up here, I thought I'd better investigate. Was it something in that letter? You aren't leaving, are you?" Funny, I've become so used to having her here, the thought of her leaving has me distraught.

"Leaving? Now why would I do that? And where would I go?"

I sweep my hand in an arc, gesturing to the mess she's making. "Then what is this all about?"

"This? Oh. Do you remember how Martha Lenger's children had no jackets? Well, today Minnie Sadler came in with her brood, and they were in the same situation. The girls' dresses are made from flour sacks, as is Minnie's. And they didn't have on any jackets." She turns back to her trunks and pulls out a wool suit. "Well, I have clothes I don't need that will make jackets for those babies."

Joy that she isn't leaving washes over me, followed by a bit of pride. My sister is the sweetest woman God ever created. "I'll help you. And I'm sure Sadie will too. Maybe we can make some clothes for Pinkie's baby too."

"That's on my to-do list." She pulls a beautiful buttery-yellow satin gown from the trunk, telling me a wistful story about how Mr. Alden bought it for her. "I plan to make a nightgown for the baby out of it, then a dress for Helen Ivey's youngest daughter.

The color will suit her perfectly."

How did I miss Duchess taking these children so to heart that she knows what color suits each one? Together we pull out most of the clothes in her trunk. I drop onto her bed. With a pile next to me, I separate them by material type.

She holds up a rich, dark wool coat. "This is for Barry. We'll make him a suit out of it."

"Are you sure you want to do that now? He's growing so fast, he'll be out of it in six months."

Duchess folds the coat over her arm and sits on the Pinkie's bed. "I hadn't thought about that. There wouldn't be enough material for when he's bigger." She fingers her earlobe. "I know. I'll turn it into a lap robe for Faylene. That way, she can sit outside on mild winter days and keep warm."

"She'll love that." We go through the clothes, keeping out what we want and packing away the others.

"Mama?" Barry slides into the room in his stocking feet, skidding to a stop just before he slams into me. "Mr. Wade wants to take us all to the movies for New Year's Eve. *Coconuts* is playing, and I want to see it really, really bad, Mama. I've wanted to see it for my whole life." He stops for a breath and eyes all the clothes laying out. A frown creases his forehead. "Whatcha doing?"

"Getting ready to make my old clothes into new ones for some of the less fortunate than us, sweet boy." Duchess folds the coat on her bed. "Now, I think Mr. Wade has a splendid idea. What do you think, Maggie? Should we say *yes*?"

"I say we could use a night of fun." Barry squeals and races out, but I call after him. "Barry, wait. Tell Wade and Ozzie to join us for supper."

Pinkie will like that. I've got to find a way to ask Wade if he has any interest in her. But how does one do that with appearing to be pushing him?

"Okay, Mama." The door slams.

I need to go back down and check the roast. "Want to come

help me with a salad?"

Duchess stretches her back, twisting first to the left, then the right. "Sure, and I'm glad you said yes, sugar. You need an evening free from worry. You're getting a frown mark between your eyebrows."

On my way down the stairs, I raise my fingers to my brow to feel if she's right.

Duchess chuckles as we file into the roast-scented kitchen. "I'm just teasing you, Magnolia. But I do think you need to trust the Lord more." She waltzes over to the fridge.

Easy for Duchess to say. She's never had to worry. Her husband took care of her, and now I am. I bite my tongue even though I hadn't spoken out loud. Where is my ugly attitude coming from? Did I need to remind myself how much of a boon Duchess is to me?

I glance at her on the other side of the kitchen table, tearing lettuce for a salad. She never complains about working. Well, except when we have to get up at four in the morning like yesterday to receive a shipment.

"What are you smirking at?" My sister shakes her knife at me.

"Only that I'm glad you didn't have that in your hand when I woke you yesterday. I might be missing a body part." I open the oven and pull out the pork roast. The thermometer needle points to medium. By the time it rests, it will be well done and perfect. The apples lining its top are golden-brown and smell divine. I'm looking forward to this evening. It's been a long while since I took time out for fun.

As we set the table, I ask Duchess for her opinion about Pinkie and Wade.

Arms akimbo, Duchess stares at me as though I have two heads. "Are you just noticing? The way he looks at her isn't—how can I say this? He doesn't see a wanton woman. He sees a sweet young woman who is very pretty."

"Really? Why haven't I noticed that?"

"You've got the weight of supporting a family on your mind, sweet sister." She snaps her fingers. "I forgot to tell you." She retrieves the letter from her pocket. "I got a check from my lawyer. After all the creditors and the attorney were paid, there was a little money left." She holds out the check. "Go on, take it, sugar. It's not a lot, but we can put it toward the tax bill."

I hate to take it, but I don't have a choice. The forty-six dollars and twenty-seven cents will lower what we need to just over two hundred dollars. Still a fortune.

I'm up before the sun. It's now 1930. I hope this year will be a better one, although the newspapers give a gloomy outlook. Gloomy or not, our laughter from the movie last night still rings in my ear as I dress and go down to open the store. Shipments of Quaker Oats, cornmeal, and sugar are arriving. Thankfully, yesterday's receipts will cover the new arrivals. I hope sales are better today. *Dear Lord, I'm trying to trust You.*

In the office, I pull out my column articles notebook. The one for this week is due to Zeke over at the *Farm Whistler.* I add a couple of sentences and then edit it once more. When done, I lay it on the corner of the desk to take over after my suppliers leave.

A key rattles in the front door and Pinkie enters. "Morning, Maggie. I didn't hear you leave this morning."

It's already six-thirty? "I'm expecting supplies, but they're late. I'm going over to the station and place a call. Will you open up?"

"Sure." Pinkie moves slowly. The baby is large now. I can't help but wonder if Doc's calculations are right about when she's due. He did say late February or March. And Pinkie wasn't sure of the date when she … when she got pregnant. I'm guessing it will be more a late winter baby.

"How are you feeling?"

She lays one hand on her lower back. "Fat." Her disgusted tone makes me laugh.

"Pretty much all expectant mothers feel like that."

"The baby is so active at times I think it's playing pom-pom pull away or red rover inside me."

That's a good sign the baby's healthy. I pat her belly and leave the grocery. I never did get to finish that conversation with her about Wade. But right now, I need to keep my mind on the supplies. I can't imagine where they are.

In the station, I have to wait while Wade finishes a call. The train station is busy this morning. Well, busy for Rivers End. Andy Simmons drops a stack of newspapers on the edge of the counter, while Fanny Herman's husband, William T., opens his shoeshine stand next to the newspaper stacks. Malcom Connor, the bank president, is seeing off his sister and her husband after their holiday visit.

Wade hangs up the phone. "It's all yours, Maggie."

"Thanks." I tap the phone's button and wait for the operator. When she answers, I give her the number in Baxley and wait.

"Heskot Distribution." The man's voice is deep and a bit garbley, as if he was chewing on the end of a cigar.

"This is Parker's Grocery in Rivers End. My deliveries haven't arrived this morning. What happened?"

"Hang on." The phone clunks onto a desk, and I wait again. "I show that delivered this morning at five-thirty."

CHAPTER 19

Delivered? "Not to me, they weren't."

"I've got a signed bill of lading. You ain't trying to get out of paying, are you?"

It's a good thing I haven't eaten breakfast yet. My stomach churns. "I always pay the day my deliveries arrive. If it's your driver, I pay cash."

"Hold on. I need to look something up." The phone clunks again as he drops it.

I tap my foot while I wait. Malcom waves at me on his way out of the station. How did he manage to keep the Rivers End bank open when so many others closed? I've been operating with cash, but maybe I should go see him. After the break-in, I don't want to leave money in the safe—not with Cal and Big Jim still having the combination.

The man returns to the line. "Miz Parker? Your account is current except for this shipment."

I heave a sigh and roll my eyes. "I could have told you that. What am I going to do? I need those supplies today. I'd also like to see the signature on that paperwork. Did the person who took the shipment pay for it?"

"No."

"Who could have done this?"

"I don't know, ma'am. I got a driver out sick, so I used a commercial carrier. Things happen in hard times."

At least he dropped the fierce tone. "Can you reorder for me? I've got the cash."

He sighs. "All right. I'll bring it myself and that bill of lading.

Maybe we can figure this out."

My knees almost buckle with relief. "Thank you." At least he didn't mention making me pay for the stolen shipment. I nod at Wade and cross my fingers on my way out.

Out on the street, I glance across at the bank but don't see Malcom. It's too early for him to open the doors, so I suppose he went home or—hmm. I wonder … I turn and go into the small café attached to the train station.

I'm right. Malcom is sitting at the counter, talking with Paul Simmons. I hate to interrupt them, so I take a seat a few stools away. Funny, I've lived in Rivers End for going on nine years and never been in here. And it's right across the street from the grocery.

Paul's daughter, Nancy, saunters over. "Hey, Maggie. What can I get you?"

I reach in my pocket to see if I even have any money. I feel a nickel and a couple of pennies. "I'll take a cup of coffee, thank you."

She plops a mug on the counter in front of me, reaches behind her, and grabs a pot. The aroma of the fresh brew makes me wonder why I've never done this before. I add a little milk and stir in a spoonful of sugar. It tastes wonderful. If every nickel weren't already spoken for, I'd love to come in here every day for a moment's quiet and a cup of coffee.

"Maggie, it's unusual to see you outside the grocery." Malcom stands, picks up his coffee, and drops onto the stool next to me. His hair is a mix of sandy-blond and gray, making it hard to determine his age. However, he's in his late forties or early fifties, judging by the middle-age spread. Malcom's face invites trust—a good trait for a banker.

"That doesn't say much for my social life, does it?"

"How are you doing? I heard about the trouble last week." He nods as Nancy refills his cup. His hands are banker's hands, without calluses except for one on his middle finger, where a pen would rest against it.

I glance at my right hand. My callus is more pronounced. "It's a loss that's going to hurt for a while."

"Do you need a loan?"

I'd love one, but I'd have to own some collateral. The store is all I have, and it's for Barry. "No, but I did want to talk with you. Do you think the bank's going to stay open?"

"Yes."

"How do you know that?"

"What's this all about, Maggie?"

"I usually pay cash for my supplies, but this morning, someone stole a shipment that was supposed to come to me. With times so hard, what's to say a delivery man won't pocket my money and say I never paid?"

"Are you thinking of using bank drafts? You know—" He stops and peers at me. "Your husband had a checking account that was never closed. You could use that. Normally, women can't *open* a checking account, but in your case, we can simply have you take over Jimmy's old account. I'll just change the name to yours. There's still money in it."

"What?" Coffee sloshes over the edge of my cup onto my hand and the counter when I startle at his statement. I mop it up with my napkin. "Why don't I know about it? And how much is in it?"

"It's not much that I remember. The statements went to the house. That's where Jimmy lived when he set up the account."

And that's why I've never been told about it. Jimmy never included me in business, and Big Jim certainly would never mention it to me. Trying not to get my hopes up, I have to ask, "Has anyone taken anything out lately?"

"No. Only Jimmy's name is on the account."

"And Big Jim couldn't take it as his father?"

"Maggie, as his widow, you're the only one who has the right to it."

"More coffee?" Nancy has the pot ready to pour into my cup.

"No, thank you." I pull out the nickel and pennies and lay them on the counter.

Malcom pushes them back to me. "I've got this." He lays two quarters beside his cup. "Thanks, Nancy. Tell your daddy I'll see him this afternoon."

We walk out together. Malcom holds the door open. "Why don't you come in later this morning? I'll pull a statement for you."

"I will. And thank you."

Can this be real? I want to pinch myself to see if I'm dreaming. I know I'd like to wring Big Jim's neck for letting me struggle if there's money in the bank. *Sadie*. Sadie worked at the bank. Not for Malcom, but she might know something about it. I need to ask her.

I hurry back to the grocery. "Is Sadie here?"

Pinkie hunches over the table, working on a recipe poster. She looks up, rubbing her lower back. "Not yet."

"You should sit to do that, sugar. Carrying the extra weight of a baby is hard on your back." I go to the office and pull out a spare chair. "Use this." I place it at the table for her.

"Thanks, Maggie." She sits and scoots up close to her work. "Where have you been? I thought you'd be back sooner." She glances up, and her cheeks infuse with pink. "I'm sorry. That didn't come out right. But I almost came looking for you. I was worried."

"No offense taken. I stopped in the café to talk with Malcom Connor. He's the president of the bank." I decide not to mention the money until I know how much. "This was after I found out our supply delivery has been stolen."

Pinkie gasps. "Who would do such a rotten thing?"

My supplier's words echo back. "Well, people will do drastic things in hard times. Which reminds me, have you caught a glimpse of Big Jim lately?"

She shakes her head, but intent on her work, she doesn't look up again. "Duchess and I are demonstrating a new recipe today. We hope it will draw people back in. I'm making a sign to put out on the sidewalk." She shows me how it will go on a sandwich board. "We thought we'd ask if Andy Simmons could wear it and walk up and down the street."

It's a clever sign with a picture of the finished dish, and Pinkie colored the black-and-white image with Crayolas, making it look delicious. "I love it. Where did you get the picture?"

"From Zeke at the paper."

"It's a fantastic idea. How did you come up with it?"

"Last time I was in Uvalda to see the lady doctor, Duchess and I saw a man wearing one. We decided to try it."

"I've never seen anything like it."

"My granny talked about seeing them when she was a kid but said they died out. I guess with the country in a money bind, they're coming back. It's a cheap way to advertise."

"It's brilliant." I thought of that money in the bank. Even if there is only a little, I can afford to hire the Simmons boy for an afternoon. "Go ahead and hire Andy. Tell him he can earn a quarter if he'll walk up and down from ten to noon. Then I'll let Barry and Ozzie take turns after school. Now, I've got a column to write. Call me if Sadie comes in, please."

I set aside my desire to run to the bank and instead pump out an article on stain removers, window cleaners, and the like, using inexpensive household products. I need to try the one for removing the odor from canvas shoes. Barry has the stinkiest feet. Setting it aside for the ink to dry, I'll come back in a bit and take it over to Zeke.

It's after nine-thirty, and the grocery has several customers when Sadie enters the store. She's not working today, so I head toward her. "Have you got a minute?"

Her eyes spark with curiosity. "I do. Where?"

"Let's go into my office." As soon as I close the door, I tell her about what's happened this morning and about the bank account. "Did you know about Jimmy's account?"

Sadie scratches the side of her head, dislodging a few shorter hairs from the bun at the nape of her neck. "I remember he had one. I didn't pay attention to whether it was ever closed or not."

I hoist myself up onto the corner of my desk. "It curdles my gravy that Big Jim never told me about it after Jimmy died." I peer at Sadie to gauge her reaction when I tell her this next part. "There's money left in it. How much I don't know yet. I'm going over to see Malcom in a few minutes."

Sadie schools her reactions better than most people, but her eyes widen slightly, and her nostrils flare. "But what about when you got a statement—wait, they went to Big Jim's house, didn't they? If your husband was alive, I'd throttle him. And obviously, his daddy never told you about it, did he?"

"No. And apparently, he didn't let Faylene know either. She would have told me."

"So what are you going to do?"

"Right now"—I jump down from the desktop—"I'm going to see how much is in the account. And get a checkbook. With the supply gone missing, I've decided my days of paying for shipments in cash are over."

Sadie gives me a sharp nod. "Good. Let me know if you have any questions."

"Thanks." We leave the office together and drift toward the rear of the store by the demonstration table, where Pinkie positions the sandwich board on Duchess. Granny Belle Jackson pauses in her shopping to point at them and laugh. Grays hairs escape her bonnet, still worn in favor of modern hats. She's stooped by years of working beside her husband in the fields, but Granny Belle never complains, and her eyes twinkle with mischief.

Sadie selects an apple from a bin, while I wander over to see what has Granny Belle so tickled.

"Hello, Maggie girl. Did I ever tell you when I was a little bitty thing, my daddy came back from a visit to Atlanta and told me about a sandwich man? I had a nightmare about a pulled pork sandwich with legs and a hat chasing me. Daddy finally had to draw me a picture so I'd understand and not be afraid anymore." Her laughter is contagious.

"I can see how you misunderstood. I've never seen one, but I think it's an ingenious way to advertise."

Granny Belle nods. "And that Pinkie is so artistic. She makes the dish look much better than when Zeke ran it in the newspaper. My Herb would like that. I'll try to come back for the demonstration." She shuffles off to shop.

"Oh, Granny Belle," I call after her. "If you don't find what you're looking for, it might be in a late delivery."

She waves over her shoulder. I guess she's seen enough trouble in her life that she isn't concerned. I turn back to my sister and Pinkie to find them staring at me.

"What?"

Duchess slides out of the advertising board. "Faith, Sister. Have faith. God will work it all out. And in the meantime, you have us to make life merry."

Pinkie grins and nods in agreement.

Duchess reads me all too well. I debate whether to tell her about the bank but decide to keep it to myself for now. Malcom's idea of a small amount could be different from mine, but if it turns out to be my version of small, I don't want it to diminish her faith. Or Pinkie's. I glance at my wristwatch. The bank will be open now.

"I've got an errand to run. I'll be back in about a half hour, I think."

They wave me away. They're used to running the grocery now. And they're good at it. *Thank You, Lord.*

Do I really thank Him, or am I merely giving lip service? My heart clenches. I truly am grateful for my sister and Pinkie. I guess I need to open what Sadie calls my spiritual eyes to what God is doing. I glance up at the sky. *Thank You.* The sun winks at me from between two clouds.

The sun or the Son?

My heart fills with peace, and I cross the street to the bank. Inside, there are only a couple of customers. Malcom sees me through the windows of his office and waves me in. He's smiling.

In High Cotton

Is it good news or just his banker's smile?

He stands, comes around his desk, and holds a chair for me. "Sit, Maggie. I have some good news."

I blow out the breath I didn't realize I held. "How much?" If it's close to a hundred dollars, I may dance a jig. That would really help my tax debt.

He retakes his seat and slides a yellow paper toward me.

"What's this?"

"It's a bank statement. From now on, you'll get one each month. See on the bottom? That's your bank balance."

I follow his finger to the bottom of the paper. At first, I can't comprehend what I'm seeing. I look up, and Malcom is grinning.

"Is that right?" I point at the numbers. "I've got $437.52?"

"Yes, Maggie."

I let out a whoop, then hunch down in my seat and glance at the bank's lobby.

Malcom laughs. "They can't hear you. The glass is too thick. Now, I took the liberty to remove Jimmy's name and put yours on the account. And the statement will be mailed to your apartment." He slides a checkbook toward me. He shows me how to write out a check to my suppliers or anyone else, how to record it in the register, and how to balance it.

"Malcom, can you add my sister to this account? If anything happens to me, I want her to take care of Barry and the store. I don't want her without any money."

He nods. "I'll do it right now." He writes a note in his book and has me fill out a card and sign it. "That'll do it for now. I'll get more checks printed that will have her name on them too." He hands the checkbook back to me. "Do you have a lawyer to write out a will for you?"

"No." He doesn't realize even the word *lawyer* makes me think of Big Jim's threats and cringe. "I don't know one."

"I do. Would you like me to help you with that, Maggie? It should cost around six dollars and will give you some peace of mind. You can name Duchess as Barry's guardian if anything happens to you and have her run the store in trust for him until he grows up."

"Now that I have some money behind me, I can afford to do it. Yes, please. And I appreciate the help, Malcom." I rise.

Malcom stands and comes around the desk. He takes my hand. "I'm delighted to have seen you this morning, my dear. I'm sorry I never realized you didn't know about the account. I should have taken some initiative before this."

I don't know how to answer that, so I smile instead and tuck the checkbook into my pocket. I have a lot of thinking to do. And talking to my sister.

As I cross the street, I wonder if Faylene has ever seen the bank statements. Immediately, I dismiss the thought. Of course, she hasn't. Big Jim would have made sure of that. I thank the Lord properly for this windfall. Now, I don't have to worry about Big Jim or his threats.

CHAPTER 20

Today is an odd day, to say the least. Instead of bustling around the grocery, Duchess, Pinkie, and I gather in my office. Mama Faylene is joining us as soon as Bessie Mae can wheel her up here. That scoundrel, Big Jim, should be doing it, but once again, he isn't home.

The office door creaks open. Duchess jumps up to help a huffing-and-puffing Bessie Mae push Mama Faylene's wheeled chair inside. The space isn't overly large, but it holds two desks and room for a couple of visitors. Earlier, Sister and I pushed one of the desks up against the wall to make more room.

Today we are five. It's cozy but not too cramped. The closeness lends an air of frivolity. We'll have ourselves a fine time, turning my sister's dresses and coats into usable clothing for the poorest of farm children. It warms my heart—and breaks it at the same time to see Duchess pare down her beautiful wardrobe to only a few practical dresses.

Mama Faylene catches me rubbing a cashmere coat's softness against my cheek. "Dear, why don't you keep that one?"

Temptation pulls—but my sister's frown pulls harder. A chuckle escapes. "Duchess would have my hide. No, we don't need such luxury." I wink at my sister. "Besides, my skin would burn if I saw a cold child while I wore it."

Sadie, who says she can't wield a needle and opted to stay out in the grocery, sticks her head in the door. "I need Pinkie. You four can sew, but we've got customers."

"Go ahead, dear," I tell our protégé. Her eyesight isn't good enough for fine stitching, anyway. The glasses that doctor in

Baxley prescribed will help once she gets them, but he said her vision would never be perfect. Still, she says she'll be happy with any improvement. For now, she can see well enough to work the register while we sew.

After she leaves us, we stitch and chat, cut and sip sweet tea for an hour or more. I'm enjoying the camaraderie.

Mama Faylene bites off her thread. "There, this one's done." She holds up a red and green plaid dress any little girl would love. From the stack of material on my desk, she picks the back section of a wool coat. "This will make a good pair of serviceable pants for a boy."

Bessie Mae eyes the scraps that litter the floor. "Don't none of you throw any of those away. They'll make fine quilts."

Duchess stops stitching. Her hands lie still in her lap. "When I think of how large my wardrobe was and I never gave it a thought, it plain mortifies me."

"Don't let it, dear." Mama Faylene pats her hand. "You're passing on the blessing now, and that's what counts."

"Hmm, I never thought of it that way." Duchess picks up her work again. "I just hope nobody is offended by—"

Sadie opens the door and beckons me with a crooked finger. With a glance at the others, I lay down the boy's shirt I'm sewing and excuse myself. Outside the office, I stop.

"What's the problem?"

She points to Pinkie, who is talking to a woman I've never seen before. By the stylish suit she's wearing, it's obvious she's not a farm wife.

"Who is she?"

Sadie shakes her head. "I only heard her ask Pinkie her age. That's when I came to get you."

"Okay, thanks. Let's go see what this is about." I cross to where this woman has our Pinkie cornered near the rear of the grocery. I step between them. My eyes fasten on her hat, which is adorable. I move my gaze to her blue eyes.

"I'm Mrs. Maggie Parker. How may I help you?"

Blondie gives me the once-over and must decide she likes what she sees because she smiles and holds out her hand. "I'm Miss Irene Eldridge, with the Child Protection Agency."

My mind flies to Barry, and my palms turn sweaty. I take her hand but release it quickly. "Child Protection?" My stomach churns. "What's this about?"

She has a small notebook in her other hand, which she consults. "We got a telephone call about you harboring an underage expectant mother."

I lock gazes with Sadie. *Big Jim?* "Am I allowed to ask who made the call?"

"I'm sorry, no. I have some questions I need to ask both of you." She glances around the store and at Sadie, who is hovering. "Is there an office or somewhere we can go that's private?"

"I'm afraid my office is filled." I gesture to the storeroom. "We can go in there."

She nods and takes Pinkie's arm. Sadie gets drawn off by a customer with a question, but I follow, and as soon as we're near the cooler, Miss. Eldridge stops.

"Miss Yates, how old are you?"

Pinkie's chin raises. "I'm sixteen, going on seventeen."

That's a stretch, but technically truthful. We celebrated her sixteenth birthday right after Thanksgiving, so she's heading toward seventeen. I'm watchful of Miss Eldridge's reaction, but the woman is good at her job. She merely nods and jots a note in her little book.

"Are you married, dear?"

Pinkie turns a deep shade of red. I put my arm around her. "Miss Eldridge, Pinkie was beaten regularly by her father." I stop and glance at her. She leans her head on my shoulder. "She isn't a bad girl, nor does she have loose morals. She thought getting married would protect her. Unfortunately, the young man wasn't honorable."

Miss Eldridge sucks in her lips. "I'm so sorry." She scribbles in her little book. "Do you have other siblings? Are they at home with your father now?"

Pinkie steps back. "I have a brother, but you can't make me go back."

The social worker shakes her head. "Sugar, you're over the age of consent. I want to make sure your brother is all right. Is he younger than you?"

"Yes. He's twelve."

Miss Eldridge makes another note, closes her notebook, and slides her pencil into her handbag. She turns to me. "I find Miss Yates at sixteen is not underage, and after what she tells me of her home life, she's lucky to have found you, Mrs. Parker. There is nothing to report here."

My arms and legs go weak, and I lean against the cooler's door for support. "Thank you."

"So, Miss Yates, what are your future plans?"

I step in. "If you mean how will she care for the baby, she's part of my family now. We'll take care of her and the baby."

"Please, I didn't mean that. Miss Yates appears to be a bright young woman. I'm interested in what she wants to do with her life."

"Oh. I'm sorry."

Pinkie winks at me, then faces Miss Eldridge. "I'm going to run for the Georgia State Legislature. After all, if Jeanette Rankin could be a United States Congresswoman in 1917, I can be a state representative. I want to make a difference."

I find myself staring slack-jawed at our Pinkie. Where did that come from?

She grins at me. "Miss Sadie and I have been talking about it. Did you know that Alice Mary Robertson was the last woman member of Congress, and she only served one term from 1921 to 1923? It's about time we have another. If I start in the state legislature, I might be the next."

Miss Eldridge tucks her notebook under one arm. "My, my. Well, good luck to you, Miss Yates. I'm sure you'll do it." She shakes her head, then adjusts her hat. "I really don't understand why the person who called us did so. It makes no sense whatsoever. Well, I'm off. Good day, Miss Yates. Mrs. Parker."

Pinkie and I stand arm in arm and watch her back retreat through the front door. We turn to each other, and I can't help but smile. "Big Jim just scored a big zero. Are you all right?"

"I'm fine now, but I was surely frightened for a moment when she first came in and started questioning me."

Sadie skids into the storeroom. "What happened? I couldn't get away from Bertha Dolan. She wanted to tell me every scene from Mary Pickford's movie *Coquette*. So what did she want?"

Pinkie wanders back to work, and I take Sadie's arm, walking toward the front of the grocery. "It seems Big Jim—at least, that's my guess—is still trying to cause trouble. This should put an end to it. Pinkie's of age, and there's nothing for Miss Eldridge to report."

"Well, that's a relief. I was getting ready to let the air out of her little car's tires." Sadie peers out the front window. "She's gone now."

"Sadie, I bless the day I met you. I'm so glad you're my friend."

She puts her hands on my shoulders. "Southern women stick together. Got to lend each other some iron now and then." She releases me. "Now, I've got some other errands to run. Pinkie can handle the grocery while I'm gone."

As Sadie leaves, I rejoin the others in the office. I have them marveling over Pinkie wanting to run for the Georgia legislature someday. I pick up the shirt I'd dropped and continue sewing. But my mind is on how proud Pinkie will make us all. I'm thankful to have a part in her life. Even if she marries, I can well imagine her standing on the steps of the capitol in Atlanta.

"Maggie, will you look at this?"

"What?" I rise from the davenport and cross to my desk, where Duchess is going over the books after we came upstairs this evening.

"I brought these home to try to recreate what I remember, and I found this." Duchess points to an entry. "That's not my handwriting, and it's not yours either. You don't suppose it's Asa or Katherine, do you?"

"No. Absolutely not. What's the entry?"

"It says ten dollars have been paid out in cash to Heskot Distribution Company. I know you paid with one of your new checks for the second delivery."

Fire burns in my belly and travels through my veins. Hot enough to melt that iron Sadie says is in there. "I'll be right back." I take the stairs two at a time, nearly tumbling down the last half dozen in my rush. If somebody has played loose with my books, what about the money I have in the safe for the taxes due in a few months? It needs to go into the bank now that I have an account. I open the storeroom door, startling Asa. Water from the mop he's wringing splatters on the clean, wet floor.

"Who goes there?"

"It's Maggie, Asa. I forgot something in my desk." I try the office door, but the lock is in place. I pull out my key and unlock it, breathing easier.

Asa goes back to helping Katherine mop the floor. "Okay, but be careful on the wet floor."

"I will, thank you."

Pushing the door open, I slip inside and make fast work of opening the safe. The box is there. In the corner. Thank goodness. I lift the lid. A lone five-dollar bill lays in the bottom. My heart stops. Where is the rest? More than fifty-five dollars are missing.

Why, God? Why is this happening?

I don't get any answer for that, but I do get a nudge reminding me of the money in the bank. It can cover the taxes, as long as nothing else happens. I close the safe, still holding the box. Taking it to my kitchen will be safer than leaving it here. I'll put it and the new check I got from the *Baxley News Banner* for my household hints column. It's only five dollars, but even five helps. Stopping in the kitchen, I slip the money in the cookie jar, then go upstairs to tell my sister the money she gave me has been stolen.

Pinkie races into the grocery the next morning, waving a postcard. "It's from Mr. Foster. My spectacles are ready." She dances a little jig as well as she can, given her condition. Duchess and I both get the giggles. "When can we go get them?"

I glance up from my inventory list. "Is he open today?"

She squints at the postcard, then purses her lips. "I can't read it." She hands it to Duchess.

"He's open." Sister hands it to me. "I can take her if you want."

It's mid-afternoon, I've got work to do, and Barry wants Ozzie to stay over. "That would be nice. You two have a good time. Take the truck." Duchess has become very proficient at driving that old heap. It makes quite a picture, her so refined, sitting behind the wheel of such a dilapidated, rusty mess. But it makes our deliveries and manages to get us where we need to go. I cross my fingers, hoping it makes it to Baxley and back.

Two hours later, I'm still in the grocery, picking up what I need to make grilled cheese sandwiches and tomato soup for Barry and Ozzie when Duchess and Pinkie dash in.

Pinkie stops and strikes a pose. "Well, what do you think? Am I not the bee's knees?"

I stop and give her my full attention. She's adorable in the glasses. "I didn't think they would add a certain air to you, but they do. You look intelligent. Not that you didn't before, but somehow they lend a certain *savoir faire*."

Duchess nods in agreement. "That's what Mr. Foster said too. Well, he said she looks sophisticated."

But Pinkie isn't listening to us. She's bent over, examining the soup cans. "Who put the vegetable soup in with the tomato?" She

moves them around, then straightens. "Oh, I guess that was me."
She chuckles. "But why didn't you tell me?"

My sister and I share a glance before I respond. "I didn't want
you to feel bad, sugar. Besides, the customers mix them all up too."

She plants her hands on her hips. "Not anymore, they won't.
I'll be watching." She twirls. "Oh, Maggie, I can see leaves on the
trees! They aren't just green blobs anymore. And I can read the
labels without putting my nose to the cans." She throws her arms
around me. "Thank you so much!" She dashes toward the door,
hollering back over her shoulder. "I have to go show Sadie—and
Mr. Wade!"

Duchess and I laugh at her antics. I'm delighted she's so happy.
I pick up the box of Velveeta cheese and two cans of Campbell's
tomato soup. "Ready for supper?"

My sister links arms with me. "I am." We head toward the
kitchen. "You know, I heard Wade ask Pinkie over for supper."

"Really?"

"Uh-huh."

"Well, what do you know?"

Duchess leans her head close to mine. "I wouldn't be surprised
if wedding bells are in that girl's near future."

CHAPTER 21

I let Andy Simmons be our sandwich man for a few days, but now it's Saturday and time to give Barry and Ozzie their turn. Andy is none too happy with me for telling him I don't need him anymore. He obviously got a kick out of strutting up and down the sidewalk, announcing the sales like a barker at a carnival, and must've assumed the job was his permanently.

Barry and Ozzie are tickled pink to be sandwich men. Barry's first, and he wiggles with excitement as we drop the contraption over his head. It's a good thing Pinkie didn't make it any larger since it comes to mid-calf on him.

He reaches for my hand, but his forearms barely stick out beyond the sides of the board. "The straps are falling off."

"I'll fix that." Pinkie slips off the boards back off over Barry's head.

While she makes some adjustments, my son throws his arms around me. "Thank you, Mama. I've wanted a job for my whole life."

"Yeah, me too," Ozzie says, his ears turning pink.

An idea for a bedtime story grows with the boys' chatter. I jot down a couple of notes, then Pinkie has the straps the right length. She settles the sandwich board over Barry's head again, and he turns to his best buddy.

"Ozzie, are you sure you don't care if I go first?"

"Naw, I'll watch how you do it and then do it better." Ozzie laughs when Barry stares at him slack-jawed. "I'm just kidding."

I chuckle along with Ozzie. I'm a firm believer in boys having some work to do, but also in making it fun. "Okay, boys, go on out now. Walk up Main Street. At the end of the block, turn left and go only as far as the courthouse. Then turn around and come back here. Then let Ozzie take a turn. If you boys are still having fun, you can trade again and have another round."

I stand in the doorway as they march down the sidewalk. Ozzie dances in front of Barry, calling attention to the sign. I think he's trying to sound like Andy. They're so cute, I have to chuckle.

I also have to write that bedtime story. The demands for them are growing, much to my delight. The store is busy this morning, but not too busy that Duchess, Pinkie, and Sadie can't manage.

I slip into the office and pull out paper and pencil. As usual, when I write, time slips away. I do notice the boys come back, but Pinkie helps them change the sandwich board from Barry to Ozzie, and they leave again.

I'm in the middle of the story when the boys return. I lay down my pencil and step out of the office. "Are you still having fun, or do you want to quit now?"

They shake their heads vigorously. "We want to keep going." As usual, Barry speaks for both of them.

Pinkie switches the board back to Barry, and the boys skip out the door. Well, Ozzie skips. Barry kind of shuffles, making me laugh. I must say, they are getting people in the store. Pinkie and Duchess' demonstration area is full with women leaning forward to catch every word. This may be the difference I need to get back customers.

My bedtime story is in a place where I can leave it for a while. I want to see Duchess and Pinkie in action. Slipping around the edge of the crowd, I move toward the storeroom doorway, a good vantage point to observe them but not get in anyone's way.

It's quite funny really, watching those two. Pinkie can cook very well, but she's playing the part of an inexperienced wife, while Duchess, who never cooked until she got here, is playing the teacher. I raise my fingers to my mouth, hiding my mirth.

"I prefer to have all my ingredients measured and laid out for easier mixing." Like an expert at demonstrations, Duchess makes eye contact with several of the ladies. Then she smiles. "As y'all know, I'm fairly new to cooking. I've found I don't forget an ingredient this way. Or use the wrong amount."

From beneath the table, she pulls a bowl already filled with ground carrots and another with cooked rice. Then she picks up a stack of small bowls and sets them beside the carrots and rice.

Pinkie hands Duchess the list of ingredients, then distributes the recipes to the women watching. Sister measures the various ingredients into each of the little bowls. When they are all filled and ready, she turns a brilliant smile on her audience. Duchess was made for this.

"And now, let's assemble our carrot loaf." As my sister continues to narrate, Pinkie hands her each bowl, reciting the ingredient, and Duchess drops its contents into the large mixing bowl. "It's a delicious alternative to meat and helps save money."

Pinkie leans over the bowl as my sister plunges in her hands to mix everything together. Duchess' surprised expression as her hands make contact with the mess in the bowl further tickles me. To her credit, she only hesitates a second, then she manufactures another smile and begins to squish everything together. She catches me grinning and crosses her eyes at me.

"Peanuts and carrots are an unusual pair, aren't they?" Pinkie asks. "I mean, carrots are sweet."

"So are peas. But the other ingredients add a savory element, complementing each other. Now, ladies, we form the loaf by setting it in a"—she reaches beneath the table and pulls out a metal pan—"loaf pan. You may top it with ketchup if you so desire." She pours some over the loaf. "Like meatloaf. Now, you slip it in a moderate oven for an hour."

Pinkie goes into the storeroom and brings back a finished carrot loaf. "We baked this earlier this morning. It's still warm, and if you'd like to try a slice, step forward."

Pinkie checks the ladies' notes on how to make the dish

while Duchess slices the finished loaf and hands samples to the participants. I have to try one.

"Miss Maggie!" Ozzie skids into the store. "Come quick! Barry's been beat up."

I startle and drop my slice of the carrot loaf, staring at him frozen with shock.

"Hurry, they're still punching him." He turns and runs out the door with me right behind him.

In the street outside the post office, Barry and the broken sandwich board are down in the street. Three boys are kicking him. It's Alvin Hadley, Nelson Taggart, and a boy I don't recognize.

"Stop that this instant!" I shout, racing toward them. As they scatter, I yell, "I know who you are, and your folks will hear about this."

Barry is crying. My poor baby. His lip is cut, and he has a welt over one eye that is already swelling shut. How many other bruises will he have once I get him upstairs and undressed?

I look down the street at the boys' vanishing backs. I'm going to have some words with the Taggarts and Russel Hadley. Then I'll find out who the other boy is. This is the first time I've had an encounter with a bully—no, that's wrong. It isn't the first time. Adult bullies have been at my door since I fired Cal. I can't help but wonder if he's somehow mixed up in this.

Wade runs out of the train station and bends over, removing the tangled and broken sign from my boy. He helps Barry up, who turns and buries his head in my skirt. I gather him in my arms, tears of frustration sliding down my face. I didn't protect my baby. I failed him.

"I may need to give you boys some boxing lessons." Wade tussles Ozzie's hair.

"Yeah. We need 'em." He turns to me. "Miss Maggie, they said we stole Andy's job."

So that's what this is about. Barry sniffs and looks up. "We didn't. Mama gave the job to us. I tried to tell them. My tummy hurts." He begins to pant. I know what's coming and lead him to the gutter, where my poor son throws up.

He's pale, and his skin feels clammy. "I'm going to get Doc to come look at you." I bend to pick him up, but Wade gently takes him from me and carries him to my office.

Ozzie runs for Doc.

"Don't worry, Maggie." Wade sets Barry in my chair, then leads me out into the grocery. "I think it's just the shock of what happened."

"I hope so. If they really—"

"Every boy has to get his first black eye sometime, Maggie. Didn't Jimmy ever tell you about our first?"

"No, he didn't. And why must every boy get one? I think that's barbaric."

Wade crosses his arms and considers me, then smiles. "Barbaric or not, it's a rite of passage. I don't know a single male who has never had a black eye. Don't you remember Ozzie's? He and Nelson got in a tussle when Nelson taunted him, saying he had a girlfriend."

A smile tugs at my lips. Every six-year-old's worst nightmare. "I do remember that. Ozzie swaggered with pride over the bruise. But didn't it worry you? His eye could have been damaged."

"By fists? Not likely. Barry will be a celebrity at school—" Wade frowned. "You can't interfere, Maggie."

"What do you mean?"

"Don't talk with the boys' parents. Alvin and Nelson were protecting a friend's interest."

That made me mad. "So they can beat up a little boy? Come on, Wade."

"I understand how you feel, but if you go to their parents, it will be as if Barry snitched. That will only invite more problems."

I crossed my arms. "That's not fair." Once again, I wish Jimmy were still alive. He'd know what to do.

"No, it's not. But God didn't promise life would be fair."

And it's times like this I'm thankful for my late husband's best friend, Wade.

Ozzie skids in through the storeroom with Doc right behind him, bag in hand.

I wave Doc over. "The patient is in my office. Thanks for coming."

"It's a pleasure to doctor a young man's first black eye." Chortling, Doc walks into the office.

I throw my hands on my hips. "Him too?"

Wade's laugh is hearty and takes away my fears. Still, I hover outside the door. But my little boy isn't crying now. He's regaling Doc with his prowess and how he "got in a few licks before they outnumbered me."

I step through the doorway. "So … is your patient going to live?"

Barry snorts. "I'll be fine. And I bet I have the best shiner in the whole school."

"What about his lip, Doc? Does it need stitches?"

At that, Barry pales then squares his little shoulders. His eyes don't leave Doc's face as he examines the wound.

"No, it's not that bad. Unless you want me to sew you up, Barry?"

"That's okay, Doc. I'm good."

A knock sounds on the door. Who could that be? I turn and get a glimpse of Andy Simmons through the window. And his father. I open the door.

Andy's eyes are red, and he hangs his head. "Miss Maggie, I'm really sorry my friends beat up Barry. Is he okay?"

"Well, he's got a black eye and a split lip, not to mention some other bruises."

"Please, ma'am, I didn't tell them to do this. They asked where my sandwich board was, and I told you gave the job to Barry and Ozzie. They didn't beat up Ozzie, too, did they, Mr. Wade?"

"No, Ozzie is okay."

I watch Andy closely for signs of belligerence. All I see is sincerity, and my heart softens. "Do you understand why I gave the job to Barry and Ozzie?"

"Yes, ma'am. Barry is your son, and Ozzie is his best friend. It's natural. Like my daddy"—he looks up at his father with pride—"lets me help in the café and my Uncle Karl lets me do all the paper deliveries."

"That's right. Thank you, Andy, for understanding."

"Yes, ma'am. And I'll tell the other boys to leave Barry and Ozzie alone."

Paul nudges his son. "Tell Barry you're sorry, too, son."

After Andy apologizes to Barry, my son shows off his wounds, then when everyone leaves, I sit down with Barry.

"You're growing up, my little love. You've gotten your first black eye, and now Mr. Wade is going to teach you how to box so you can defend yourself."

Barry winces as he tries to smile. His hand goes to his lip. "Yeah. Next time, they won't get me before I get a few more licks in."

Lord, I need some wisdom here. "You aren't going to start looking for fights, are you?"

"Naw. That's not what Jesus would have done. Hey, Mama, how old do you suppose Jesus was when He got His first black eye?"

I hug my boy and chuckle. We'll discuss that during story hour tonight.

I close the office door behind us. Barry runs to show off his wounds to Sadie. She's making over him, exclaiming and oohing at all the right times as he tells the story. He may become a writer—his embellishments are pretty creative.

The front door flies open with such force, it crashes against the washing powder display, knocking boxes over. The knob punctures one, and powder spills all over the floor. Big Jim stands in front of a woman I've never seen before. Alarm bells ring in my head. Her light-brown hair is pulled back so tight, it makes her eyes slant.

Her navy suit is large and dowdy and looks as if it came from a missionary barrel. Who is she?

Big Jim stomps over and thrusts his finger in my face. "Maggie Parker, you've gone too far this time. Not only did you bring an unwed girl in the family way into your household, subjecting my grandson to her immoral ways, now he's been in a fight and injured. This"—he stops his tirade to gesture to the woman behind him—"is Miss Ferguson from Georgia Child Protection Services."

CHAPTER 22

"Where is my grandson?"

My mind screams, *Run, Barry!* But my mouth doesn't cooperate.

My baby tentatively approaches from the back of the store. "Hey, Granddaddy."

Big Jim grabs Barry's arm and shoves him toward the woman, who picks him up and starts toward the door.

"Barry!" I sprint past Big Jim, reaching for my boy.

Barry's legs kick wildly. "Mama!" His scream pierces my heart.

"Give me my son!" I reach for him.

Big Jim shoves between us. His arm holds me back. "Get him in the car," he shouts over his shoulder. The child services agent drags Barry outside as my father-in-law faces me again. "Maggie, you have a choice. Get these people out of your house and this store, or you'll never see him again. And believe me, I have ways of knowing if you listen."

I ball my fist, ready to punch him. "Now you just—"

He turns and storms out, but I'm right on his heels. I lunge for his coattail, but he shoves me hard.

I fall to my knees in the gutter.

He jumps into a dark sedan parked at the curb with the engine running, and they speed off.

I see my baby through the back window, crying and reaching toward me. I scream his name and jump to my feet, chasing the car.

Sadie runs up beside me, but at the end of the street, they turn and leave us behind. She clutches my shoulder, slowing me, until I collapse in the street, gasping for breath and sobbing.

There's no way we can catch them. Sadie stands silent for a moment, her shoulders slumping.

My heart shatters.

My tears flow in an unending stream. *Dear Lord, where are they taking Barry? And why?*

Sadie straightens, reaches down, and helps me up. I limp back toward the grocery.

Nellie marches out and plants herself square in front of me. Arms akimbo, she stares down her nose at me. "You just got your just desserts."

"And you"—Sadie is in Nellie's face—"are about to get yours. I'm leaving your boarding house this afternoon." She spits a chewed clove onto Nellie's shoe.

Nellie turns white, then so red I think she may have a heart attack right there on the street. Sadie has boarded with her for thirty-some years.

Sadie spins around and helps me inside. My dress is torn, and my knees are bloodied, but they're not half as bad as my heart. This is my fault. I thought money would keep me safe from Big Jim, and I let my guard down.

"Now don't you fret." Sadie puts her hands on my shoulders and looks me in the eye. "That child whatever-it-is-agency is brand new. They can't keep Barry for long. Find your iron, girl, and pump it into your veins. We'll get him back."

I'm not sure I have any iron. Nor am I sure I believe her this time, for God has surely turned His back on me.

Fog hovering over the river obscures its dangers, and that's where I am. Lost in a fog, not knowing where my baby is. *Why, God? Why?*

I've cried for four days. I didn't cry this much when my husband died. All I want to do is sleep, yet I haven't slept at all. Every time I close my eyes, I see my frightened little boy crying and reaching for me. I keep asking God for an answer, but I don't think He's listening to me.

Faylene didn't have any answers, either, when Sadie told her what happened. Big Jim hasn't been home. How I hate that she had to learn what her husband did. Barry is the delight of her heart. I've never heard her utter an angry word, but Sadie told me she was so mad at Big Jim, she swore.

"Maggie?" My sister pokes her head in my bedroom door. I roll over and burrow beneath the covers. I don't want to talk. Words aren't going to help me. I just want my baby back.

Duchess yanks off my blankets. I curl into a fetal position.

"Magnolia Parker, you need to get up. Pinkie and I found out where the office for that child agency is."

It's futile. Without hope, I ask, "Where?"

"Atlanta."

Duchess pulls on my arm until I'm standing. Pinkie riffles through my closet. She pulls out my old gray suit and holds it up for my sister's decision. Duchess nods. I couldn't care lesswhat I wear. I just want to see my baby.

"Stand still, Maggie. You need to be dressed to go find Barry." Pinkie slides the blouse over my head.

A tiny seed of hope plants itself in my heart. "Do you think Barry is there? Can we bring him home?" But how—Sister turns me to button the back of my blouse. "How are we getting there?" It's impossible. I don't have a car, and the grocery truck won't make it that far.

"Mr. Wade is giving you and Duchess vouchers for the train," Pinkie says. "He's a gentleman and a good friend." She holds my skirt while Duchess supports me as I step into it.

"Oh."

Pinkie zips my skirt and hands my jacket to Sister. "I want you to know how sorry I am, Maggie. I know I caused this and so much mo—"

Her words light a fire inside me that burns away the fog. "No, you didn't! It's Big Jim's stone-cold heart that's at fault." I glance back and forth between them. "What I want to know is *why*. He knows I take good care of Barry. So why did he do it?"

Pinkie narrows her eyes. "You can't see it? I recognized his jealousy and greed the first time I met him. He wants the grocery for himself. I overheard him muttering to Cal that he never should have given it to his son. Said his son left it to you in the throes of dying when it should have come back to him."

Big Jim is a lot of things, but greedy? Wait—I frown. "When did you hear that?"

"On Friday." Pinkie is wearing one of my old maternity dresses. It reminds me of being pregnant with Barry, and that brings my father-in-law's duplicity into sharp focus.

I turn my eyes on my sister. "He took Barry on Thursday. Wasn't he still gone Friday?"

Pinkie folds her arms. "He's a skunk, that one. He was in town and talking to Cal. I'd gone to Trey's gas station to get a Co-Cola from the vending machine. When I heard Cal's voice, I hid. He gives me the creeps. And that's when I heard Big Jim say that. Trey was putting gas in a car, and I heard Big Jim say it was his."

"He doesn't own a car." Does he? I'm also searching my mind to remember the last time he was home. Faylene said he hadn't been there in over three weeks. "He's sneaking in and out of town, but he doesn't go see his wife? What is wrong with that man?"

Duchess helps me put on the jacket. "We need to have all that information and more to tell the people at the agency. We'll write a list on the way. Pinkie, please get me a pad and pencil." Sister throws a coat at me. "Your gloves are in the pocket."

I slap my hat on my head, and we hurry out the door. It's dark out. "Duchess, what time is it?"

"Four forty-five and our train is here. It leaves in thirteen minutes."

"What about the store?"

Pinkie shoves a pad and pencil into my hands. "Sadie and I will take care of that."

I hug her. "Thank you. You're a brave girl." I know many of our customers look down on her.

Duchess and I run across the street. I can't believe I'm going to see my Barry in a few hours. Wade is waiting and hands three ticket vouchers to us.

"One is for bringing Barry home. Now, have a safe trip. I'll be praying God opens doors and ... brings Big Jim his own just desserts." He gives me a hug.

I lean against his strength for a moment. "You're a good friend, Wade. I know you love Barry too. Thank you for praying."

Sister and I board the train and drop into our seats. We barely settle when she pulls the pad and pencil from my hands. "Now, what do we know?"

I stare out the window at the station. The whistle blows, and we begin to move. I remember standing in Mobley's Dry Goods two months ago, hearing the train whistle. Barry and I watched it from across the street as it passed through Rivers End. I wanted to be on that train going somewhere exciting. And now I am but going to Atlanta to find my missing son isn't a romantic journey.

I turn my gaze back on Duchess. "My father-in-law confuses me. I don't understand him."

"Why not?"

"His prejudices, for one. He's so narrow-minded, his brain only has one side. Sadie told me she once was sweet on him. Then he called her a savage and said she didn't have the brains to get an education. But later, after she graduated with honors, he tried to date her. Now he and so many others look down on her. It's crazy. Why?"

"I don't know about the others, but maybe Big Jim's pride was hurt."

The train picks up speed, and the conductor comes to punch our vouchers. After he moves on, I slip off my coat. "I'm sure you're right, but what I really want to know is why he's hurting his own grandson. It's not like he wants Barry around him. He never spends any time with him. And why is he never home? Where does he go? Why does he stay away so long?"

Duchess writes every question down. "If he's gone all the time, he has no idea of how Barry is being raised. He's accusing you of neglect, yet he neglects his wife." The pencil scratches against the paper. Then she looks up. "Did I tell you Barry told me that Big Jim is mean to Faylene?"

The whistle blows, and the train crosses the Ocmulgee River. "What did he mean by that? How?"

"She asked Big Jim to wheel her into the necessary room, as she calls it. He got up but walked out of the house instead, completely ignoring her request. Barry got Bessie Mae for her, but he told me he thought his granddaddy was a mean man."

"There isn't a sweeter and less demanding person on this earth than Faylene. How can he do that to her?"

"Didn't you tell me theirs was an arranged marriage?"

"Yes, and apparently no love ever grew."

My eyes grow heavy as the train lulls me. I lay my head back, letting my sister's discussion of arranged marriages swirl around me.

"Maggie, wake up, sugar. We're here. Terminal Station." My sister's voice breaks through my dream, and I'm glad to be free of it. An older, grown-up Barry was accusing me of not finding him. My cheeks are damp from tears. I gather my handbag and slide my arms into my coat. It's even colder up here in Atlanta than at home.

"What time is it?"

"Three minutes past ten." She squeezes my hand. "We've got plenty of time. Our return train doesn't leave until four-fifty-eight."

We step off the train and go into the station. People scurry in all directions, their voices blending into a discordant concert. After obtaining directions to the agency, Duchess charms the counterman into letting her use his phone. She places her call, smiles sweetly at the man, and hangs up.

"Come on. Sarah Jane is picking us up in ten minutes."

"Who is Sarah Jane? Why aren't we taking the motor bus?" I hurry after my sister. She seems to know this train station well. I guess she and Mr. Alden were here often with all their travels. We go outside and wait. It's so different here. I've been to Lawrenceville and once to Buckhead for a short visit with Duchess. But I didn't see Atlanta proper. The city is huge. How had my sister ever gotten used to it? One can hardly see the sky for all the tall buildings.

"Sarah is a friend, and I've never been on the motor bus. I don't know where it goes. This is easier."

A few minutes later, a young woman pulls up in a Chevrolet. It's not brand new, but I'm impressed, anyway. She hops out and hugs Duchess. She's wearing a beautiful coral suit with the cutest hat that tilts charmingly over one eye. Her light-brown hair is jelly-rolled in the latest fashion.

"I was afraid I'd never see you again. How are you holding up, dear?" She notices me and grins. "Oh, Maggie!" I'm enveloped in a hug. "I remember you from when you visited. My, you've grown into a lovely woman. Now, where can I take you, and how long are you here for?"

Duchess winks at me and takes Sarah Jane's arm. "Just for the day, I'm afraid. Sugar, you wouldn't believe it. My sister's father-in-law is a horrible man. He wants her store and called that new Child Protective Services agency to take her son away. We've come to get him back."

Sarah Jane looks at me, horrified. Will she still give us a ride?

"That rotten man."

Relief is sweet.

"If you have any problems, you let me know. I'll have Charles make a phone call."

I don't know who Charles is, maybe her husband or brother. Whoever he is, I'm glad he's on our side. We get into her Chevrolet. She and Duchess chatter as she drives us a few miles. Each building we pass resembles the next. How does one distinguish between them? It's like a forest of concrete. It isn't long before we pull up to an austere-looking building.

Sarah Jane points to the granite front. "The office is in there." She lays her hand on my shoulder. "I'll wait out here, but come get me if things don't look good."

Duchess and I climb the steps. Sister smiles. "Did I tell you her father-in-law is a judge? He and Mr. Alden were close friends."

My spirits pick up. With any luck, we'll be taking Barry home with us. We enter the building. It's a sorry-looking place with institution-gray walls and peeling paint. I hope they don't keep any children here. The poor babies will feel like they're in prison.

We pass several doors until Duchess stops. "This is it, sugar. Deep breath."

I inhale.

"Good. Now, blow it out."

I do as she says.

She nods once. "Okay, let's go."

Inside, three chairs line the wall. The room, if you can call it that, is maybe ten feet long and no more than four feet wide before a half wall with and counter. Except for the closed window, frosted-glass partitions hide the rest of the place. There's a bell on the counter. With a glance at my sister for support, I tap it with my finger.

The window slides open. It's not that woman who took Barry from me, thank goodness. This woman has iron-gray hair, cut in a modern style. Her eyes, magnified behind her glasses, are gentle.

"May I help you?"

"I hope so. My father-in-law ... he ..." No matter how I say this, it isn't good. I look helplessly at my sister. She steps up.

"My sister is a wonderful mother, ma'am. She's a widow who has done a marvelous job raising her son. Her father-in-law thinks for some reason that taking me in after my husband died"— Duchess stops and raises her hankie to her eyes—"is some kind of sin. He called your offices and told them I don't know what, and they came and took my nephew away."

The clerk's eyes grew sad. "Oh, dear me. Let me do a little investigating. I need your names, the child's name, your father-in-law, and if you know it, the social worker who was with him."

We tell her. Both of us. At the same time. She stops us and looks to me. "Your name, please."

"Maggie, I mean, Magnolia Parker. My son is Barry Parker. James Parker is my father-in-law, and I believe Miss Ferguson was the woman from the agency. This is my sister, Duchess Alden."

"Alden? William Alden's wife, I mean, widow? Duchess, I'm Mary Alice Cornwall's mother, Nellie Draves. My dear, I was so sorry to hear about your dear husband." She holds out her hand to my sister.

I'm confused. Duchess knows this woman?

Duchess grasps the lady's hand. "Mrs. Draves, how lovely to meet you. But why are you working here?"

She pats Duchess' hand through the window. "Dear, the stock market crash hit more than just you. And when I heard about this agency opening, I wanted to help. With those orphan trains, so many children were being used as free labor and not taken into loving families. Unfortunately, a few who work here don't fully assess a situation. They believe any accusation. Now you two sit down and let me look into this, make a few telephone calls. We'll find your son."

My knees nearly buckle in relief. I reach through the window and clasp her hand. "Thank you, Mrs. Draves."

We sit. I cross my legs, but my foot bounces so badly, I uncross them and put both feet on the floor. Duchess crosses her ankles.

"Are you sure about Mrs. Draves? She does seem nice."

"She's delightful. Better still, her daughter Mary Alice and I are dear friends." She pats my hand. "Don't you worry. She'll find Barry."

We wait as the minutes tick by. There aren't any magazines to look at. I guess they, not Mrs. Draves but the others, don't want you to be comfortable. I can't sit still. I get up and pace. I'm glad no one else is here, or there wouldn't be enough oxygen in the room.

"Maggie, you're wearing a groove in the floor. Sit down."

I can't, but I'll try for her sake. Soon, I'm plucking at a tiny thread in my skirt. Duchess lays her hand over mine, stopping me.

"How long has it been?"

Sister glances at her wristwatch. It was the one thing she couldn't give up, besides her wedding ring. It was the first gift she received from William. "It's been ten minutes. Give her time."

I don't have time to give. Time is a gate keeping me from my son. Oh, my sweet Barry. How he must be hurting. I just want to hold him and keep him from harm and fear. *Oh, dear Lord, be with him. Let him know I'm trying to find him!*

I hear footsteps. I rise and go to the window. Mrs. Draves comes around a corner. Her face—she isn't smiling. I want to scream. Instead, I hold my breath.

"Mrs. Parker, there is no Miss Ferguson in this agency, and Barry isn't in any of our facilities. He never got here."

CHAPTER 23

I'm spittin' mad. Take that and mix it with my fear for Barry, and the two could fuel this train all the way back to Rivers End. Mrs. Draves told us she telephoned all four of their facilities that house the children, but Barry isn't in any of them. Then she went through all their personnel records, not that it took long—the agency is only a couple of years old. They've never had a Miss Ferguson employed.

However, she did find where Big Jim had tried to lodge a complaint against me. That must have been when that social worker came and questioned Pinkie. Lucky for me, Duchess knows Mrs. Draves, and she believes us. I need someone outside the family to help me.

As we take our seats, I'm not looking forward to the trip home. I'd hoped to have Barry with me. "My only conclusion is Big Jim has kidnapped Barry. His own grandson. But why? And who is Miss Ferguson? Did Big Jim hire her to make me believe the state agency has Barry? I don't understand this one bit. It makes no sense."

After pulling out a hankie, I set my handbag on the floor beneath my seat.

My sister removes her hat and lays it next to her, then smooths her hair. "I'm glad no one is sharing the seat across from us." Duchess stretches her legs between the two seats and rests them on the opposite side. "Anyway, part of it *does* make sense. Mrs. Draves told me when he lodged that complaint, he found out they house the children in group facilities. He wanted to withdraw his charge then." She raises her hands as if asking why. "It's my guess he wants to keep Barry in order to get what he wants from you. The agency told him once a complaint is lodged, they must investigate. But now that Mrs. Draves knows it's you, she will tell them to close the case. There's no neglect or abuse here."

"Well, thank the good Lord for that, but I still don't have my son. And what does Big Jim want? It can't be Barry. He never takes him anywhere or spends time with him. I just don't get it, Duchess. I've got a headache from trying to figure it out. I'm so mad at him for putting Barry through this, I could—well, I don't know what."

My gracious lady of a sister snorts. "He wants the store. I'm so angry at him I could wring a chicken's neck and pretend it's his."

Coming from Duchess, that's saying something. And it makes me smile. I guess God hasn't left me alone. He brought my sister to me. *Did I say thank you?* I don't receive any answer, but peace settles over me, and I hold onto it tightly. I think I'll need it in the days to come. I have to believe Big Jim will take good care of Barry. *Please, Lord, don't let my Barry be afraid.*

"So, what are we going to do?" I don't know if I'm asking my sister or God, but I'll take any suggestion either one has to offer.

Duchess closes one eye and pulls a grin like that cat in Barry's *Alice in Wonderland* book. "I say we tell the sheriff that Barry has been kidnapped. We don't have to tell him it was Big Jim. He wouldn't believe it, anyway. We'll simply say a woman grabbed him and dragged him into her car …" She adds an eyebrow raising to her statement. "It's the truth."

My sister has grown into a strong woman in the few weeks she's been with me. I admire her so much, but I have to admit I'm a little jealous. I lean my head back and close my eyes. The long day and my emotions are taking their toll on me. I only hope my sweet boy knows his mama is trying her best to get him home.

A tear seeps out through my closed lid and trails down my cheek. I haven't the strength to wipe it away.

Clouds hide the sun the next morning as I slip on a jacket and leave my sister and Pinkie to run the store. I'm going to see the sheriff as Duchess suggested. The jail and Sheriff Jubal Lee's office is across the road and down at the corner of Main and Church Streets. They built it close enough to the saloon that it never takes the sheriff long to jail any drunks. The only habitual drunks in town are Nellie's husband, Harry, and Asa Hopper the barber, which probably explains why Big Jim won't let Asa trim his nose hairs.

I open the door to the jailhouse. The small office is thankfully in front of and not in sight of any of the cells. Jubal sits at his desk. Rivers End isn't large enough to warrant a deputy. In times of need, Jubal deputizes Wade or a couple of men in town.

He looks up as I enter. "Maggie? What can I do for you?"

I never have been able to judge our sheriff's thoughts. He has a good poker face, keeping his thoughts hidden behind a blank expression. It unnerves me. I open my mouth to say Barry's been kidnapped. I stop, realizing he'll ask me when, and why I didn't come to him on Thursday when it happened. Then I'll have to tell him Big Jim is involved, and one thing I know for certain is the good ole boy network is alive and well in South Georgia. He'll never believe me. I turn to leave.

"Maggie."

His commanding voice stops me. He rises and comes around the desk, putting his hand on my shoulder. "What's bothering you, girl?"

"I—" I swallow and try again. "Barry. He's …." That's it. I can say he's missing and won't need to say anything else. Except if I say that, it makes me look like a bad mother—like I don't keep an eye on my son. And why I did I wait so long to tell him? No matter which way I try to do this, Big Jim will come into it. Or win.

"I was passing and thought I'd let you know—" What? Jubal isn't married, so I have nothing to tell a wife. He boards with

Nellie Taggart, so he doesn't shop for groceries. There's no reason for me to— "Please tell Nellie I'm running a special on stew meat." I turn and scurry out of his office and onto the street.

Stew meat? After butchering all those hogs, I say *stew meat*? I stop mid-stride. But now what? I can't find Barry on my own. I don't know where to start looking. I need help. The weight of my loss nearly doubles me over. Tears blur my eyes, and I swipe my nose with my sleeve.

Doc's wife, Clara, turns the corner. I step back and flat against the corner of the bank. Clara enters the grocery and thankfully doesn't see me. I look up and down the street. There are few people out and about today, and nobody notices me. That's good because I can't talk to anyone right now. Pinkie and Duchess will be fine without me for a time.

I follow my instinct, and, turning, I head out behind the station and past the shanties. I'm drawn to the woods, where the forest with its sweetgum and Georgia pines has always been my special refuge. I go when I need to think. When I'm drawn to connect with God in a special way. When I'm troubled. And I have troubles. The path before me blurs as my tears flow unchecked.

As I enter the forest, it gives up its scent with each step on its floor of pine needles and dried leaves. I button my jacket against the cold air. Soon I arrive at my favorite sweetgum tree. With my foot, I brush its spiny balls aside and sink to the ground.

"Lord, my troubles are bigger than I can carry alone. I need your help."

The sweetgum's familiar trunk gives me support like an old friend. This is where Barry found Pinkie. Silence surrounds me, except for the sounds of the forest. Crickets, birds, squirrels scampering up and down the trees. I'll wait, though. I refuse to leave without hearing from God.

All that breaks the silence is a pine warbler's song, rather unusual when the skies are overcast as they are today. Sadie can imitate any bird's song and have them answer her back. Barry and I love to sit in the woods with her and tell her which birds to mimic. We have yet to find one she can't. Next to my sister, she's my best friend.

I strain to listen for God's soft voice, but my thoughts scatter like cockroaches when a light goes on. How can I find Barry? Why did Big Jim take him? Why does he hate me so much? Who is Miss Ferguson? If only Jimmy hadn't died.

My thoughts are overtaking me again. "Oh, Lord, how long do I have to wait for an answer? Where is Barry?" My sweet boy. I pick up a handful of pine straw, letting it fall through my fingers.

I turn my wrist to glance at my watch. I need to get back to the store. It looks as though God isn't giving up any answers today.

Right now, I need to find that stew beef I bragged about to the sheriff.

Barry has been gone a week, and we are no closer to any answers. Each morning, I pray for God to help me find him, and I fight the darkness that wants to suck me under.

This afternoon, Duchess, Sadie, Pinkie, and I gather around Mama Faylene's dining table to put our collective brains into a thinking cap and figure out what Big Jim is up to. Whatever it is, it can't be legal. Bessie Mae brings in a tray with coffee and slices of her heavenly caramel cake. I've barely eaten anything in the past week, but this smells divine.

"Thank you, Bessie Mae." My sweet mother-in-law takes a cup and a small slice of cake. "After everyone is served, get yourself a slice, and please join us in here."

Bessie Mae's eyebrows move upwards as she considers Faylene, but she doesn't contradict her request. She continues around the table. When she gets to Sadie, she turns the tray so the largest slice is within her reach. There's always been a connection between those two, both having seen the uglier side of human beings. Sadie licks her lips and takes the plate. A chuckle rumbles in Bessie Mae's chest. Finally, she takes her own plate, sets her tray down, and sits between Sadie and Faylene.

I'm glad she's here. She helps fuel my faith. "Bessie Mae, when was the last time Big Jim was here?"

She shoots a quick glance at Faylene, who nods. "Well now, Miz Maggie, that would depend on where you mean by *here*."

Is she being evasive? "I mean here at the house."

"Ah. That'd be five weeks and two days ago. But I knows for a fact that he's been in town. I seen him with my very own eyes goin' intah Sheriff Jubal Lee's office just last Thursday."

That's no help. I know he was here then. That's the day he took Barry. "Have you seen him since then?"

"Yes, ma'am, Miz Maggie. I've caught glimpses of him lots of times before when he was supposed to be up in Macon or wherevah. But last Friday, he was a-sneakin' 'round the saloon. I was on my way to get Miss Faylene some medicine from Beau Hampton with the money you gives me. I knows it was Big Jim, but to be sure, I peeked in the windah. He was sittin' with Cal Llewellyn, arguin'." She looks at Faylene, puts her hands on the table, and pushes herself up. "Now, I've got dishes to wash."

I wish she could be comfortable sitting at the table with us. I know that's from Big Jim, not Faylene. I swanny, Rivers End is the strangest town, rife with convoluted prejudices. Why, even Sadie's move into Fannie's boarding house caused an outcry in the town. One would think Nellie and the folks at her boarding house would have been happy to be rid of "that Indian half-breed." But they're more incensed about her going to Fannie's because Fannie and her boarders are Negroes. It's just plain hinky and makes no sense whatsoever.

We finish our pie in silence.

Sadie takes a good long sip of her coffee then sets the cup back on the saucer. "If Barry isn't in one of the Child Protective Services facilities, then it stands to reason that Big Jim has him with him. That means Barry isn't in school." She wags a finger at my sister. "Put that on your list, Duchess. That's a strike against him. Now the question we need an answer to is where Big Jim has him."

"I knew he was up to something early last month." Faylene folds her napkin, sets it beside her plate, and sighs. "I only wish I'd had an inkling of what it was. I might have been able to stop it. He asked me where the clothes I have put away for Barry's birthday were. Said he wanted to see what I bought for the boy. At the time, I was grateful he was taking an interest." She shifts in her chair.

I reach over and adjust the pillow behind her back. "Is that better?"

"Yes. Thank you, dear. I have a feeling Big Jim took those clothes. Bessie Mae?"

We wait until she comes back, wiping her hands on a dish towel. "Yes'm?"

"Would you please go see if those clothes we got for Barry are still in my dresser drawer?"

"I'll go, but why wouldn't they be there? I hasn't moved 'em, Miz Faylene."

"I know that, Bessie Mae. I'm afraid maybe Big Jim took them."

She shuffles toward Faylene's room, muttering as she goes, "Why in heaben's name would that man want the chile's clothes? He's nothin' but a scoundrel, that's fo' sure."

I hate that my mother-in-law is tied to Big Jim. She's so sweet, and he's so ... not sweet. A drawer scrapes open in her room.

"They's a'gone, Miz Faylene. You was right."

Faylene's jaw muscles twitch, then set. She folds her hands on the table and steeples her forefingers. "I've suspected that man of miscreant behavior for some time. Being in this"—she pats the arm of her wheeled chair—"makes me invisible. At times, that's beneficial."

It may well be, but it breaks my heart. From the day Jimmy brought me to Rivers End as a new bride, his mother welcomed me into her heart and home. She's an example of graciousness to me every day.

"He seems to think that the polio stole my hearing along with the use of my legs. Lately, I've been out in my lovely garden." She stops and reaches over to squeeze my hand and looks at Sadie. "Maggie and Barry fixed the ramp so Bessie Mae can push me out there. I sit under the wisteria arbor out of sight but not out of earshot. I've heard Big Jim and Cal talking about the grocery, and it sticks in Big Jim's craw that you're making a profit, Maggie."

"Not for long, though." I reluctantly tell her about the problems with suppliers. But that is neither here nor there. I want my son home. "Pinkie, you said you saw Big Jim after he took Barry, is that right?"

"I did." Pinkie glances at Bessie Mae. "It was the next day. I think I saw him before Bessie Mae did. He was at the gas station."

"And you're sure he didn't see you?"

"No, ma'am. I'm sure." She turns to Faylene. "He and Cal don't like me one bit. I stay away from them."

Faylene pats her hand. "Those two don't like too many people."

Pinkie grimaces and turns back to me. "I was going back over what I'd heard and thought of something. When I overheard them, Big Jim was grousing about not being able to get any more money. Do you suppose he was blackmailing Cal?"

That's a new wrinkle. Could Cal have been caught stealing money before Duchess caught him? If so, how would he have been found out? Scenarios play out in my mind. "What if Cal has been stealing from me since Jimmy died? Maybe Big Jim discovered it, but wanting me to give him back the store, he didn't tell me. Maybe he told Cal to keep it up but give him the money, and he wouldn't tell the sheriff." Sadie and Faylene know him best. I look to them. "Do you think that's possible?"

Faylene and Sadie share a glance, then Sadie nods. "I truly am sorry to say yes, I do think that's a possibility, Maggie. What's your feeling on it, Faylene?"

"I wouldn't put it past him. Before Maggie started paying Bessie Mae's wages, he shorted her more times than you can imagine, telling her it was for broken eggs and silly things like that. No,

I'm afraid Big Jim is obsessed with money. He wasn't always like that, though. Only since I got back from New York." She smiles at Pinkie, who's looking confused. "I caught the polio up there in the epidemic. I had to stay there for eighteen months before I could come home. I noticed a marked change in him when I returned. I couldn't put my finger on what the change was, but he *was* different."

There's a clue in there, I know it, but for the life of me, I can't think what it can be. "Given the transformation in Big Jim and the fact he kidnapped his own grandson, we need to be very careful. I can't say he wouldn't harm any of us or Barry." I turn to Sadie. "How are we going to trail Big Jim? What with you being half Yamasee, Pinkie in the family way, and Faylene in that wheeled chair, none of y'all could hide in a haystack."

My sister reaches for our cups and pours more coffee from the pot Bessie Mae left on the table. "You left me out, Magnolia." She lazily stirs the cream into her coffee. "I'm thinking with my hair tied up in a turban-like bandana and wearing overalls, I could pass for a farm wife."

That intriguing image makes me laugh. Whether from tightly strung emotions or the mental image of Duchess in overalls, I can't stop. Not for several moments.

"You laugh, but he'd never suspect it's me who's following him."

"It could work, Maggie," Sadie says. "There's only one problem."

I can think of several. "And what is that?" I ask, mopping my eyes with my napkin.

"When he leaves town. We know Barry isn't anywhere in Rivers End. We've searched every house and business and backyard storage shack. Wade has even been in every shanty looking for him. So we'll need an automobile."

I shake my head. "I've got the only one, and it's the delivery truck. Big Jim's driven it many times. He borrows it anytime I'll let him. He knows not only every inch of it but every truck and automobile in Rivers End." I look around the table at each of them so willing to help me, but we are without a way. "He has the advantage."

"Not so fast." Sadie drums her fingers on the table. "I have an idea." She pushes up from the table. "I'll see you tomorrow."

Sadie's like that—often close-lipped until she's sure of her plan. I don't know what she's got in mind, but a sniglet of hope lights the darkness inside me. I'm going to think positive thoughts. An image rises again and drags a snicker out of me. "I can't wait to see Duchess in a bandana and overalls."

Faylene laughs. "And I can't wait to see Big Jim Parker outfoxed by you girls."

CHAPTER 24

Rays from the sun slice through the Venetian blinds, tickling my eyelids. Time to get up, but I lie there not moving. I'm finding it harder and harder to get out of bed in the morning as each week slips by without my boy. I can't sleep at night. Instead of tree frogs and night birds, I hear Barry crying for me. I'm as close as I can be to sending a message to Big Jim telling him he's won. The only thread holding me back is wondering what will happen to us if I lose the grocery. How will I feed us? Sadie hasn't yet told me the idea she's hatching.

By the noises coming through the floorboards, Duchess is in the kitchen. I could use some of the coffee she's brewing. I throw off the covers and slide on my robe, but my fingers catch and tear through the sleeve's worn material. Can anything else go wrong? The desire to wad up that old robe and throw it in the burn barrel is strong, but I can't afford to replace it. I drop onto the bed, doing battle with the equally strong desire to climb back beneath the covers, pull them up over my head, and cry.

The bedroom door opens, and Pinkie waddles in. "Maggie, I—" Eyeing my robe, she picks it up. "What happened?"

"It's so old, the material gave way. My hand went right through the seam."

Watching her carefully examine the sleeve with focused eyes lights a spark of joy for her deep within me. We did a good thing, Sadie and I, getting her those spectacles. Is God telling me to hold on? There's hope for Barry too?

She finally folds the robe over her arm.

"I can fix this. I'll tell Duchess to hold breakfast for another few minutes while you dress." She opens the door to leave.

"Thank you. Now, why did you come in? Is there something you wanted?"

She stands for a moment, thinking. I can't help but smile, remembering how being in the family way seems to rob a woman of her brains.

"Oh yeah. Sadie's here and says to plan on a day trip tomorrow. She'll explain over breakfast." Pinkie closes the door.

Day trip? I'm not sure I want to go anywhere or be away at all. What if Barry gets free and runs home? Or if Big Jim relents and brings him here?

I hurry my morning ablutions at the washbasin, throw on one of my three workday dresses, and hightail it down to the kitchen. I'm anxious to at least hear what Sadie has to say.

Duchess is at the stove, and by the aroma, she's frying smoked pork belly. A bowl of eggs sits on the small table by her elbow. That table brings back a sweet memory of when my Jimmy made it for our first anniversary. He put casters on the legs so I could roll it around the kitchen. My husband was a visionary is some ways and stuck in the past in others.

Pinkie has the sewing kit out and is mending my robe. Sadie is at Duchess' elbow, watching her every move. She glances back at me as I sit at the table.

"Your sister has discovered a talent she didn't know she possessed." Sadie grabs two cups from the stove's top shelf, pours coffee into them, and brings both to the table. She slides one toward me, then adds milk and sugar to hers.

My curiosity refuses to wait another minute. "What is this day trip Pinkie said you want us to go on?"

She may be half Yamasee, but Sadie's other half is pure Georgia peach ... cunning as a snake and sweet as Southern tea. She smiles and raises one eyebrow.

"Remember how we talked about getting Duchess in disguise to spy on Big Jim? Our only pickle was transporting her into Baxley without being noticed, right?" She picks up her cup and takes a sip.

My leg bounces while I wait for her to swallow. Even Duchess moves the frying pan off the hot spot and turns to listen. When Sadie talks, we all listen.

"Early last week, I sent a letter to my brother." She tilts her head to Pinkie. "He lives in Brunswick. He's a shrimper ... and ... he owns an automobile. A nice, old, nondescript 1919 Model T Touring car. It's black and it's got some rust here and there, so it's nothing to attract attention." She winks at me and takes another sip of coffee.

I think I see where she's going. Apparently, we can borrow his car. But how are we going to get it here? Duchess adjusts the stove's draft, slides the pan back on the stove's hot spot, then slaps a spoonful of lard into another pan and moves it over a hot spot. It begins to sizzle, and she breaks eggs into it.

I motion for Sadie to get on with it.

She sits forward in her chair. "We're going to get Barry home, Maggie. My brother said we can come get his car."

Using a spatula, Duchess slides an egg on a plate. Pinkie lays two rashers of pork belly next to the egg. She turns and holds out the plate to me.

I nod thanks to Pinkie and take the offered plate. "And how are we going to do that?"

Sadie takes the other plate from my sister and forks a bit of pork belly before answering. She momentarily closes her eyes, savoring it. "Delicious. All right, here's the deal. Wade is lending us his car. We're taking it as far as Everett. Wade has a cousin there, Justine Rowntree. We're trading Wade's auto for hers. That way, nobody in Brunswick knows the car. We'll bring my brother's back, leaving Justine's with him." Sadie is apparently finished explaining and dives into her breakfast.

I dip a slice of toast into my egg yolk, scooping up its golden goodness. A new thought hits me as I chew. "What if we don't find Barry that fast? Wade's car is in Everett. What's he to do without it?"

Duchess points her fork at me. "He said not to worry about that, there's another he can borrow." She butters her toast and dips it.

"Wade's a wonderful man." Pinkie knots and bites off the thread. "There. Good as new. Well, almost." She folds and lays my robe over the back of her chair.

As we finish our breakfast and chat about the day's work, a tiny spark of hope ignites. I glance at my wristwatch as I rise. It's almost seven o'clock. I set my plate in the sink. "I need to get the grocery open. Sadie, what time do we leave—wait. How do we leave without drawing attention?" I pause in the doorway. "It will be noticed if we all miss church."

Sadie pushes up from the table and carries her plate and cup to the sink. "Not if we lay the groundwork today." She squints her eyes, crossing her arms and cupping her chin in one hand. Suddenly, her eyes pop open, and she snaps her fingers.

"I've got it. I've got a cousin on my mother's side in Allenhurst. Her son is a new preacher, and he's preaching tomorrow. It's in the opposite direction, but it will serve as a good deflector."

"I'm not comfortable with lying, Sadie."

She shakes a finger at me. "We won't lie. He *is* preaching tomorrow. We just won't be there to hear him. I can't help it if people *think* we're going there."

I consider, mentally searching for places in the Bible where God let people think something other than reality. Then it hits me. "That's exactly what God *did* do to aid His people in the Old Testament. He let the Philistines think there was a huge Israelite army surrounding them. In their confusion, they killed each other."

Sadie laughs at me. "You're a study, Maggie Parker. Where do you think I got the idea in the first place?"

I head downstairs and into the grocery. After unlocking the front door, I check the shelves for any restocking I need to do. It appears Pinkie did it last night before she locked up. She and Sadie enter through the storeroom and go behind the meat counter, ready for the Saturday crowd. Duchess pulls out the change bag from the safe and puts the money in the till. A moment later, customers begin to arrive, first in a trickle, then a stream. Thankfully, they herald the start to a busy day.

By noon, most of the town knows we're taking a day trip tomorrow. When Preacher Gordon comes in to get a chicken quarter to make soup for his sick wife, I make him privy to our plans. He concurs that we didn't tell any lies. He blesses our venture and prays with us to find Barry.

He leans his head close to mine before he leaves. "I'm also praying Big Jim receives the Lord's discipline for what he's doing."

Our pastor is another good man.

The sun is up and climbing to the treetops when Wade hands the keys to Pinkie with a smile—a rather intimate smile. I'd like to talk to him about that, but we want to get going before church starts. My sister collects the keys, puts the picnic hamper on the floor in the back seat, then takes the driver's seat. There are three of us who can drive. Wade prays a blessing over us, and we wave goodbye. I know today won't see Barry home, but I can't help but feel hopeful. We're doing something positive instead of sitting and stewing.

Our first stop is Faylene's. She deserves this outing more than any of us. She's dressed in a cheery yellow dress with sunflowers printed on it. They suit her mood. Bessie Mae, who declined to join us, saying she would visit her daughter instead, helps us load Mama Faylene into the back seat and strap the wheeled chair into the trunk, which is actually a wooden box Wade built and attached to the back of his car to transport trunks to and from the train station. The wheeled chair fits in quite nicely with the top half sticking up above the box's sides.

Her eyes sparkle with anticipation for an adventure. "If there's any problem, Maggie, we can always give me a tow rope and pull me along the highway. Might be fun."

I stop tying down the chair to stare at her. She can't be serious, can she? My horror must have shown because she laughs at me. "Well, it might."

I climb in, sandwiching Pinkie between us. Sadie rides in the front passenger seat. A few people wave at us as we leave town. Fortunately, nobody follows us, so when we get to the highway, we don't have to turn toward Allenhurst but head straight for Everett.

Staring out at the passing scenery, I pray for Barry, asking God to hold him in His hands.

"Maggie?" Pinkie nudges me. "You were helping Duchess get things in the car when Wade handed me the keys. He asked me to go to a movie next week."

"Just you? As in a real date? How do—?" Silly question. I can see by her shining eyes, she's thrilled. I pat her hand. "I'm delighted for you, sugar. He's a fine man."

Nothing like her daddy. I'm happy for Wade. He's never taken an interest in any of the girls in Rivers End. And for him to show any interest with her in the family way raises him to hero level in my mind … and apparently in Pinkie's too.

After close to an hour, we arrive in Everett. It's a small rural community. Mostly farms and a few shanties. The town is tinier than Rivers End, with only a general store and gas station. Sadie reads Wade's directions, and soon we pull up to Justine's house. The door opens, and she runs out, waving her hankie. She's rail thin with light-brown hair, pulled back in a bun.

"I'm so excited to be involved in helping you get your little boy back," she says, every inch of her wiggling as she speaks.

I shake hands with her. "And you don't mind being without your car for a bit? This may take a couple of weeks." I hope it's at least that fast.

"Not in the least. This is the most excitement I've had in years." She gestures back to an old white Victorian, with faded pink and cranberry trim. One of its shutters is loose and hangs slightly askew.

"I help my mama run the boarding house." Her eyes roll. "It's not much fun, as I'm sure you can imagine."

She directs us around the side of the former carriage house, where an old motorized depot wagon waits in the shade. It's actually a smart choice for picking up boarders and their luggage. I raise an eyebrow at Justine.

"How did you come to buy this?"

"We didn't. It was left by a man we thought a traveling salesman. He turned out to be a flimflam man. We kept it in lieu of the rent he owed us."

"There's plenty of room in here, and even though it's unusual, nobody knows us in Brunswick, except Sadie's brother. It will serve us well." I take her hands in mine. "Thank you, Justine. You really are helping me get my boy back." I swallow the rising emotion before I start to blubber.

"Oh, it's my pleasure. I feel like Ellery Queen—or at least his assistant. Good luck, ladies!"

We trade keys, situate Faylene, stow her chair, and get on our way. Sadie sits behind the wheel now.

"We'll go halfway and stop to eat. That will give my brother a chance to get back home."

Pinkie leans forward and taps Sadie's shoulder. "Does your brother only fish for shrimp?"

Sadie chuckles. "No, and they don't *fish* for shrimp in the regular sense. They drag a large bag, shaped a lot like a slingshot made out of netting, behind the boat. But when it isn't shrimping season, he fishes for whatever he can catch. Do you know how oysters are harvested here in Georgia?"

"No." Pinkie shakes her head.

Sadie adjusts the rear-view mirror. "In the coastal waters and in the mouth of the river, the oysters are exposed to the air twice a day at low tide. R.W.—that's my brother—takes his boat out to the oyster beds and stays there." She grins at Pinkie. She's enjoying telling this story. "When the tide goes out, he steps out of his boat and just picks 'em up. Then he waits till the tide comes back in and lifts the boat so he can come home."

Faylene tells us her favorite recipe for oyster stew, which sparks a discussion on the best ways to shuck them. Soon we're all hungry, and Sadie pulls over to the side of the road for our picnic. There's a nice flat field to eat in and a stand of trees not too far away for our necessaries. Sadie and Duchess pull out a light fare of cheese, bread, and fruit.

"If I know my brother," Sadie says, "he will be preparing a feast of oysters for us."

Since Bessie Mae isn't with us, I help Faylene. Soon enough, we're back on the road. This excursion is good for me. It's the doing something instead of waiting that fuels my faith and hope. The good Lord knows I'm a doer. I know I need to learn faith in the waiting, but oh, how I chafe at that.

Forty-five minutes later, we pull into Brunswick. Sadie navigates the traffic and streets as though she lives there. We end up near the water, which isn't hard to do since between the river and the ocean, it's all around. She turns on P Street, then onto Reynolds, and into the third driveway. A small house is nestled in the trees.

Sadie honks, and the front door opens. A man runs out. He looks so much like Sadie, I know it's her brother. They hug long and hard. Then she brings him to meet us.

He bows elegantly. "Sadie has told me much of you, Maggie. I thank you for being her friend and champion."

What has she said? "It's she who is my mentor." I like him immediately.

"Well, don't just stand out here jawin'. Come on in. I've got oyster bacon pot pie waiting for you." He disappears into the little house.

"My brother is a strange mixture of Yamasee and redneck." *He is indeed.* Sadie laughs as she ushers us inside.

Even with large windows, the tree covering keeps much of the sunlight out. I suppose with Georgia's hot, muggy summers, that's a good thing. The colors of the wallpaper—which is peeling a little at the edges from the ocean moisture that permeates everything—is a deep sea-green. The furniture appears old but comfortable. There are a few pictures on the wall, one of Sadie and R.W. as youngsters. I stand in front of it, trying to get a better feel of my friend's family.

"Is your brother married?" I whisper to Sadie.

She nods with a fond smile. "Doreen works at the grocery in town."

R.W.'S voice carries from the kitchen. "She's a good provider of meat and canned goods."

I glance at Sadie, whose laughter joins her brother's. "He's got amazing hearing and is a horrid tease. Doreen will be home to eat any minute."

She walks in as if Sadie's statement was her introduction. She's short and round with the jolliest face I've seen anywhere. She puts me in mind of a Yamasee Mrs. Clause.

Dining on the hot oyster bacon pot pie is divine. Doreen's biscuits are the lightest I've ever eaten, but my heart isn't into socializing. Sadie's eyeing me, and I give her a little shrug. She nods and pushes up from the table.

"As much as we'd like to stay here, we need to get back. We're of a mind to catch a varmint and return Maggie's little boy home."

We pull into Rivers End after dark. Sadie drives behind the station, out of sight of the town. Since we don't want anyone catching a view of this car, Sadie will take it into the woods by a trail she knows. As long as it doesn't rain, we'll get it out easily enough. Duchess and I push Faylene home in the wheeled chair while Pinkie goes to bed. She's worn out.

"It's a bit late for a stroll, isn't it, Maggie?" Jubal's voice startles me from behind.

I stop and glance over my shoulder. "Is there a problem, Sheriff?"

He folds his arms across his chest and considers me. "Yes. There is. Where's Barry? I've been alerted that he's missed school for more than a week."

My heart drops to my toes.

Duchess looks at me, and Faylene twists her neck as best she can to see over her shoulder.

"Well? Where is he, Maggie?"

My mouth opens, but nothing comes out. Faylene maneuvers her wheeled chair around to face the sheriff. "Jubal, I can't tell you *where* he is, but I can tell you why he isn't here. My husband kidnapped him."

The venom Mama Faylene infused into the word *husband* could kill Big Jim if it struck him.

"What?" In the dark, the question sounds like an explosion. "Just what are you accusing Big Jim—the boy's own grandfather— of? And why wasn't I told sooner?"

I awaken from my fear-induced stupor. "I'll tell you why. The good ole boy network. You wouldn't have believed me."

Jubal pushes his hat back on his head and scratches above his forehead. "I may have a problem believing it, but I can't ignore what Miss Faylene says."

Thank God for my mother-in-law.

Jubal takes the handles of her chair and begins to wheel her toward her house. He stops and looks back at Duchess and me. "Well, come on. Let's get Miss Faylene out of the night air. Then maybe Bessie Mae has some pie left. And some coffee. I have a feeling this story will take a piece o' time."

CHAPTER 25

We gather around the table in Mama Faylene's dining room. The coffee is fresh and hot, and the apple pie is warm. Jubal takes a huge forkful, slides it in his mouth, and closes his eyes as he chews. I glance at Duchess and wink.

"Bessie Mae, you still make the best pie in Rivers End." He swallows and opens his eyes. "All right. Let's hear it."

We all begin to talk at once. Jubal holds up a hand and turns his gaze on me. "You go first."

"Big Jim has been threatening me for a long time. I don't know why, except Pinkie thinks he wants the store back. For the money. Why he needs it is the question."

Jubal turns to Faylene. "Y'all having money problems?"

She shakes her head. "No. Maggie keeps us in food and buys my medicine."

"What about other bills? The mortgage? Bessie Mae?"

"I don't have a mortgage. Contrary to what James let people think, this house was a wedding gift from my father. We did not buy it. There is no mortgage. And Maggie pays Bessie Mae's salary."

For the first time since I've known him, the sheriff's expression shows surprise. Big Jim has let everyone think he bought the house.

Jubal's brows draw together. "All right. For now, let's move to Barry. Maggie, what happened?"

I tell him how Big Jim and that Ferguson woman—if that's really her name—snatched Barry. Duchess jumps in and explains about Atlanta and Mrs. Draves at the Child Protective Services office.

He pulls out a small notepad from his pocket and with a stub of a pencil writes down her name. "And she didn't find Barry at any of the homes that shelter the children? Do they all have telephones?"

"Yes," Duchess says. "Mrs. Draves told us when they set up the homes, telephones were installed in each."

"Hmm. So Ferguson isn't an employee of the Child Protective Services office? What about one of the homes? Could she work in one of them and the main office not know that?"

Duchess shook her head. "I doubt that, Sheriff. They all work for and get paid by the state. And Mrs. Draves said no one knew of her at any of those homes."

"Has anyone seen Big Jim since he took Barry?"

Thank the good Lord, he believes us. "Pinkie saw him the next day, talking to Cal at Trey's gas station. He was bragging on how the car they were filling with gas belonged to him. But he never came into town or showed his face anywhere else."

"Did he come home, Miss Faylene?"

"I haven't seen him since Christmas Day."

That surprises Jubal. His eyes narrow. "Are you telling me he hasn't been here in almost a month?"

Faylene sets her fork on her plate and looks Jubal in the eye. "That's exactly what I'm saying. I realized something was stirring in that black mind of his at the beginning of December." She reaches over and puts her hand over mine. "I only wish I'd known how rotten he's become." She turned back to Jubal. "Apparently, he's been planning this, because he stole the clothes I'd put away for Barry's birthday."

"When was that?" Jubal poises his pencil over the notepad.

"I believe it was December third. Yes, it was December third. Bessie Mae and I were sorting through the Christmas decorations."

Bessie Mae comes in with the coffee pot and refills our cups. After Jubal adds cream and sugar to his, he stirs it slowly, takes a sip, then sits back. "I know the men in this town tend to stick together. After the War of Northern Aggression, it was us against the carpetbaggers. Those scalawags would steal anything a Southerner had. Food. Money. Land. There wasn't any law but what those scoundrels decided on. My daddy told me drawing together and keeping secrets was how they survived."

He drew in a long breath and let it out slowly. "That's not saying it's right or wrong. It just is. But I can tell you those good ole boys don't cotton onto this kind of behavior."

He pushed himself up from the table. "I'm puttin' out a call to the police in Jesup, Baxley, Uvalda, and a couple of other towns. I don't suppose Pinkie got a license plate number, did she?"

"No, I'm afraid not. She probably didn't think of it. She was hiding. He and Cal don't like her, and she's a bit afraid of them." I push my chair back and stand to walk him to the door. I decide to tell him about our searching. "Big Jim has been spotted in Baxley. My sister and Pinkie caught a glimpse of him once when they were at Pinkie's doctor. We plan to take a few trips there to look for him."

Jubal quirks his mouth and doesn't say anything for a moment. Finally, he nods. "But y'all be careful and let me know the minute you find him. Kidnapping is a federal offense, even if it's a family member."

I put my hand on his arm. "Thank you, Jubal. I can't tell you what having you believe us means to me."

He gives me a half smile. "You're a good woman, Maggie. A bit wild in your ideas, but a good woman, nonetheless." He opens the door and takes his leave.

On my way to the dining room, I spy Bessie Mae in the kitchen doorway, tears falling down her cheeks. Tears of relief? She's been listening to us. I stop and give her a hug.

"I know you've been grieving Barry, too, Bessie Mae, and I love you for it. You're part of our family. Now, come on in and sit with us."

She nods and follows me, wiping her eyes with her Christmas apron. Back in the dining room, we finish our pie and talk about the change in the sheriff.

"I can see how their network got started," Duchess says. "But I'm glad Jubal found a hole in it. I hope he keeps a more open mind about other things in the future."

With a wry smile, Faylene shakes her head. "I wouldn't count on it."

The rising sun finds me already in the kitchen and on my second cup of coffee. A terrible nightmare woke me earlier than usual. I went to sleep hopeful that it was only a matter of time before Barry's home. But in the dream, we found Big Jim but not my baby. Or that woman. They were gone. The sheriff arrested Big Jim. Under interrogation, he admitted not knowing the woman. Then he said he thought maybe she was part of a ring of people stealing children for adoption in other countries. What if Barry was in another country? Or worse … what if … I awoke fighting to breathe.

Now, my hope is dying. I'm struggling to keep my faith. And I know well enough that God doesn't owe me any answers. I may never know one for the why of this. But … what if I never find Barry?

A verse from Job comes to mind. "The Lord gave, and the Lord hath taken away. Blessed be the name of the Lord." But can my heart truly bless the Lord? It's not for me, but for my Barry. How my child must be grieving … be frightened.

A soft knock on my back door arouses me.

It's Sadie. She opens the door and comes in. "I saw your light on across the commons and figured you needed me."

I sigh. "How do you keep your faith? I'm angry at God for letting this happen. Poor Barry. My heart is breaking, Sadie. I'm losing the will to go on. I can hardly breathe. All I hear or see is my little boy crying for me. He's scared and alone." I tell her about my dream.

"Maggie." She stands and moves to the stove to get the coffee pot. "When Sam Hardee took me in, I'd had six long years on my own as a small child, scavenging for food and clothes, finding shelter at night, fighting off men who thought to use me. It wasn't until later when I looked back on how God protected me even when I didn't know Him, that I realized how much He loves us. How He watched over me."

She pours our coffee, sets the pot down, and reaches across the table and takes my hands. "He's watching over Barry too. Your son has faith beyond his years. You've taught him well. Now draw from his example. Believe, Maggie."

A flicker of hope dawns within me once again, and a small smile tugs at my lips. She's right, this friend of mine. Beautiful Sadie, with her wrinkled skin and her sage advice. How I thank God for her.

"You're a good friend, Sadie. You're right." I drain my cup, rise, and pull out a cast-iron skillet. "I let a nightmare get the best of me. I'm going to believe." I open the icebox and pull out a bowl of eggs. "One or two?"

"Two, thank you. And I'm thinking of going to Allenhurst today. I have a theory. If Big Jim is living in another town, which he surely is, he's probably trying to look like an upstanding citizen. One who goes to church every Sunday. So I'm thinking I should start with my nephew. Tell him our story and have him watching for Big Jim. I've got a photo from Faylene to leave with him. We're going to do this in all the towns around until we find him."

I slide a thick slice of ham into the pan. It sizzles and sends up a lovely aroma. "That's a wonderful idea." It's Friday, so he can ask around on Sunday morning. "You can take the farm truck. We planned for Duchess to get into disguise and go to Baxley tomorrow. She'll look where she and Pinkie saw him before."

"Who did I see?" A sleepy Pinkie waddles into the kitchen, followed by Duchess.

"We're talking about finding Big Jim. And breakfast. How many eggs?"

"One," Duchess says, pouring herself coffee.

Pinkie's nose turns up. "I've got a yen for flapjacks and maple syrup."

Using a serving fork, I pull the ham from the pan and set it on a plate, then break the eggs into the skillet. There's something different about our little mother-to-be. What is it? She's standing in front of the icebox, her hand resting on top of her belly. That's it. Her belly. The baby has dropped. Oh my. I'm the only one who notices, but that doesn't surprise me. Neither Sadie nor Duchess has ever had a baby.

"When is your next appointment with the lady doctor, Pinkie?"

"Uhm, I think it's next week sometime. Why?"

"Because by the look of it, you are getting very close to having that baby. It's dropped—getting into place to be born."

"Oh." Pinkie turns a little green. She puts the syrup back on the shelf.

"Now, don't worry. It's not going to be today. In fact, it could be a few weeks still. But that baby thinks it's ready." I pick up a spatula and lift out the perfectly cooked sunny-side-up eggs. After I cut the ham into servings, it joins the eggs on the plates. "Let's eat."

While we have breakfast and Pinkie nibbles a slice of toast, we lay out a plan for our sleuthing. Sadie will go to Allenhurst today and Duchess tomorrow to Baxley. Sadie's is the easier of the two. She'll see her nephew, leave a photo, and come back. Duchess will have to find a spot to wait and watch … and not be obvious. Maybe she could play bill collector and ask if anyone has seen this man, then show a photo of Big Jim. Of course, she couldn't dress in overalls and a turban, and I know she wants to.

I lay down my folk and stare at my plate. What's Barry eating this morning?

"Ladies?"

Wade stands in the doorway. His station master's uniform gives him an air of dependability. Pinkie blushes when she hears his voice.

"Good morning. Coffee?"

"Love some. You've got a phone call. Mr. Alexander in Lawrenceville."

I jump up. I don't want to keep him waiting. Phone calls cost money. I hope he hasn't changed his mind about my stories or the column. I hurry to the train station office, leaving Wade to enjoy a cup of coffee with Pinkie.

I close the station office door and pick up the phone. "Hello, Mr. Alexander."

"Zeke, please, Maggie. Now, listen carefully. I've shown your work to a friend, who's an editor at Lippincott in Philly. He's intrigued by your premise and wants to see your novel. How far along are you on it?"

A big publisher like Lippincott, interested in me? "I'm about three-quarters through it."

"How soon can you be finished? And can you send me what you have? I'll have my secretary type up a copy and send that to Grey."

If I found my son, I could keep my mind on my story. Then I'd get it done quickly. "I haven't talked to you in a while, but my son was kidnapped by his grandfather. I can't think beyond that right now."

"What?" His words explode in my ear. I jerk the phone away. "That's despicable. When did this happen?"

I tell him the details of all that has taken place.

"I had no idea, Maggie. Your columns arrive on time."

"They're short and unemotional. I can manage those, but as soon as I get into my novel, the main character's emotions draw my heart back to Barry."

"I can imagine. Well, Grey is highly intrigued. I'll explain, and I know he'll wait. He loves your bedtime stories. He even mentioned a book of those. In the meantime, I'll pray you find your little boy quickly."

His words are a soothing balm to my heart. "Thank you, Zeke."

I hang up.

Like a hungry dog, depression nips at my heels as I cross the street. I should be excited about a publisher as big as Lippincott's being interested in my novel, but all my heart longs for is Barry. I'd give up everything to get him back. If Big Jim showed up in town right this minute, I'd tell him he's won.

CHAPTER 26

Pushing back curtains, I peek out the window. A light rain falls against the panes. All the better for my sister's disguise. She can hide beneath an umbrella. There's no aroma of coffee this morning. What time is it? I pick up my wristwatch from the dresser. Oh my. It's after seven. I slept late. I splash water on my face from the bowl on my dresser, dry it, then grab a workday dress from my closet and throw it on. For the first time in two weeks, I'm feeling expectant. Maybe we'll find Barry today.

Please, Lord.

I open the door to my sister and Pinkie's room to wake them. We have to get a wiggle on, or we'll be late opening the grocery. Their beds are empty and made. Where are they? I hurry down the stairs to the kitchen.

Duchess looks up as I enter. "Good morning. I hope we didn't wake you." She's wearing the overalls we bought for her.

"No, but I wish you had. We're running late."

"Sadie said she'd open the grocery and can handle any early customers. Nobody ever gives her any trouble."

I have to laugh. She's right. Sadie could handle a glowering mob. With one fierce look, she'd have everyone waiting quietly in line like they were schoolchildren.

Duchess hands Pinkie the coffee can. "Will you make the coffee so Maggie can help me wrap this turban?" She tosses the folded swath of material to me.

"Didn't we get one that was already made up?" I unfold the length of fabric, trying to determine which end is the beginning. It puddles at my feet.

"Uh, yes."

"Well, where is it? I've never *made* a turban." I wad the material and drop it onto the table.

"Uhm … that's it." Duchess's grimace is sheepish.

"What do you mean, this is it?"

"I … sort of … took it apart. To see how it's made, but I couldn't put it back together. I'm sorry, Maggie."

Oh, for pity's sake. My sister has done some dumb things, but this one takes the prize. A vision of her unwrapping the turban and her horror as the small chapeau disintegrates into a very long piece of nothing makes a chuckle bubble up.

Duchess stares at me, and her lips pull into a tentative giggle. I point to the chair, and she sits, as I compose myself, holding one end of the long blue cloth.

"I've never wrapped one of these, but—oh, Pinkie, would you get me the new *Woman's Way Magazine*? It has an article on how to wrap a turban." She nods and waddles out. The exercise is good for her. She's been sitting a lot lately.

"I remember thinking we should know how to wrap these. It's cheaper to buy material than a finished turban." I place one end of the material at Sister's hairline.

She glances over her shoulder at me, dislodging the material from her head.

"Hold still, Duchess. I'm trying to start this. I think they said to place one end at the forehead. Or maybe it was the back." I move the end to the back of her head. "Applesauce. I'd better wait until Pinkie gets back with the magazine." I drop the cloth into my sister's lap. "I'll pour us some coffee."

Five minutes later, the magazine is open before us. Pinkie reads as I follow her instructions.

"No, Maggie, wind it the other way. Counterclockwise."

"But why? That shouldn't make any difference." But I undo what I just wrapped around Duchess' head and turn it around. "Okay, let's see." I move to the front of my sister. The turban sits catawampus, covering her right eye and ready to slide off her head. Pinkie laughs. Sister rolls her eyes—at least, the one I can see rolls—and makes me laugh. It feels good to laugh. I haven't done much of that since Barry … my heart squeezes, and the mirth dies. Duchess and Pinkie blur.

Will I ever get my boy back?

I fall into a chair and bury my face in my hands as my heart shatters. Arms embrace me, and my sister whispers in my ear, "Shh, Maggie. Don't cry, sugar. We'll find Barry. I promise. I've never broken a promise to you, have I?"

"N-no." I draw a stuttering breath. "But how can you promise that?" I drop my hands, taking the hankie Pinkie holds out to me.

Duchess cradles my face between her hands and looks me in the eye. "Because I saw it in a dream two nights ago."

That stops my tears. Sometimes, my sister's dreams are visions from God. "Why didn't you tell me?"

"Because I don't know when it will happen, but"—she steps back, arms akimbo—"I *know* it will happen."

Lord, I need her faith. I dry my tears, letting my prayer fly to Heaven and hoping for an answer. Squaring my shoulders, I pick up the magazine. "Why don't I read, and we let Pinkie wrap your head?"

Our mama-to-be takes the turban cloth. It goes much better, and soon, Duchess looks like the magazine article's picture, ready to drive over to Baxley. After I hand her a wrapped sandwich for her lunch, she heads out to retrieve the borrowed vehicle from the woods where we have it hidden. Wade is helping her.

"Now, Miss Pinkie, it's your turn. Let's get your hair washed and curled for your date tonight."

I set the small tub on the table and fill it with water from the stove's reserve tank. Draping a towel around her shoulders, she bends forward over the tub. I dip a pitcher into the reservoir and pour it over her head. I love the smell of Mulsified Coconut Oil Shampoo. I squirt some into my hands and work into her hair.

"Ohh, that feels so good, Maggie."

"We should do this more often for each other." I rinse her hair and lather it again. Finally, I pour a pitcher full of warm water over her head to rinse out all the soap, then wrap her head in a towel.

Once she's in the chair, I use the towel and briskly rub her head. "Now, I'm going to try something I learned about from a reader of my Helpful Hints column. She sent *me* a hint." I open the Crisco and swipe a tiny smidgeon onto my finger. I rub my hands together and massage the oil on them into her hair. "If I use too much, we'll have to wash your hair all over again. But if this works, we should be able to comb out your tangles easily." I pick up the comb.

"I'm nervous about tonight. I've never been on a real date."

"Never?" I work the comb through her hair. Apparently, I used the right amount of Crisco because the comb is gliding through and untangling her hair. As Pinkie chatters and I work, my mind slips to Duchess. I pray she finds Big Jim. She took some change so she can make a phone call to the sheriff if she sees him.

Pinkie picks up the hand mirror and watches me. "Wow, the Crisco really works." She lays the mirror back in her lap. "Wade said we're going to the movies in Uvalda. He said the film is *The Virginian*, starring Gary Cooper." She sighs. "He's so handsome."

I can't help teasing her. "Who? Gary Cooper or Wade?"

She blushes. "Well, Gary Cooper, but Wade is nice-looking, isn't he? I hadn't thought about it. I just like how nice he is."

Wade's one of the few eligible bachelors in town. When his wife died, he suddenly became the Big Cheese, and half the county beat feet to his door. But she's right, he's not handsome in the movie star sense. He's nice-looking, though.

"Besides, looks fade, but nice only gets better."

That's quite profound. "Where did you hear that?"

"I didn't hear it anywhere, but I notice it in people. My grandpa wasn't a handsome man, but he was so nice. I saw a daguerreotype of him when he was young." She stifles a giggle. "He wasn't handsome then either. My daddy took after his mama and was a looker when he was young, but he isn't nice. I'll take nice over looks."

Tangles out, I pat the chair next to the stove for Pinkie to sit. Then I open the firebox and toss in another log to help her hair dry part way before I curl it. It should only take a few minutes. I pour us each another cup of coffee. By the time we finish, her hair is ready for ragging.

Pinkie holds up a rag curler. I'd love to get some of those new metal kind or the leather ones, but that's an expense we can't afford. For now, these strips of rag do the job. I wrap a small section of her hair and tie it off.

She holds up another. "Do you think Duchess will find Big Jim today?"

I tie the rag in place and take the next one she hands me. "I'm praying so. It can't happen soon enough." I twist and tie that rag then hold my hand out for the next one. After a few minutes, her hair is all tied in the curling rags.

"Thanks, Maggie. I'll go get dressed."

"Afterwards, come right back here to sit until your hair's dry. You don't want to catch cold. I'll go help Sadie."

In the grocery, traffic is picking up, but Sadie's handling it just fine. She seems to be having fun—at least, she waves me off. I'll use the time to work on my novel. I've need to finish it for Mr. Edwards at Lippincott.

I step into the office and pull out my manuscript. By simply reading the last chapter, I slip into my story world, leaving the everyday one behind. Words flow like water from a pitcher as my character searches for clues to solve the mystery. She's on the trail of a clever art thief.

"Maggie!" Sadie is gesturing through the window.

I jump up, knocking over my ink bottle. Oh no! The thick black liquid pours over the pages I've written, destroying my morning's work. I grab a towel to blot it.

"Maggie, come quick! Someone spotted Barry!"

I drop the towel and fly out the office door. I can always rewrite words. "Where? Who? When?"

"A phone call at the train station." Sadie pushes me toward the door. "Go!"

I take a quick glance up and down the street. Not that we get many cars here, but right now isn't when I want to get hit by one. Someone has seen my baby! I run across the street and into the station. Wade hands the phone to me.

"Hello?"

"Mrs. Parker?" A man's voice, young by the sound of it.

"Yes. Have you seen my son?" *Please, God!*

"This is the police department in Reidsville."

How—? I guess Jubal spread the word farther than I realized. Reidsville is a good forty-five miles from Rivers End.

"I got a call from a woman who claims to have seen your boy here in town. We're doing a door-to-door search."

"Who is the woman?"

"I'd rather not say."

"Oh. All right. I suppose that's not important, anyway. I'm on my way."

"All right. Check in at the police station when you arrive."

I hang up the phone and run back to the grocery, hoping the truck will get me that far. What would Big Jim be doing in Reidsville? There isn't anything there in which he's ever expressed an interest. But I'm not waiting for any answers on that. I wish there was a way to get hold of Duchess. That car would be better. I grab the truck's keys from my office.

"I'm going to Reidsville," I call to Sadie. "Tell Pinkie, and pray we find Barry."

Sadie shoos me out. "Done."

I run back out front and jump into the truck. The engine grinds and sputters a few times. "Start, you old heap of junk." Thankfully, the engine finally catches.

To get to Reidsville, I have to go toward Henderson and past Faylene's house. I'll make a quick stop and ask her to pray. I leave the truck running, zip into the house, and back out after telling her what's happening.

This old truck won't go any faster than thirty miles per hour. It's going to take me at least an hour and a half. Oh, how I wish I could fly. *Hang on, Barry, Mama's coming.*

With nothing but trees and creeks with the occasional farmhouse, the drive is monotonous and seems so long. It's too bad Duchess chose today to go play detective. In the borrowed truck, I'd get to Barry faster.

Oh no. Up ahead, I see a farmer or rancher—whatever—herding cattle across the road. I put my foot on the brake and come to a stop. *Hurry up.* The rancher tips his hat to me. Okay, he's a courteous rancher, but can't he hurry? I can't even see the end of his herd—oh, wait. There it is. Bringing up the rear is a dog, barking and nipping at the cows' heels. Thank goodness. The cowboy slaps the reins against his horse's flank and waves at me.

I ease the truck into gear and—it sputters and dies. "Oh no! Come on, you old thing, start." But the engine refuses to cooperate. I turn the key and pump the gas pedal. That grinding doesn't sound good. Why now? "Please, don't give out on me now."

I open the door and look down the path that rancher took. There's only dust now. "Hello? Can anyone hear me?"

Silence answers my call. Blast! I turn in a circle. Tears fill my eyes. I'm so close to finding Barry. I pound my fists on the truck's hood.

"It's all your fault." My tears mix with the dust in the air, making my face gritty when I wipe it. I have no idea where I am, except for I'm in the middle of nowhere. The only thing I can do is try to find that rancher or a farmhouse or something. I grab the keys and my handbag from the truck.

Stepping onto the wide swath of dirt between the trees where the rancher drove his cattle, I'm praying leads to his place—and to help. The dirt is churned up and soft from all the cows' hooves. It isn't as easy as walking on hard dirt. My heels aren't made for this.

"If I'd known I was going to have to hike through a forest, I'd have worn my boots." I have no idea if I'm talking to God or not, but it's so quiet out here, I'm a little spooked. My stomach growls, reminding me I haven't had more than a cup of coffee this morning. "Why are You doing this to me, God? I'm trying to have faith, but every time I get close to finding Barry, something gets in my way. What have I done to make You mad at me?"

Oh great. The path splits up ahead. I stand at the fork. "Now what, Lord? I could use some help here."

The dirt in the left fork is soft like what I've just come through. But the right—wait. I squint and watch. Yes, up the right fork, dust clouds the pathway. I've almost caught up. *Thank You.*

If I run, I may be able to catch the rancher. I'm going to twist my ankle if I run in these shoes, but if I take them off, I'll ruin my last pair of stockings. But I've got to hurry. Barry's waiting for me. I yank off my shoes and start running.

Cows must not move fast because the cloud of dust is getting closer. If I can keep up this pace, I'll catch them. After a few minutes of running the best I can without twisting my ankle in a hole or stepping in a cow pie, I'm huffing and puffing and nearly out of breath. The path curves up ahead. I round the curve and stop. Oh what a glorious sight. A house and the rancher getting off his horse.

"Help, please!"

He turns at my call. "Ma'am?" He looks around. "Didn't I see you up on the road a while ago? How did you get here?"

"Yes, about a half hour ago. I followed you. I'm Maggie Parker. My old truck broke down, and I have to get to Reidsville because my little boy was kidnapped and someone spotted him there."

The rancher—I gauge him to be around thirty—cocks his head and gapes at me.

"Can you help me? Or at least let me use a telepho—do you

have one out here?"

He pulls off his cowboy hat and slaps it against his thigh, causing a smaller cloud of dust to rise from it. Then he scratches his head. "It sounds as if you've got a heap o' trouble." He blows out a breath. "I don't have a telephone, but I can help with your truck." He holds out his hand. "Name's Jeff McCarthy."

"Oh, thank you, Jeff. It's nice to meet you. I don't know what's wrong with my truck. It's got gas in it."

"Well, let's go take a look." He eyes my straight skirt. "You can't ride a horse in that. My wife can lend you a pair of her trousers."

Despair threatens to overwhelm me. "Don't you have a truck or car?"

"Oh yes, ma'am. We sure do."

"Can't we take that?"

"We'll get back to your truck faster on horseback. The road winds in the other direction before it hits a crossroad. That would take us an hour. On horseback, fifteen minutes."

No contest. "Horses it is, then." What an adventure to tell Barry.

After meeting his wife, I explain what I'm doing out in the middle of nowhere asking to borrow her trousers.

"Oh, my stars," she says. "Well, you follow me. We'll get you ready to go in a jiffy." She turns to her husband. "Jeff, saddle Chloe for Mrs. Parker." She takes my arm and guides me to their bedroom. "Chloe is my horse, and she's the gentlest of our mares."

"I can't thank you enough for your help." But I do wish she had a telephone.

Considering I haven't been on a horse in over twelve years, I manage to stay in the saddle. Jeff's wife—I never did get her name—was right. Chloe is gentle and patient, and twenty minutes later, we arrive back at the truck. It doesn't take Jeff long to figure out what's wrong.

He points beneath the hood. "The distributor is cracked. This truck's not going anywhere today."

"What'll I do? I've got to get to Reidsville or at least telephone the police there."

Jeff wipes his hands down the front of his jeans. "That's not hard. There's a general store about ten minutes down the road. The proprietor is my brother-in-law. We'll ride there, and you can make your telephone call."

I'm so tired of crying all the time, but between his kindness and my frustration, I can't stop the tears. I turn away so he won't notice and climb back up onto Chloe's back. "Thank you."

As soon as we arrive at the store, I slide off Chloe and run inside to make my call. Once Jeff explains the situation, the proprietor, whom he introduces as Davey, won't let me use the pay telephone. He reaches beneath the counter and pulls out his private telephone.

"You use this one."

"Thank you so much." I tell the operator I want the Reidsville police department. After a moment, the call is connected.

"This is Mrs. Parker. Y'all are searching for my little boy, Barry. My truck broke down, and I can't get there yet. Have you found him?"

"No, ma'am. I'm sorry. It turns out to have been a false sighting. The child in question is the son of the Methodist minister in Claxton. He looks remarkably like your son, so the mistake was understan—"

I can't listen to the rest. I put the receiver back in its cradle and burst into tears.

CHAPTER 27

Jeff pats my shoulder in unending, rhythmic regularity as I cry. When he shifts from one foot to the other, his hand moves from my shoulder blade to its edge and back again. The sentiment, while sweet, does nothing to comfort me. I reach in my pocket and pull out my hankie, forcing myself to stop weeping. It's not helping anything. I raise my head and wipe the tears from my face.

"It wasn't my son, Barry. It was merely a boy who looks like him."

Jeff thankfully stops his incessant patting and moves back. Frankly, he looks relieved, making me almost laugh. I suppose laughter and tears are close together the nearer one draws to hysteria.

"I'm so sorry, Miss Maggie. What are you going to do now?"

I turn to the store's proprietor. "May I make one more call? I'll need to have someone come get me." The thought crosses my mind that I have absolutely no idea where I am. "And I need your address."

The ever-gallant Jeff steps up beside me. "You could wait at our house. Why, Jenny would flay me alive if I left y'all here to wait for two or three hours."

So that's her name—Jenny. "That would be nice but unnecessary."

I place my call to Wade. After telling him what happened, I ask him to come get me when Duchess arrives home from Baxley. I'm about to hang up when I remember.

"Wait, Wade? I forgot your date with Pinkie." I glance at my wristwatch. "If you come get me, you'll miss the movie. Maybe you could arrange for Sadie to borrow a car from Trey."

"I'll do whatever needs to be done and call you back here as soon as I know who is coming to fetch you and when."

"Thank you. I don't want you to miss your date." I hang up.

"Well, it appears I'm stuck here until my friends find a car to come get me. You've wasted enough of your time on my problems, Jeff. Tell Jenny thank you for—" I look down at the trousers I'm wearing. "Applesauce. I left my skirt at your house, and these"—I pull on the pants' pockets—"are hers."

What a mess this day is. It's so mired in tangled-up details, it would even depress the devil.

Jeff pushes his hat back on his head and grins. "Well, now, Miss Maggie, I'm fixing to make a suggestion that might just work." He raises his gaze to the store clerk. "Davey, why don't you plan to come to supper after her call comes in? Jenny'd be delighted to have you. Then you can tell Miss Maggie who's coming for her and when." He grins at me. "And I won't face Jenny's ire for leaving you here."

I must say it's better than standing around the general store for hours on end. With nothing to do, I'd probably start reorganizing Davey's shelves. They could sure use it. And he's making the error of keeping all his merchandise behind the counters. I thank him for allowing me to use his telephone and leave a dime on the counter to pay for the two calls. He shakes his head and pushes the dime back at me.

Men are strange. They have their good ole boy network that can give a woman fits, and at the same time, they're gallant and heroic.

Outside, Jeff gives me a leg up onto the mare.

"You're pretty comfortable with Chloe." Jeff taps his heels against his horse's sides, and it starts walking. Chloe follows.

"I grew up on a farm about thirty miles from Rivers End. I rode all the time, but I haven't in at least a dozen years. I'd love to have my son see your ranch."

I take my eyes off the trail and turn them to his face in time to see him brighten. "We'd both love to meet your Barry and have him come learn to ride. We have a couple of ponies just for that purpose." His words hold a hint of wistfulness, and his generosity touches me.

"I plan to take you up on it."

Another few minutes and his house comes into view. Jenny is outside, hanging some laundry on the clothesline. She waves in welcome, we dismount, and Jeff takes both horses reins, leading the mounts to the barn.

Jenny hangs the last sheet on the line. "Let's go see to supper. You can help me if you'd like."

"Thank you. I'd feel much better with something to do."

By the time we have supper ready, Davey arrives with the news that Sadie is on her way and should arrive by seven o'clock.

"Would y'all like to stay the night? That's a bit late to start driving back, isn't it?" Jenny looks between me and her husband. "Sunset is about seven-thirty this time of year."

I don't know their sensibilities when it comes to the Yamasee side of Sadie. But she and I will do fine driving home alone.

"I'm anxious to get home. We'll be fine but thank you."

My concerns were groundless as far as Jeff and Jenny went. They were only slightly uncomfortable. And that because of Davey, I think. He glared at Sadie and wouldn't speak to her. Being used to it, she ignored him. We accepted Jenny's offer of a thermos of coffee for the drive home. Davey promised to order a new distributor for the truck. Jeff said he'd install it for me. So with another trip out here in our future, we were soon waving goodbye.

"I'm glad to be on the way home. They were nice folks and helped me out, but after the letdown of that boy in Reidsville not being Barry, I was having a hard time being sociable."

Sadie glances at me then back at the road. "Duchess didn't have any better luck than you did. She didn't catch sight of Big Jim at all."

"Lord, have mercy on us. Sadie, I can't seem to climb out of this pit. My baby's not here, taxes are coming due in a few months, and now the truck. If I can't make deliveries, will I lose those customers too?" I sigh under the weight of it all.

Where are You, God?

"Well, now, I can solve one problem. That money you have in the bank from Jimmy will just about cover the taxes. I can make up any difference."

Over my dead body. I turn in my seat to face her. "Sadie, you work for me and don't let me pay you. How could I in good conscience take money *from* you?"

She brakes the car, slowing for an upcoming stop sign. Then she looks right at me. "When I came down with the Spanish flu in 1918, you didn't hesitate but took me in and nursed me through it and back to health. The rest of the town would have let me die. Nellie tossed me out at the first sign of sickness." She crosses the empty intersection.

"I'm surprised you went back to her boarding house after that."

Sadie's grin flashes. "I wanted to rub her beak in it that I survived. But what I'm saying is, I owe you my life. What's a little money? Besides"—she reaches over and pats my knee—"you're the only family I've got. Who else should get my money?"

She has me there, but there's a lot of living left for her money to cover. "All right. If—and it's a big *if*—I need it when the time comes, I'll let you help me out. But right now, our biggest need is Barry."

It's nine-thirty when we pull up at Trey's gas station. It's closed, but we leave the key under the front seat. Sadie bids me goodnight and walks on toward Fanny's, and I climb the stairs with leaden feet. The entire day has been a loss.

Duchess meets me at the door and folds me into her arms. "Oh, sugar. I heard what happened. I'm so sorry. To get your hopes up like that, and then have them come crashing down without me there to help you—well, it's just awful."

I lean into my sister's love and strength. I'm weary to my bones. It's getting harder and harder to find the will to fight.

She leads me to the davenport. Two mugs of steaming tea await us on the coffee table.

"How did you know when I'd be home?"

"Wade figured it out for me. As long as you and Sadie started back shortly after she arrived there, and you didn't run into any trouble, he said it would be around nine-thirty. And it was." She hands me my mug.

I take a grateful sip. "Mmm, this is good. Did you put in honey instead of sugar?"

Sister nods. "Do you like it?"

"I do. It's like being home." We sit in comfortable silence for a bit, drinking our tea. I'm close to falling asleep. I set my now-empty cup beside me and lay my head back, closing my eyes.

Duchess' hand is soft on my shoulder. "Remember my dream, Maggie. Don't lose hope or the will to fight. We're going to find Barry." She moves my cup to the coffee table.

Maybe it's being home, or maybe it's being with my sister, but my hopes rise again. "Tell me about your day. Did you have fun, playing detective?"

She wrinkles her nose. "I walked all over downtown Baxley. I have memorized the location of each store. Then I walked a few of the streets adjacent to downtown. I tried to see inside some of the houses, but all I saw was my own reflection from the sidewalk. I didn't dare get any closer than that." She blows out a sigh. "It was so frustrating. I know Pinkie and I saw Big Jim that one time."

I pull my feet up beneath me. "That doesn't mean he's staying there. He could have just had business there, although I don't know what business he could have."

Duchess snorts, making me laugh. "Monkey business, that's what."

The door opens, and a radiant Pinkie enters. Wade salutes us, then steps out and closes the door behind him. Pinkie emits a long sigh and leans dramatically against the wall. I don't want to let my own emotions spill over to her when she's so obviously happy.

"So, I take it your date was a success?" Duchess asks.

That's a silly question, gauging by her sappy smile. Come to think of it, Wade's matched hers for sappiness.

"Come sit, and tell us about it." I could use me some happy right now.

Pinkie drops onto the davenport then jumps right back up and paces as she talks. "It was wonderful. First, he took me to the café across the street for burgers. Do you know I've never eaten in any kind of a restaurant? It was scrumptious. Then, in the movies, partway through, Wade reached for my hand and held it. He never let go until we got home." She sighs.

This girl is completely smitten. I'd deeply thankful it's with someone like Wade.

Duchess, forever the romantic, leans forward. "Did he kiss you?"

"No! That would be wrong. Not on a first date." Pinkie nods toward me. "Maggie told me that."

CHAPTER 28

The past two weeks have been a flurry of fruitless espionage by my sister and dates between Pinkie and Wade. He's speeding up the courting process since Pinkie's baby dropped, determined to have his name on the birth certificate. My emotions are like a whirligig, blowing dark and oppressive over Barry, then the next minute to joy over Pinkie and Wade. Then before I can grab hold of some of their enthusiasm, my thoughts swing back again to Barry.

"Here, Maggie, take this with some coffee." Duchess hands me a pill. "Doc said to give you one each morning for energy."

I stare at it lying in the palm of her hand. A little wonder of modern medicine? But my sister is getting a permanent worry line between her brows, so I take it and swallow it with the coffee.

"Are you going to Baxley again?" She's dressed in her overalls and turban.

Duchess shakes her head. "I'm going to Surrency, and Jubal's going to Hazlehurst. He got calls from both areas, saying Big Jim was seen there." She sets the coffee pot back on a warm spot on the stove. "For some reason, he seems to be visiting farmer's markets. At least, that's where he was sighted. Anyway, we're each going to stake out a town."

Pinkie enters the kitchen. My sister's gaze goes back and forth between us as Pinkie opens the icebox, pulls out the milk bottle, and pours a glass.

Duchess frowns, then her lips turn down. "Maggie, you need to eat. You're letting worry rob your appetite, and you've grown downright thin, sugar. When we find Barry, you'll be too sick to do him any good."

"She's right, Maggie. Here." Pinkie pours milk into my empty cup, then sits. "At least have a glass of milk."

"And some faith," Duchess adds.

I drink the milk down, knowing they're right. I'm not blind to the glow of health on Pinkie. In contrast, I look like one of the poorest, malnourished farm children.

Lord, I need a faith booster. I paste a smile on my face. "I'm trying. I really am." Their love helps. I push up from the table. "I'd better get to work."

"Not before you eat something. Have a bowl of oatmeal." Pinkie jumps up—well, as fast as she can haul her belly out of the chair—and scoops out the oatmeal into a bowl. "Granny Belle brought us a jar of honey from her bees." Pinkie dips a spoon in and pours a generous amount over the oatmeal. "I can't imagine having pet bees. I love the honey, but keeping them seems strange to me."

"Our groundsman kept bees on our place in Atlanta." Duchess slides her spoon into her oatmeal. "It's not that unusual. Our friends used to compete for the best honey."

While Pinkie stares wide-eyed at my sister, I take a bite. Whether it's the honey or the love from these two women, I find myself hungry and take another bite. A glance of satisfaction passes between them, making my heart squeeze. I don't know what I would do without them. I give myself a mental shaking. For their sake, and for Barry's, I need to be strong.

Duchess lays her hand over mine. "Lean on the Lord, Maggie. He's strong enough for all of us. Now"—she pushes away from the table—"I need to go. I'll see you this afternoon."

My sister reads my thoughts all too often. It's uncanny. I look at Pinkie and raise one eyebrow. She simply smiles, and after we clear the table and do the dishes, we make our way into the grocery. Sadie is already stocking the shelves.

"It's about time you two got here. Pinkie, Wade wants you to come over at noon for dinner at the station. Maggie, you go work on your novel. The store is quiet today. I'll come get you if we get busy."

"Thanks, Sadie. I could use the time. I'm almost finished with it."

I step into my office and close the door, shutting out the world for a short while. I'm quickly absorbed in my heroine's topsy-turvy world. My vacillating emotions from this morning will serve me well for her story. Soon, I'm inside her head. It's like watching a movie. As my fingers pound the typewriter keys, her friends gather around her to help after a devastating flood. I stop typing. Just like God surrounded me with strong women to help carry me through this time. I need to take a moment to thank Him. In my heart of hearts, I know now, no matter what happens, Barry and I will be all right.

The office door opens, and Sadie pops in her head. "Are you at a stopping point?" She holds out a sandwich, making my stomach growl.

I stretch out the kinks in my back from hunching over the typewriter. "Yes. Guess what? I just typed *the end*."

Sadie zips behind me and peers over my shoulder. She sets the sandwich beside my elbow. "Really? Can I read it?"

She's been reading for me as each chapter is completed. I pull out the last page from the typewriter, adding it to the stack beside me. "Yes, please. It's the first draft. I'll make some notes, then retype it, but I'm pretty pleased." I peek at the ham, sticking out from between slices of bread. My stomach growls a second time.

"I'll take it home tonight and have it back to you in the morning. After you eat that, I could use your help."

I take a quick bite of the ham, lettuce, tomato, and bread. The added mustard gives it a snap. "This is wonderful. Thank you, Sadie. I'll nibble more between helping people."

In the store, traffic has picked up. Sadie has four customers waiting at the meat counter, her preferred place to work. I take over the cash register and helping anyone in between. Pinkie is out, eating dinner with Wade.

During a lull, I walk to the front window and peer across the street at the café next to the train station.

Sadie comes up behind me. "Do you think he's asked her yet?"

I don't take my eyes off the café. "No. He'll wait, I'm sure. Oh, look. They're leaving."

Wade holds the door for Pinkie, then takes her hand. He walks her past the station, and they head into the woods.

I grin at Sadie. "Actually, I think he's going to ask her now." We turn away from the window. "Sadie, do you ever regret not marrying?"

She doesn't answer right away but reaches for her tin of cloves. After popping one in her mouth, she smiles. "I never met a man who made me even remotely interested in giving up my independence." Her gaze grows tender. "I realized after you saved my life, you were my family. When Jimmy died, I knew you needed me more than ever. Then Barry came along. He's been the joy of my life. No, Maggie girl, I've got a family *and* my independence. Why would I ever feel any lack?"

Why, indeed?

Ida Clare and Alice stroll into the grocery together. Alice waves and heads to the meat counter. Ida Clare stops to chat.

"Did I see Pinkie and Wade holding hands?"

She's been supportive of their budding romance, and her words hold hope, not judgment. I smile. "Your eyes aren't deceiving you."

"Well, I hope he hurries up and proposes. That baby needs a daddy and a name. Besides, I've seen the way he looks at Pinkie." Ida Clare chuckles. "There's no hiding it."

She leaves me and wanders over to the shelves where the cleaning items are located. I glance back out the window. Yes, I've seen Wade's heart in his eyes too. It makes me yearn for love again, but like Sadie, I'm not sure I'd want to give up my independence. It would take a very special man—one who supported women who work. Why, even Wade approves of Pinkie's dream to run for the Georgia legislature. There's only one Wade, though. It's funny that I never had any romantic feelings toward him. He's as close to perfect as they come. And perfect for our Pinkie.

Although, I have to admit, sometimes late at night, I wonder if God has someone out there for me. I turn away from daydreaming. Ida Clare and Alice come to the register, and after totaling their purchases, they pay but don't leave.

Alice sets her box of groceries on the counter, pretending to check the items inside. "How's your novel coming along, Maggie?"

Knowing she's stalling to see if Wade proposes, I can't cast blame and indulge her. "I finished it. I have to edit it, but I should be able to send it off to the publisher within two weeks."

Her eyes leave the window and latch onto mine. "Really? You actually finished it? Oh, how thrilling." She turns to Ida Clare. "And we knew her before she became famous."

Sadie wags a finger at Alice. "Finishing a book doesn't make one famous."

She pats my hand. "You're already published in the newspaper, my friend. You'll be famous one day. Just you mark my words."

Ida Clare nods. "I quite agree. Most dubiously."

I quickly bite my lip against the giggle that threatens to erupt. Dear, sweet Ida Clare loves to try new words on me. If she only knew how she's misusing that one, she'd be mortified. I shan't tell her. I love her too much. "Thank you, my friend."

Myrtle Davis pushes open the door and winks at Ida Clare as she passes us. What is she doing here in the middle of the day? Don't tell me. Known well in town for her matchmaking activities, my guess is she's taking ownership of Pinkie and Wade's.

Clara Barlow and her sister, a teacher over in Uvalda, walk in. All we need now is—oops, here she comes. Rosa from the bank. All these ladies, standing around the grocery as if this was a normal

Tuesday afternoon's activity.

The church bells announce it's one o'clock. Chatter stops, and all eyes turn to the front window. A moment later, Wade and Pinkie round the side of the train station. Walking arm in arm, they cross the street.

Suddenly, all the ladies scatter, each to a different corner of the grocery. This time, I can't stop my giggles. Pretending they're here for anything but groceries isn't going to work. Wade opens the door for Pinkie, gives her hand a squeeze, and nods to all of us. He then whispers in Pinkie's ear, and she smiles as color spreads into her cheeks.

As soon as the doors close, we all surround her. She isn't frightened this time, knowing all the ladies here love her. Having seen a glint when she walked in, I grab her hand. A small diamond, set in a gold band, sparkles on her finger.

"He proposed." That man's a hero in my mind. "When are you going to want the wedding?"

"Quickly." Pinkie laughs and lays her hand on her belly. "Wade wants us married before the baby comes. He's insistent on it having his name." She sighs. "He's coming over after supper tonight with Ozzie to plan it. It's just our true friends—" Her gaze takes in the ladies in the grocery. "All y'all are invited."

The ladies all start talking at once.

"We need to give you a shower," Ida Clare says. "I'll give everyone a discount on anything they buy at our store." My heart swells with love for my friend.

"Yes, but what kind of shower?" Alice asks.

Sadie smirks. "Wedding on Friday and baby on Saturday." A shocking statement, but by the laughter, they're all enjoying being a little bit incorrigible. Everyone has an idea of what games to play, what to get Pinkie, and what a baby needs. Eventually, we decide on our apartment and the times, and the ladies leave.

I put my arm around Pinkie. "Are you happy, sugar?"

"Very." She lays her head on my shoulder. "I've grown to love him so much. He puts me in mind of God's grace, never looking down on me and loving me even in my condition. He's amazing."

"I couldn't be happier for you. We'll make it a pretty wedding in the yard. The violets are blooming, and so is the winter jasmine. We can decorate a bower for you two to stand under. Duchess can probably make over one of her dresses for you—"

Pinkie holds up her hand, stopping me. "Simple, Maggie. I want things simple, please. I don't want photos to show me looking like … well, what people think I am. I don't want my baby ever to think that he or she was an accident. Whatever the circumstances of this baby's conception, my child is wanted and loved. And I'll fight anyone who wants to—"

"Oh, sweetie. We'll never let anyone speak badly of this wee one." I reach out and pat her tummy. "This baby will be so well-loved, he or she will never notice if someone turns up their nose. Besides, the baby will have Ozzie—and Barry—to defend it."

While Pinkie sits in front of the mirror at my dressing table, Duchess sets a hat on her head. She adjusts the angle, then inserts a hat pin to hold it in place. Pinkie turns her head to each side, watching her reflection.

"I adore the hat, Duchess. Thank you so much." She inhales deeply and blows it out slowly. "I'm so nervous."

One corner of her collar turns up. I step closer and smooth it down. "Why? You're only going to get a marriage license."

"What if they turn us down? Or tell Wade he shouldn't marry me?"

"They wouldn't dare. He has a wonderful reputation in the county." I hold out gloves for her.

Pinkie hesitates before pulling on the first glove. "That's just it. What if they tell him I'm a—"

"Stop right there. If anything, they will think he jumped the gun and is doing the right thing." I laugh at her open mouth and wide eyes. "Well, they will. No one in Hazlehurst knows you." I put both my hands on her shoulders and lock eyes with her reflection in the mirror. "All they will see is how much he adores you. They'll wink at your condition. People tend to turn a blind eye to a whole lot when in the presence of true love. And isn't that what the Bible says? 'Love covers a multitude of sins.'"

Pinkie pulls on the other glove and finally stands up. She holds out her hands to the side and poses. Honestly, she looks so sweet in lavender. The soft material from one of my sister's old gowns has pleats at the shoulders and drapes in a becoming fashion. It's so chic, and the overall effect hides how close she is to giving birth.

There's a knock at the door. I give Pinkie a quick hug. "That'll be Wade. You look lovely. Now go." I follow her into the living room.

She opens the door, and Wade steps inside to help her with her coat. He stops and stares at her. His Adam's apple bobs as he swallows hard. His mouth opens, but nothing comes out. I turn away to keep from laughing.

"You … wow. You're beautiful." He shakes himself. "I mean, you've always been beautiful, but you look especially pretty today."

I step in to rescue my friend. He's blushing more than Pinkie is. "And so she should. You two are going for your marriage license. Have fun. And I have a special supper at Faylene's planned for when you get back."

While Wade and Pinkie are in Hazlehurst, Sadie, Duchess, and I close the store early and head to Faylene's to offer our services in the kitchen. Bessie Mae has been busy all day with preparations for supper. I sent down a ham with pineapple rings and cherries on top of it. She'll have basted it with brown sugar and molasses as it cooked.

"I'm honored you're allowing us to help, Bessie Mae." Duchess is setting the table, while Sadie and I sit at the kitchen table with

Faylene, a bowl of green beans before each of us. We pick up one, snap the ends off, and pull the string, then toss them into my mother-in-law's bowl. She's cutting them into bite-sized lengths to be cooked with bacon. My mouth waters just at the thought.

"This a new way o' cookin' a ham. Never seen one wearin' piney-apple rings." Bessie Mae shakes her head. "It's a luxury for sure."

She's right, but the two cans of pineapple have been sitting on the shelf in the grocery for nearly a year, and nobody would buy them. I figured we may as well use them. Oh, Barry would love this.

I snap and toss the last bean into Faylene's bowl. "Shall I start the bacon, Bessie Mae?"

"I've already done that, Miss Maggie. But I'd appreciate you pickin' some fresh flowers for the table." She picks up the bowl from Faylene and tosses the beans into a pan of boiling water. "Supper'll be ready in an hour. Them two lovebirds will be coming back soon."

Faylene dries her hands on the towel I hand her. "Then we'll leave you to finish your preparations, Bessie Mae."

I push the wheeled chair into the living room so Mama Faylene can watch the birds come to the feeders in the backyard while I go pick the flowers. After finding a nice variety, I bring the flowers in and put the vase on the table as Duchess lays out the eight plates and silverware. Mentally counting, I start to tell her it should be nine. Barry should be here for this. After all, Pinkie's his Good Samaritan project. I raise my eyes, meeting my sister's gaze. Her expression of sorrow makes me realize she's seen mine. We'd both like to strangle Big Jim for robbing Barry of this.

My fists ball at my sides, and I clutch my skirt. I'm struggling to keep my faith alive, but sending up a quick prayer for strength helps. I nod at Duchess and go join Mama Faylene in the sunroom.

"Shh. Look." She points at a suet ball feeder we made and hung for the birds. A pair of red-headed woodpeckers are having a meal. "They're pesky on the trees but so pretty."

Duchess peers out the window at the birds. "I thought they were looking for bugs and helped the trees."

Faylene shakes her head. "They're looking, but actually, the holes they leave allow harmful insects into the tree. See that big oak in the back corner? The one on the right side of the yard." She points to the rear of the property. "One woodpecker pecked his holes so close together, the bark fell away and left the tree vulnerable to disease. I had Bessie Mae smear grease and tie a rag around it. I'm hoping that helps."

I peer at the tree. "Is that why you hang the suet?"

"That's it. If they eat that, they'll leave my trees alone."

Too bad I never hung one at the store. Might have kept Big Jim from pecking into my business.

The front door opens. "Yoo-hoo, we're here," Pinkie calls. She and Wade walk in. Ozzie is holding Pinkie's hand. He is thrilled to be getting a mama, and by the happy flush on Wade's and Pinkie's faces, they got their license.

How I wish Barry was here too. But if he were, he would most certainly not want me to put a damper on their spirits. With that thought soothing my broken heart, I allow a genuine smile to greet them.

"Come in! Ozzie, I'm delighted to see you." I pull him into a hug, breathing in his little boy scent. It will have to do me for now. "I've missed you. Have you been avoiding me?" I whisper in his ear.

He solemnly nods. "I didn't want you to feel bad or miss Barry more."

"Oh, you sweet boy. I need to see you to remind myself that Barry *is* coming home." One day.

His red eyebrows rise and disappear beneath his curls. "Really? When?"

"I don't know yet, but his Auntie Duchess saw it in a dream, and that dream came from God." And in that moment of speaking it, my heart knows it.

Thank You, Lord.

"Now, let's all have supper."

I help Bessie Mae get all the dishes but the ham on the table. When she carries it in, Pinkie's reaction is worth every penny of the canned pineapple.

After supper, we gather in the living room to discuss the wedding plans.

"What we'd like"—Wade glances at Pinkie—"is a small gathering in the common yard. Just our friends and neighbors."

A snort escapes my oh-so-ladylike sister's nose. "You realize that will encompass the entire yard? Every family who lives around that yard has claimed Pinkie as their own. And they all love you both—three—four."

Faylene laughs at Duchess' verbal stumble. "She's right. It won't be quite as small as you thought. The Mobleys, the Wiggins, Beau Hampton, Asa and Katherine Hopper, Doc and Clara, Malcom Connor, Rosa ... why, the list goes on and on. They either live on the common yard or they are attached to the train station in some way. Half the town will have to be invited."

Pinkie gapes and hides her face in Wade's shoulder. He strokes her cheek and whispers to her.

"Pinkie, sugar." I wait for her to look up. "The best way to put everyone on your side and have them protect that baby is to make them part of your story. Make them *want* to protect you and the baby. If they are included in your wedding day, they will be family forever."

I catch Faylene's frown. I know what she's thinking. That didn't work with Big Jim. I almost hope he shows up for this wedding, thinking it's his duty to stop it. That would be so like him. But then Jubal could catch him and bring Barry home.

CHAPTER 29

The next morning, we're still trying to iron out the wrinkles in planning Pinkie's wedding. I set the coffee pot back on the stove's hot spot and join Duchess, Sadie, and Pinkie around my kitchen table.

"Okay, so the wedding will be Saturday afternoon. That gives us three days to get ready. Not that there's that much to do. Everyone coming is bringing something for the wedding supper. Doc and Beau Hampton are in charge of setting up the tables." I take a sip of my coffee. "Am I forgetting anything?"

Pinkie pulls off her glasses and breathes on a lens, then wipes it on a napkin. "I wouldn't know. I've never been to a wedding. Do people always bring food?"

"They do in Southern farm communities. At least since the War of Northern Aggression." Duchess' nose wrinkles whenever she mentions that late unpleasantness. "Our maternal grandmother, Cora, the one who was raised on a plantation, was only nine years old when the war broke out. She lived the humiliation of going from landowner to sharecropper. Meemaw Cora filled Mama's ears with tales of the Old South that grew in scope with every telling."

With a wry smile, Duchess shakes her head. "I bought into the tales. Why, Mama could make us hear the music from a ball and smell the barbecues." She tilts her head toward me. "That's where Maggie gets her storytelling talent." Duchess rises, sets her cup in the sink, then turns and leans against the counter. "I'd look out the window at Daddy plowing behind a mule, barefoot Maggie following him, dropping seed into the soil and covering them up. And I'd think we sure fell a might far from Mama's stories. It made me wonder if they were really true."

"What? I thought you always believed them. You fell in line with Mama's wishes for you."

Sister crosses her arms. "Well, of course, I did. For me, it was the makings of daydreams and pretending. You wouldn't play tea party with me. You were always playing with the animals if you weren't working with Daddy." She shrugs her shoulders. "Mama and Meemaw loved to have tea parties. Through playing with me, they taught me to be a good hostess. I went to my husband with some accomplishments, frivolous as they were."

"Still, he saw the good mind in you. He didn't treat you like you didn't have one." I shake a finger at Pinkie. "Don't you ever let me hear of Wade treating you like you aren't intelligent. I loved my husband, but he didn't think I had enough brains to understand our finances. Why, I'll bet Cal was stealing from Jimmy too."

Pinkie sits up straighter. "Wade isn't like that. He's already told me about his ... I mean *our* finances."

"Has he said anything about Louella?" Sadie asks. She and Louella were schoolmates through fifth grade. Then Louella had to go to work.

"He said he's going to keep her on since I want to work at Parker's. But I'll work just while Ozzie is in school. Louella will do the housekeeping and cooking."

I have to ask. "Is Wade all right with you bringing the baby into the grocery?"

Pinkie puts both hands on the table, palms down. "Wait a minute. Maggie, you *said* I could bring the baby to the grocery like you did Barry. You haven't changed your mind, have you?"

I cover her hand with mine to reassure her. "No, I haven't changed my mind. I just wondered if Wade agreed."

Pinkie sniffs. "He'll have to. All y'all are the baby's aunties."

She fairly glows with happiness. And she's right. Before Wade said anything about loving Pinkie or marrying her, we'd all decided we were going to raise this baby with her.

I push up from the table. "That's the truth, sugar. Now, it's time to get to work. For you, little mama, you need to rest. I've got a pot pie for dinner ready to go into the oven. Slip it in about ten-thirty, then come into the grocery."

We'd been working for a couple of hours before Pinkie joins us. I'm glad she rested for a bit. It's a busy morning for a Thursday, and Pinkie relieves me at the cash register and greets Ida Clare. Duchess is in the office, getting statements ready to go out, and Sadie is filling orders at the meat counter while I restock shelves.

"Maggie, come quick!" Pinkie's harsh whisper hints at disaster.

I set down an armload of boxed macaroni and hurry over. "What is—oh my." She's standing in a puddle of water.

"I … I …I've wet my pants." She's puckering up, ready to let go a gullywusher.

Ida Clare is gaping at us.

"Now, don't cry. It's natural. A little early, but your water's broken."

"Broken? Can we fix it?"

I laugh and take her arm to pull her into the storeroom. "No need to. You are about to become a mama. You're in labor." I grab a towel from beneath the counter. "Wad this between your legs, and if you can manage it, get upstairs. I'll get Doc." I call back over my shoulder, "Ida Clare, will you let Wade know?"

Ida Clare flaps her hands at us. "Yes. Get her upstairs. I'll get Wade." Her words trail her flight out the door.

Pinkie starts to wail. "I can't have this b-b-baby yet. I have to g-get m-m-married."

I help her get the towel beneath her skirt and between her legs. "Now clutch it with your thighs. Keep your knees tight together when you walk."

"I'll try. Hurry, please!" She duck-waddles out of the storeroom toward the stairs.

I stop at the office and open the door. "Duchess, we're about to have a baby. Pinkie's water broke."

Sister jumps up. "Oh my! What about the wedding?"

"Right now, we have to worry about a baby. Ida Clare went to let Wade know."

Duchess shoos me away. "You go to Pinkie. You're the only one of us who's ever had a baby. I'll get Doc and take care of things down here."

I'm climbing the stairs when a white-faced Wade pounds up behind me. He isn't alone. He's dragging Preacher and Emma Gordon behind him.

I stop him at my door. "Wade, we don't need an audience. We need to get this baby born."

"And that child needs a name."

Hero Wade isn't backing down. My heart melts. "All right. Y'all wait in the living room. Let me check Pinkie first."

In the bedroom, I find our girl sitting on the side of the bed in a pretty nightgown.

"Are you all right?"

"Yes. Nothing else is happening. I've heard it's supposed to hurt, but it doesn't."

Not yet. "That's good, because your fiancé has brought the preacher, and he's determined to become your husband before this child is born. Can you stand up?"

Her smile lights the room like the sun. "Yes. Let's go."

"Wait a minute, honey. We need a robe for you."

She looks down and blushes. "Oh."

I pull out the beautiful robe Duchess and I made for Pinkie's honeymoon. She may as well wear it for her wedding. I hold it out for her, and the two of us start to giggle.

"This will be one funny story to tell this child someday," she says.

"Then again, maybe just you and Wade should share it."

She slips into the robe. The door bangs open, and Sadie and

Duchess fly into the bedroom.

"Ida Clare is closing the grocery and pinning up a sign." Sadie breathes heavily. "How're you doing?"

Pinkie pats her hair, tucking one wayward strand behind her ear. "I'm fine. My water broke, but nothing has happened yet. Now, let's get me married before the baby decides not to wait any longer."

We all step into the living room, where Wade and Preacher Gordon have rolled back the rug and moved the furniture out of the way.

Wade hurries to Pinkie's side. "Are you all right, sweetheart?"

"Yes. Where's Ozzie? He needs to be here."

Sadie hurries to the door. "I'll get him and Louella."

"All right. Wade?" Preacher Gordon opens his Bible. "Do you have the license?"

"It's next door. In my apartment."

"That's fine. Emma, will you get it, dear?"

"Certainly." Emma nods but stops, looking back. "Shouldn't Pinkie sit down until we're ready?"

Duchess and I take Pinkie to the davenport. "Wait!" I stop her from sitting. "Let me put a towel down. Just in case."

Wade talks with the preacher while we get Pinkie situated on the davenport. Sadie returns with Louella and Ozzie, followed by Emma, waving the license in her hand. My living room is full.

With everything as ready as it can be, Preacher Gordon nods at Pinkie. We help her up, and Wade takes her arm. His tender gaze brings tears to my eyes. Pinkie will be well-loved.

"Dearly beloved, we are gathered somewhat hastily here ..."

My eyes are on Pinkie as Preacher Gordon drones on. Under the satiny robe, her belly visibly contracts. He'd better hurry up. Pinkie's head turns to Wade. Her eyes open wide, and her jaw drops.

"Ah ..." She hunches her shoulders and bends forward. "Ohhhh!"

255

The color drains from Wade's face, leaving him as white as the dead. Preacher Gordon starts talking so fast, I can hardly understand a word he says.

"Pinkie, do you take Wade as your husband?"

"Yes. Yes. Ahhh-ow!"

"Wade do you—?"

"Yes. Get on with it."

"Where's the ring?"

"Here it is."

"Well put it on her."

"Oh. Right. Sugar, give me your finger."

Pinkie flings her hand up, and her thumb hits Wade's eye. "Ow."

Bless his heart, he hangs onto the ring and manages to get it on her finger.

"I now pronounce you man and wife. Get her to bed. I mean—oh dear!"

Everyone bursts out laughing. Well, all but Wade and Pinkie. He has her up in his arms, and he's kissing her as he carries her to the bedroom. Doc meets them at the door and shoos Wade back out as he beckons to me and Emma. We join him in the bedroom.

Pinkie is in true labor now. Sadie brings hot water from the stove's reservoir.

I take the bucket from her. "Ask Wade to put another bucket on to boil. And tell him to make some coffee. We're going to need it, and besides, it will give him something to do."

After Doc examines Pinkie and declares it will likely be suppertime before the baby is delivered, Emma has her up again and walking to help her labor.

"I think she can rest for a bit now." Emma and Sadie lower Pinkie to the bed.

Sadie reenters the room and sits beside Pinkie. She hands our little mama a fat stick, the thickness of a man's thumb, wrapped in cloth and tied with a leather thong. "You bite on that when the pain gets too bad."

There's fear in Pinkie's eyes but resolve in her face. She takes the stick.

"Remember," Sadie says. "There's iron in your veins. Use it when the time comes to push that baby out."

As the hours progress, the room becomes hot and sticky. I open the window a bit to let in some fresh air. Wade knocks on the bedroom door every thirty minutes or so. The poor man is inside out, he's so worried. It's understandable. His first wife died trying to birth Ozzie's brother. Little Walter died with his mama.

I go down to the kitchen to boil more water and to make some coffee and sandwiches.

Wade wanders in, sniffing the air. "I could use some of that coffee."

While waiting for another bucket of water to boil, I attempt to reassure Wade, reaching between our coffee cups on the table to pat his hand. "Pinkie is built to give birth, Wade. She isn't narrow in the hips. Doc is confident. If he had any doubts, he'd have taken her to the hospital in Hazlehurst."

Wade rakes his fingers through his hair. "I know that. I trust Doc. I'm just … she's so young."

I smile. "You should see her, Wade. She's ageless right now. Instinct, maybe? But she's strong. I'm amazed at her. She hasn't cried out once." The water on the stove bubbles, and I pull it off the heat. "We need to get this upstairs."

He jumps to his feet and reaches for the bucket handle. "I'll carry it."

Just as we open the bedroom door, a flurry of activity is going on. Emma grabs the bucket from Wade and shoves him out. Sadie sits behind Pinkie and Pinkie leans into her. She's pushing now.

"Maggie, help her," Doc says, positioning himself at Pinkie's feet. "Hold her right knee."

Sadie reaches over Pinkie's shoulder, wraps her hands beneath her knee, and pulls. I sit in front of Pinkie and push up on her right one. She grunts and turns red with the exertion. Doc arranges the sheet to prepare for the delivery. Pinkie pants.

"Okay, my dear. On the next contraction, I think we'll have us a baby."

A few seconds later, Pinkie's panting picks up. Then she holds her breath and pushes. Sadie and I push at the same time.

"Hold it!" Doc's command is sudden. "There, just a moment. I see the baby's head." Doc unwinds the cord from its neck. "Aannd … there. Okay, push again."

We lean into it, and a lusty cry breaks out.

Doc holds up the wiggly newborn for all to see. "It's a girl!"

Emma takes the baby and cleans out her mouth and nose, then lays her on Pinkie's chest. Tears blur the scene before me as I think of my baby boy. Pinkie checks her little girl's fingers and toes and cuddles her. "Look, Maggie, her little eyebrows aren't white! She doesn't have albinism." Tears of joy stream down Pinkie's face.

I take the baby, wash her, and wrap her in a soft blanket while Doc finishes with Pinkie.

As I return this new life to her mama, Pinkie looks up at us. "Thank you. Wade and I decided if it's a girl, her name is Magnolia Duchess Sadie."

Love for my namesake and her mama wells up. "Oh, my goodness. I think there's a nervous daddy in the living room, waiting to see his wife and Little Maggie."

My sister sticks her tongue out. "I think you mean Little Duchess."

Sadie snorts. "I'll tell him Little Sadie is ready to meet her daddy." She beats us out of the room.

Pinkie stares wide-eyed at us, then chuckles. "I think we may have created a problem. My poor girl won't know which name to answer to."

"Sure, she will. By whatever name she hears, she'll know who's calling her," Duchess says, laughing.

We leave the room and send in Wade. I collapse on the davenport, Duchess beside me and Sadie on the other side. We are too tired to talk, which is saying something. I close my eyes, smiling at the image of that pretty little girl.

Wade comes out of the bedroom a few minutes later, Little Maggie is in his arms. "She's so beautiful. Just like her mama." His voice is hushed in reverence and awe.

That baby will never wonder who her daddy is.

Wade turns and moves back into the bedroom.

Duchess chuckles. "When Little Duchess grows up, methinks her daddy will be her hero."

Sadie raises her chin. "You mean Little Sadie."

"She means Little Maggie."

Sadie pulls out a clove and pops it in her mouth. "I guess we can let everyone know we'll hold off the wedding supper for a couple of weeks."

I nod and, crossing my fingers, look heavenward. "And maybe … just maybe, Barry will be home in time."

CHAPTER 30

There's a knock on the door the next morning. It's early for callers, but I answer it. First, it was Sadie, then Alice Wiggins and Ida Clare Mobley. This time it's Bessie Mae, and she's holding a small package.

"Come in. Is that for the baby?"

"Yes'm. And there's something in there for Mistah Wade and Missus Pinkie." She holds out the gaily wrapped box. "Part of it is from me."

I won't hurt her pride by telling her she shouldn't have but hug her instead. "Pinkie will be touched. So will Wade. Go on in and see Little Maggie."

Bessie Mae's right eyebrow raises while the left pulls down. "Lil' Maggie? Your sister said her name's Lil' Duchess."

"To be honest, her name is Magnolia Duchess Sadie Rowntree."

Bessie Mae's laugh rumbles through her whole body. "I sees the way of it." Shaking her head, she lets me usher her into the bedroom where Pinkie is holding court. "Lotta name fo' a body so tiny."

As I return to the living room, Duchess is closing the front door behind Rosa Perez and Myrtle Davis with more presents. Sister shoos them into Pinkie's room. Through the door, I catch a glimpse of Wade, holding his baby daughter. A prouder man couldn't be found.

"Rivers End is filled with the most generous people." Duchess joins me on the davenport and pours herself a cup of tea. "The presents aren't lavish—nothing like I gave to friends back in Atlanta." She glances sidelong at me and sips her tea.

While true, it's an odd statement for her to make. "I'm sure they aren't. But y'all had money then."

Duchess sets her cup and saucer on the coffee table and turns, facing me. "No, no, I wasn't comparing them like that. I'm saying these are given out of loving sacrifice, not duty. More often than not, we'd send the maid out to purchase a baby gift or call the store to deliver a wedding present. There was little thought put into it, other than how much to spend to keep up with the Inmans, the Calhouns, or the Rhodes."

Her answer surprises me even more. "You sent gifts just to keep up?"

"No, but the thought was always in the back of my mind. To keep our position in society, we had to measure up." She pulls up her feet, tucking them beneath her. "I only meant that in comparison, these are actually ... oh, fiddle. What's that Bible verse about the widow's mite being more than the wealthy gave? That's what I mean. Bessie Mae gave Pinkie a dollar. That's a huge sacrifice for her. But she gave it willingly and I'm sure without any thought of what anyone else gave. Pinkie will love it more because of the sacrifice it represents."

My admiration and love for my sister soar. If I can become even half as wise as her, I'll be pleased.

The last of the visitors leave, and Wade strides into the living room. "Pinkie wants to go to our apartment. Do you think it's safe to move her?"

I begin picking up the coffee cups. "Yes, but I'd wait until you get off work. She needs someone with her for a while yet."

"I already arranged for time off."

Smart man. "Then sure. She shouldn't lift anything heavier than the baby, though. And get her right into bed. You can put her clothes away for her."

Sadie hands me her cup. "I'll help them." She follows Wade back into the bedroom. It only takes a couple of minutes for them to gather Pinkie's things and take them next door. Then they come back. Wade sweeps his wife into his arms, and Sadie holds the baby.

"Wade, please." He pauses at the door at Pinkie's request. "Maggie, how can I say thank you? I don't know where I would be if it hadn't been for you. Certainly not married to this sweet man." She smiles lovingly at her husband.

I'm going to miss her presence in the apartment. "Sugar, you blessed us from the moment we brought you home. Now go on. It's not like you're leaving Rivers End."

I close the door behind them. Duchess picks up the last of the coffee cups and deposits them on a tray to go back down to the kitchen. "It's going to be quiet around here." She stares at the bedroom door and sighs. "I'm going to change the bedding. I've got something else to do today, but I'll do the wash tomorrow."

"Do you want help?"

"No, thank you." She doesn't elaborate, and I don't ask. If I want to move back into my own bedroom, then I need to go to work.

After she deposits the soiled bedding down the laundry chute, she sets her hat on her head and pulls on her gloves. "I'll be back in a couple of hours. I'm taking R.W.'s car."

Duchess walks out before I can ask her where she's taking it. She's not wearing her sleuthing disguise, so she's not looking for Big Jim.

I cross to the front window and, slipping my fingers between two slats of the Venetian blinds, I part them and peek out. Duchess crosses the street and disappears behind the train station. For the life of me, I can't think where she'd be going or what she's up to.

There's been a steady flow of customers today, but nothing I can't handle. Most want to chat about Little Maggie. Sadie came in around ten, saying she felt like Wade was handling things fine. "After too many games of Go Fish with Ozzie, I felt like a third spot on the two of clubs."

"Well, I'm glad you're here. I've been lonely." I pick up an apple from the bin and wipe it with a towel.

Sadie looks around the store. "Where's Duchess?"

I shrug my shoulders, set down the apple, and select another. "She took R.W.'s car and went somewhere."

"Oh. Well, we all need to get away now and again. Maybe seeing Pinkie's baby made her a little sad."

Of course, that has to be what it is. Sadie is so intuitive. Poor Duchess.

Sadie grabs a rag. "Are we going to polish all these apples?"

"Just the top layer, so the barrel looks inviting." They were merely a time passer. "Something is wrong with me today. I feel out of kilter. I don't know what it is, but I can't concentrate, and I don't know why. Poor Granny Belle bought ten pounds of flour and four apples. I charged her for four pounds of flour and ten apples. Thankfully, instead of getting mad, she laughed and asked what made my cheese slide off my cracker." I grimace.

Before Sadie can offer me any wisdom or reassurance, Emma Gordon strolls in for some coffee and eggs. "Oh, and give me a pound of bacon, too, please, Maggie."

We grow busy and over the next hour stay that way. I run the register, and Sadie is working the meat counter.

"Maggie!" Duchess races in the door. "Grab Sadie and come. I've found him! I'm going for Jubal."

I blink at my sister. She's talking so fast, I can't understand her. "Who have you found, and why are—" Understanding dawns. "Big Jim? You found Big Jim?" I turn in a circle, searching for help as Duchess runs back out. "Emma! Please, will you mind the store or close it? Duchess found Big Jim! Somebody let Faylene know. We're about to find Barry! Sadie? Let's go."

Sadie meets me at the door, and we race out. The car is on the street, and Duchess is in the driver's seat. "Come on. Get in. We've got to get Jubal."

We jump in. My heart is racing, and I can hardly catch my

breath. Duchess guns the engine, throws, the car into gear and it stalls. Sadie jumps out and cranks the motor again until it catches. She leaps back in, and Duchess lets out the clutch. This time, it doesn't stall. We're off.

At the sheriff's office, she stays in the car with the engine running. I zip inside.

"Jubal!" The office is empty. No, not today. "Jubal? Are you here?"

A voice comes from the area where the cells are located. "I'm back here. Hang on."

"Hurry! It's Maggie Parker. Duchess—"

"I know your voice, Maggie." He walks in from the back, drying his hands on a towel. "Now what has you in such an all-fire dither?"

"Duchess found Big Jim. Come on."

He grabs his hat from a peg by the door. At least he didn't dawdle asking me questions. "I'll take my car and follow you." He stops by R.W.'s car for a moment to ask Duchess where she saw Big Jim.

"In Baxley." She slides out from behind the steering wheel. "Maggie, you drive, and I'll ride with Jubal."

I gape at her. "I don't know where we're going."

"No, Sister. You follow us. I need to tell Jubal what I found out. I'll tell you later. Come on, we're wasting time."

That makes sense. I turn to hop into the Model T, but Sadie is in the driver's seat. Thank goodness. I wouldn't be fit to drive, anyway. I run around to the passenger's side, and off we go.

"Don't lose Jubal."

Sadie has her eyes glued to the back of the sheriff's car. "No need to worry, girl. I wonder what Duchess found out."

Is Sadie nuts? "She's found Barry. I'm sure. At least, I think I'm sure. Oh, Sadie." I turn to face her, keeping one hand on the dashboard. "What if she found Big Jim, but Barry isn't there? Oh, I don't think I could stand that."

"Stop it. You're borrowin' misery you don't need. Trust, Maggie-girl."

I feel a holy nudge. "You're right. Step on the gas. I'm going to see my boy!"

The next hour creeps by as we go as fast as we dare on this road.

"I wonder what Duchess is telling Jubal. It's hard to be so close and not hear her." I lean forward. I don't know why—I can't make the car go faster.

Finally, Baxley city limit comes into view. Jubal pulls over onto the grass at the side of the road and parks. We park next to him and jump out. Jubal and Duchess wait for us.

The sheriff lays out the plan. "Duchess made an important discovery." He glances at her with admiration in his eyes. My, my. That's the first time I've ever seen an emotion from him. "Rather cleverly, I might add. She went to a realtor's office near where she last saw Big Jim and talked about renting a house in the area. She'd been looking at houses with this realtor for a couple of weeks when she finally spotted Big Jim again."

Aghast, I gape at Duchess. "Why didn't you tell me?"

"It was day before yesterday. But before I could tell you, Pinkie went into labor."

"Okay, so what happened?"

Duchess leans back against the front fender, her elbows resting on the hood. "Well, I casually asked the realtor if he knew him, as the man looked familiar—at least, that's what I told him. He tells me he sure does. That's James Sullivan. He sold him and his wife their house. I asked where that was. He never suspected anything but gave me their address. I came this morning and saw that Miss Ferguson go in the house. A while later, Big Jim came out."

I'm hardly able to take this all in. "His *wife*? That's bigamy! More important, did you see Barry?"

"No, but I did see a toy truck in the fenced yard."

I look around us, but there's nothing but stores. "Where's the house? And how are we going to do this?" I don't bother to ask more about the wife. Not yet, anyway. But I figure I now know why he's been after money. Dirty, rotten, no good …

Jubal holds his hands up. "You're going to stake out the house first. I'm going to get the local police chief in on this. Duchess, you drive to the street and park down the block at least five houses away. Stay low, but watch to see if anyone comes out or goes in. Don't anyone go to the door. We don't want to risk them leaving out the back or hurting Barry. I'll be back directly."

"Do you think they'd really hurt Barry?"

Jubal puts his hand on my shoulder. "I don't know, but we can't risk it. Desperate people act crazy."

Jubal leaves, and we pile into R.W.'s car. Sadie cranks the engine, Duchess revs it, and Sadie jumps in the back seat. We drive to a normal-looking street. How can people who live near this house not know they have a kidnapper in their midst?

A couple of minutes later, Duchess pulls to the curb and stops. She points down the street. "It's that one."

I squint at the non-descript brown bungalow. "You said the realtor told you he sold this house to Big Jim and his *wife*? How does he know it's his wife?"

"Because he goes to the same church where"—she locks gazes with me—"they got married."

Sadie gasps. "Married? Are you telling us Big Jim really married this lady? He's already married."

"Married and—duck!" Duchess squeaks. We duck.

"What's happening?" I try to peek and stay hidden at the same time.

"The door opened, and I saw Big Jim coming out." A little way off, a car engine starts. Duchess pulls off her hat and raises her head so she can see between the steering wheel's spokes. Now she sits up. "He's driving the other way. Come on. We're not waiting."

We scramble out and run up the block. At the house, I ring the doorbell, my stomach clenching and palms sweaty.

Duchess steps in front of me.

The door opens, and it's the "social worker" with the mousey brown hair pulled back—the same woman who snatched Barry. "Yes? May I help you?"

"Are you Mrs. Sullivan?"

"Yes." She eyes Duchess with icy reserve. "Who are you?"

I push forward. "You have my son." Her eyes open wide in recognition, and she tries to close the door, but I shove her aside and run into the front room. "Barry? Where are you?"

My baby's voice answers from down a dark hallway, high-pitched with excitement. "Mama? Mama! I'm here."

Fergie grabs my arm, but I yank free. Duchess seizes hold of Fergie's shoulder, draws back her fist, and slugs the woman. Fergie goes down like a prizefighter with a glass jaw. I gape at Duchess, who, rubbing her fist, sits on Fergie while Sadie yanks the drape's tiebacks and ties the woman up.

"Mama? Where are you?"

I run to where I hear the sweetest voice. The door's locked. "Hang on, baby. I've got to get a key."

Back in the front room, Sadie is also sitting on Fergie, or whatever her name is. She's regained consciousness and is crying and babbling.

I lean down into her face and make mine as menacing as possible. "Where's the key?"

"Jimmy has it."

Jimmy? "Does he lock his own grandson up every day?"

"The kid keeps trying to run away."

"What do you expect? You kidnapped him. You realize you're going to jail, right?"

She responds by dissolving into torrential tears.

I want to punch her like Duchess did, but right now I want Barry more. I run back to the room. "Stand away from the door, Barry. I'm going to try to break it." I back up as far as the small hallway allows. I throw myself at the door but bounce off.

In the other room, the front door slams open, and a forceful command rings out. "Don't anyone move."

"Jubal!" I run back to the living room. He's got three policemen with him. "Barry's here, but the door's locked, and Big Jim has the key. He's not here."

Jubal shoos me toward the hall. "Show me where."

The sheriff leans close to the door I indicate and speaks in a soothing tone. "Barry? This is Sheriff Lee. Stand back, son."

Wringing my hands, I raise my voice. "Do what he says, Barry. I'm here, too, baby."

"It's okay, Sheriff. I'm in the closet." My smart boy.

Jubal leans his shoulder against the door and pushes. Testing it? The wood groans. Then he takes a step back and rams the door with his shoulder. It splinters and flies open. Jubal and I leap into the room. Barry bursts out of the closet and into my arms.

"Mama! I knew you were coming."

I can't talk. All I can do is hold my baby. I run my hands over his curls. They let his hair grow too long. But he looks all right. I pull him into my arms and hold him tight. Then I kiss him. His little arms go around my neck, and he's hugging me so hard I can scarcely breathe. When I do, I smell a horrible odor.

"Barry, didn't they let you use the bathroom?"

"Only when Granddaddy was here. I had to use that bucket when he was gone."

I turn to Jubal. "When that man gets here, I'm going to personally strangle him."

"You won't need to." Jubal covers the bucket with a large book. "I'll have him put away for the rest of his life."

The warmth of the sheriff's reassurance fades when a gruff voice makes a demand from the living room. "What's going on here?"

Big Jim! Jubal flies out the door. I hold Barry tighter and fight the urge to flee. We crouch together behind the bed.

"James Parker, you're under arrest for the kidnapping of Barry Parker."

In High Cotton

Feet scramble and glass breaks.

Fergie screams.

A loud thud makes the walls rattle.

A loud crack, and a man grunts.

I hold Barry tighter. Then it goes quiet.

Metal clicks against metal.

"You're done, Parker." Jubal has him.

Barry and I creep out of the bedroom. I hold him behind me and peek into the living room. Big Jim is on the floor next to Fergie with his hands cuffed behind him. One of the Baxley policemen helps Duchess and Sadie get up. Another slips handcuffs on that woman. It's finally safe.

I lift Barry onto my hip and edge up beside the sheriff. "They're evil. I don't know why he did this to his own grandson. You saw how they kept my son locked up like an animal."

Jubal nods, his eyes never leaving my father-in-law. "They're going away for a long time. Big Jim, not only are you being charged with kidnapping, but bigamy too."

Big Jim glares at Jubal then at me. He sits up. "I'll get—"

Jubal plants his boot on Big Jim's shoulder and pushes him back down. "Shut up. There are a lot of things the good ole boys will overlook, Parker. But kidnapping and bigamy aren't included." He turns to the local police chief. "Lock him up. I'll have Hazlehurst send a paddy wagon for him in a few days."

The chief salutes Jubal. "At your leisure, Sheriff. We've got a nice cold cell waiting for a scumbag like him."

I grab Jubal's arm. "Don't forget his *wife*. She's part of this too. She knew Barry is my son and helped Big Jim."

Jubal nods at the cop who pulls "Miss Ferguson" to her feet. "Lock her up too. The charges are kidnapping, child abuse, and neglect."

Holding Barry tight with one arm, I run my hand down his cheek. "Did either of them hurt you, sweetheart?"

"Nobody hit me, but she"—he points at Miss Ferguson—"can't

cook good. I'm hungry."

Thank you, Lord. "Then let's go home."

Jubal ruffles Barry's hair. "Maggie, you come to my office tomorrow. There's paperwork we need to fill out."

I nod. "I'll be there. But right now, I want to take my boy home." I carry him to the car, my heart full. "I've got so much to tell you."

EPILOGUE

Six months later

"Happy birthday, dear Barry, happy birthday to you."
Bessie Mae enters the living room with Barry's birthday cake, with its eight candles lit. All his family and friends are gathered to celebrate.

After Big Jim was sentenced, Mama Faylene asked us to come live with her. She has more than enough room. Duchess, Barry, and I each have our own bedroom. I offered Sadie the apartment above the grocery, and she loves it. She says she has Little Sadie close by, and I have to admit, she gets to babysit more than we do.

Barry's grin rivals one of those new, high-powered Klieg lights. When he blows out all his candles in one puff, Bessie Mae claps her hands, then slides the cake to one side and cuts it.

Proudly carrying each slice to its recipient, Barry pauses beside Wade. "Can Baby Girl have some?"

Six-month-old Little Maggie sits on her daddy's lap, tasting everything he allows from his plate.

Barry fell in love with her the day he came home. While he wasn't here for the wedding, my words were prophetic, and he *was* here for the marriage celebration supper. And the fact that *his* Pinkie married his best buddy's daddy thrilled him. As for the baby's name, I think Barry got tired of us all vying for top billing and provided her a nickname.

Baby Girl adores her *two* big brothers.

Wade ruffles Barry's hair. "I think she'll stick her fingers in it, anyway." The instant the words leave his mouth, she makes a grab for the cake, and before he can pull the plate away, she stuffs a handful in her mouth. Her wide-eyed expression changes to a delighted squeal. She dives for another handful. Wade leans back, and her face turns to sorrow.

Ozzie sneaks his baby sister another taste.

Beside him, Pinkie, who has lost all her baby weight and is more slender than we have ever known her to be, stays his hand. "That's enough now. We don't want her to get a tummy ache, do we?"

"No, Mama."

Pinkie nearly melts every time Ozzie calls her *Mama*, which he started right after his daddy said "I do." I think she loves him as much as she loves Little Maggie.

Back in his chair, Barry leans close to me. "I love you, Mama."

I hug him. I can't hug him enough these days. "I love you more than life itself, Barry."

He's stuck close to my side since he came home. He's getting a little better but still wants me in sight. Thankfully, his nightmares have become fewer and farther in between. I pray he gets over all that soon. When we were driving home from Baxley, he told me the one thing that kept him from being afraid was Jesus told him I was looking for him.

"Is it time to open my presents yet?"

Mama Faylene's eyes twinkle. "I do believe it is. Let's go into the living room. Bessie Mae, you leave this table alone. We'll pile the plates on my lap later and wheel them to the kitchen. Right now, it's time for more fun."

With the permanent absence of Big Jim, Bessie Mae is relaxing and, when asked, joins us without any coaxing. We're all more relaxed now that Big Jim and his other *wife* are in prison. He got more years than he has life left in him. She got fifty and will be a very old lady and harmless by the time she gets out—if she ever does.

We parade into the living room, where there is a small but respectable pile of presents on the coffee table. I can hardly wait for Barry to open the big one. I really splurged on it, but with Lippincott publishing my novel, I got a nice advance. With Sadie and Duchess running the store, I have more time to write, and it's a good thing since Lippincott contracted me for two more novels.

I finally learned who the anonymous donor was who left money in mailboxes for folks in need. It was Sadie. Turns out she let Mr. Hardee—and later Mr. Connor—invest most of her money for years. In February of last year, Mr. Connor advised her to sell all her stocks. She did and has enough to live comfortably for the rest of her life if she's careful, which she is.

As for Barry, I'm trying hard not to overindulge him, but I hold to the belief that he's unspoilable.

I sit on the davenport, while Barry and Ozzie drop to the floor next to the coffee table. Ozzie hands him a present. "This one's from me and Baby Girl." He's picked up using Barry's name for his sister.

Barry rips off the wrapping. Ozzie is wiggling in anticipation as Barry lifts off the top. He reaches in and pulls out a piece of paper. Opening it, he reads out loud. "Go to the kitchen and open the broom closet." He looks at Ozzie with a quizzical frown.

Ozzie laughs. "Go on."

The boys jump up and run to the kitchen. The closet door opens, and Barry lets out a whoop.

Ozzie's exultant voice follows. "I told Daddy that you'd guess it if we wrapped it."

"What is it?" Sadie calls.

"A fishing pole," Barry answers, bringing it into the living room for us to see. "It's swell, Ozzie. I'll bet I can get a really big fish with this rod. Thanks!"

Next, he picks up the large box from me. He reads the tag on it. "This is from you, Mama."

"You'll see it's from Auntie Duchess and Miss Sadie, too, if you keep reading. We hope you like it." I know he will. He's been mooning over the catalogs for weeks.

When he gets the paper half ripped off, he stops, his eyes grow wide, and he gasps. "Oh, Mama. It's a telescope." His hands fly in a frenzy to get it open, then he hugs me, nearly choking me. "I love it!"

"You're welcome."

He leaps to my sister then Sadie, giving each of them stranglehold hugs.

Wade helps the boys set up the telescope on the veranda, where they can view the stars when it goes dark. Sadie and Duchess help me gather up the paper, while Pinkie goes upstairs to my bedroom and puts Little Maggie down for a nap.

I gather up the toys. "I'll take these up to Barry's room."

Twilight is falling, so we go out on the veranda to watch Barry and Ozzie look through his telescope. Though a toy, it's pretty powerful, Wade says. I take a turn.

"Look at the moon, Mama. You can see holes on it."

I peer into the eyepiece, and sure enough, he's right. I see round rings, like a shallow basin. "Maybe that's why people think the moon is made of Swiss cheese." I lean back. "What do you boys think?"

"I think this is the bestest present I've ever gotten. As good as my model airplane." He throws his arms around my neck, gives me a sloppy kiss, then goes back to the telescope.

Wade helps the boys find Orion and the Big Dipper. After a few minutes, Barry steps away and turns in a circle, looking at all the people he loves. "This is a high cotton birthday."

Maybe he's right. In all the ways that matter—love, family, and friends—we are indeed blessed and surely in high cotton.

The End

DEPRESSION RECIPES

Depression Casserole
  1½ lbs. ground beef
  1 can kidney beans
  5 sliced raw lg. potatoes
  3 sliced raw onions
  10 oz. bottle catsup
  salt, pepper, and garlic powder
  green pepper

Brown ground beef and flavor with salt, pepper, and garlic powder. In 9 x 13 inch casserole pan, layer kidney beans, sliced raw potatoes, sliced onion, diced green pepper, top with ground beef, and cover with catsup. Repeat with a second layer in same order. Cover and bake at 375 degrees for about 1 1/2 hours. Uncover during the last 15 minutes of baking. May need to add small amount of water if too dry.

Carrot Loaf
  1 1/2 c ground raw carrots
  1 c boiled rice
  1 c ground peanuts
  1 egg
  salt, pepper
  2 tbsp red or green peppers
  3 tbsp minced bacon or other fat
  1 tbsp onion juice
  1/2 tsp mustard
  Mix ingredients in order and bake the loaf in a moderate oven 1 hour. Serve tomato sauce if desired.

Macaroni Papoose

1 package macaroni, broken in ¼-inch lengths
1/3 c milk
grated cheese
small amount horseradish
thin slices raw smoked ham

Cook macaroni until tender, spread slices of ham with macaroni, horseradish, and cheese.

Roll slices and skewer or tie together. Place in shallow baking dish with milk.

Bake in moderate oven (350 degrees) for 35 minutes. Serve hot with dish of crushed pineapple to sprinkle over each "pappose" as desired.

Meatless Loaf

1 c rice
1 c peanuts crushed
1 c cottage cheese
1 egg
1 tbsp oil
1 tsp salt

Combine all the ingredients together, and bake in a loaf pan for 30 minutes or until loaf is good and set.

Hardscrabble Salad
    1 can yellow hominy, drained
    1 can black-eyed peas, drained
    1 green pepper, chopped
    1 tomato, chopped
    1 small onion, chopped
    2 ribs celery, diced
    1/4 cup cooking oil, optional (I use olive oil)
    1/4 cup vinegar
    salt and pepper to taste

Mix all the above ingredients together and serve hot or cold

Junket
    2 c milk
    2 tbsp sugar
    ½ tsp vanilla
    2 tsp rennet* or
    ½ junket* tablet
    2 tsp lukewarm water

Heat milk to lukewarm in double boiler. Add sugar and flavoring. Stir until sugar is dissolved. Add rennet dissolved in water and pour into the dish from which it is to be served. Let stand until cool and firm. Serve with cream, soft custard, fruit, or fruit syrup. Cinnamon, nutmeg, coconut, chocolate, cocoa, or other flavor may be substituted for vanilla.

    *Junket (rennet) tablets are still available at Walmart

Ginger Taffy
2 c. granulated sugar
½ c. white syrup (corn syrup)
1 rounded tbsp butter
½ c boiling water
2 tbsp vinegar
1 level tsp ground ginger

Boil all except butter and ginger, without stirring, to soft-ball stage in large saucepan. Still without stirring, drop in butter and cook to hard-ball stage. Sprinkle in ginger and turn into buttered pans. When cool enough to handle, pull with buttered hands as long as can be pulled and cut into 1-inch chunks. Wrap each, kiss fashion, in waxed paper.

MAGGIE'S HOUSEHOLD HINTS

Upholstery cleaner

Anyone who has children or pets can benefit from this upholstery shampoo. Mix together 6 tablespoons of pure soap flakes and 2 tablespoons of Borax. Slowly add 2¼ cups of boiling water, stirring well, until dry ingredients are dissolved. Allow to cool, then whip into a foam with an eggbeater. Brush dry suds onto the furniture, concentrating on soiled areas, before quickly wiping them off with a damp sponge. All evidence of sticky little fingers or paws is gone.

Pine floor cleaner

Washing soda (from the laundry section of the supermarket) is a cheap and effective way of cutting through grease and removing stubborn stains. Mix 1/2 cup soap flakes with 1/4 cup washing soda (sodium carbonate), 1 cup salt, and 2 cups water in a saucepan, and heat gently until dissolved. When mixture has cooled to lukewarm, add 2 teaspoons pine essential oil (available at health food or aromatherapy stores) and stir well. Store in a jar and simply use two to three tablespoons in half a bucket of hot water to clean floors. After cleaning, rinse floor with half a bucket of clean water mixed with a cup of white vinegar.

Window cleaner

Mix 1/4 cup white vinegar, 1 tablespoon cornstarch, and 2 cups warm water in a spray bottle, and shake well to dissolve cornstarch. Spray generously onto glass surface, then wipe dry with a clean cloth or old newspapers, buffing to a streak-free shine.

Mold remover

Here in Georgia, the humidity levels are high, and we get mold easily. Try adding a cupful of Borax, a natural mold retardant, to your soapy water whenever you wash down the walls. Alternatively, mix ½ cup borax with ½ cup vinegar and 1 cup water in a spray bottle, and spray generously on moldy surfaces before wiping clean with a damp sponge.

Stinky shoes

I find my little boy's canvas shoes are stinky from his sweaty feet. We all know sprinkling baking soda in shoes removes odors, but you have to clean them out in the morning before your child puts them on again. So here's another way for you that works well. Fill a spare pair of socks with a mixture of coarsely crushed dried herbs and spices—any combination of rosemary, bay leaves, cinnamon sticks, whole cloves, orange peel, lemon peel, thyme, lavender, and pine needles. Tie the socks at the top, and leave them in the shoes between each wear.

Stubborn stains

These need a bit of extra help, but there's no need for expensive chemicals—try these more natural remedies.

Blood, chocolate, or coffee stains: Soak overnight in a solution of 1/4 cup borax and 2 cups cold water. Wash as usual the next day.

Grease: Apply a paste of cornstarch and water, and allow to dry before brushing away the powder and the grease with it.

Red wine: Sprinkle stain with salt; let sit for several hours. When dry, brush away salt and wash, or clean immediately with soda water.

Grass: Soak stain in a 3 percent solution of hydrogen peroxide, then wash.

Ink on a white shirt: Wet fabric with cold water, and apply a paste of cream of tartar and lemon juice one hour before washing.

Scorch marks: Rub area with a cut raw onion. After the onion juice has been absorbed, soak the stain in water for a few hours.

Mildew remover

For stubborn mildew on light-colored items, wash fabric in warm soapy water, then make a mixture of 2 parts salt to 1 part lemon juice and apply it to the mildewed area. Place the item in full sun, rinsing after several hours. Repeat if necessary. Don't use on dark items though, as the lemon juice will bleach them.

Rugs

For a lovely, fresh-smelling carpet devoid of any of the stinky evidence of the children and pets who have wreaked havoc upon it, crush 1/2 cup of lavender flowers to release their scent, then mix with 1 cup of baking soda and sprinkle liberally on carpet. Leave for 30 minutes, then vacuum.

Drains taking a long time to clear?

Keep them clog-free by pouring ½ cup baking soda down the drain, followed by 1 cup white vinegar. Allow the mixture to fizz for several minutes, then flush down a liter of hot water. Do this weekly to keep drains in good running order.